CRASH
&BURN

BURNOUT BOOK THREE

ADELL RYAN

Published by Upside Down Red Umbrella
First Edition: December 2020

Cover Art by Upside Down Red Umbrella
Edited by G. Surley

CHAPTER ONE

T his is going to be a really long night.

After completing the individual group updates, we all enter into a combined meeting of sorts. I want to ask questions like "How did Jude and Crow end up in the same vehicle together?" and "Whatever happened to the meet attendees?" All those answers will come in due time, though; gear by gear. Plus, the last thing this group of testosterone needs right now is a ton of estrogen-filled questions. But, goddamn, it's hard not to word-vomit everything on my mind.

On a positive note, no one is showing any animosity toward anyone right now. I imagined the convergence of these two groups to go down a lot differently. Porter is the exception, though; his enmity is practically visible as he seethes with anger. Pinned in place by the fear that if he adjusts even an inch Jude will shoot him, he is still resting cockeyed on an elbow with his hip propped against a crate.

He has witnessed similar scenes play out in the past and evidently isn't willing to test their friendly ties under the given circumstances. *Fuck my sister once, shame on you… Fuck her twice, shame on me. Fuck her three, four, five…*

Honestly, it's amazing he hasn't been shot already.

The delay is in his benefit, no doubt, helping him to bide time. Every second that passes, he regains energy and focus, allowing him to better defend himself and come up with an epic alibi.

I'm surrounded by some pretty damn excellent minds… Porter not excluded. Sure, he was a tool for everything he did to me, but it wouldn't come as a surprise if every slander from his mouth and thrust of his cock was calculated — the abuse and manipulation part of a bigger, badder scheme.

Hayes breaks away from the Revelry crew and pulls me aside to quietly ask my permission to share the information divulged moments before Jude, Crow, and Porter made their grand entrance. I assure him that, at this point, anything I openly discussed is completely okay to relay.

However, whenever I try to join the discussion, they shoo me away. Not because I'm invaluable or they see me as a nuisance, but because they're still getting individual base stories and worry my involvement might influence someone's version since I'm blood to one and in an intimate relationship with the other three.

While waiting, I sit across from Porter and stare smugly at him for the first time in… forever…

watching as he continues to blink away the fogginess from the beating he apparently took.

He's still working on it when the guys announce they're ready to include me in the conversation. Trenton scoops an arm around my waist and tugs me in close. "Sorry, Pet, but where the four of us are concerned, you're too much of a damn distraction. We're ready for you to step onto the witness stand though, now. You good?" The sudden switch from aggressive and standoffish to caring and somewhat playful again comes as a shock to my already overstimulated mind.

A light sparks and expands in my chest as I realize that Trenton is not much different than Jude: His personality can go from hot to cold and volatile to passionate and caring, all in the snap of a finger. Everyone outside of "family" be damned.

For a short period of time, I was pushed outside of that ranking as seniority took precedence. I do not fault them at all for that decision. Being brushed aside hurts like hell, but I'm pragmatic enough to understand — to be able to roll with the punches.

As for being on the witness stand, in that they are sorely mistaken. Witness seats are for victims or bystanders. I intend to be involved in their plans in whole, not in part, and certainly not as a victim or spectator.

Before I can begin to analyze and "help," though, I want to be enlightened regarding the most recent goings-on. "To start… I need updates, if you don't mind." I try to sound as meek and humble as possible — to respect the male ego and all — but Jude just rolls his eyes at the farce.

Trenton, Hayes, and Crow let him answer. "Our Grand Opening meet went really well… considering." His gaze slants sideways toward Crow.

For obvious reasons, this particular update and the accusatory way it was delivered does not go over well with Revelry. Tension ratchets up a notch.

Ignoring their piercing glares, Jude continues, "That said, we had three arrests, twelve summonses, and nine impounds." He grimaces, much like I do at times — something that people from our past would take us as twins for if it weren't for our age difference.

Our similarity does not pass the guys' notice. The situation is serious, but that comical trait is not. The expression pulls a small smile from each — even black-hearted Crow.

Their warm reactions give me a flicker of hope. I want them to see Jude like I do: like me but way more insane and hella smarter — when grief is not in the picture, that is.

"Ouch," I respond, grimacing in return.

Jude continues, unfazed, "Yeah, but—"

"But with their turnout, that really isn't too bad," Crow interjects.

The comment was tame enough, but the three Revelry guys share nondescript looks that scream esoteric knowledge. Jude notices, catching the remnants of their silent exchange and reading the insult between the lines of Crow's comment.

Another boost of tension hisses through the circle.

Jude shifts from one foot to the other.

Hayes, Trenton, and Crow take a step back, shoulders bunching and fingers curling slightly at their sides.

The scene goes from cautious and somewhat amiable to volatile with a few narrowed glares. My hopes that Revelry will see Jude like they — hopefully — see me, crashes and burns the moment Jude pulls out his gun and rests it loosely at his side, finger hovering over the trigger.

Revelry might be into the underground street scene, but they aren't moblike — aside from the illegal racing part; none of them wield weapons or use strong-arm tactics to get what they want.

When it comes to their passions, their cold and calculative mindset isn't much different, though. They took a step back but didn't cower. The commitment to the competition, to survive, is in the set of their jaws and the determination of their locked focus.

Several actions happen in a blink of an eye:

Jude's eyes slit into harsh lines.

His gun hand rises.

I step between the two crews.

Arms wrap around my torso.

A shot pops throughout the port warehouse.

My body lands with a scrape against the concrete...

...and someone falls on top of me.

CHAPTER TWO

My uneven, rasping breaths mingle with those from the person covering me. The slight tang of engine grease mixed with sulfur from a fired gun burns through my lungs. Unwilling to let in any of the scene, I squeeze my eyes tight and give way to the blackness.

Unfortunately, my mind has other plans and projects an entirely unwanted scene behind my closed eyelids. The overwhelming senses of real life surround me, mimicking those from a few months ago — ringing echoes of a fired weapon and acrid scents of smoke and blood. I become lighter, floating, almost out-of-body as the memories of that night come flooding back.

A light sweep of warm air ghosts over my ear. "Remi? Remi, please look at me."

Shuffling resounds around me and someone applies pressure to my body again. Everything rushes back at once; the details of the night a few months ago blend with those from the present, and I jolt upward, eyes snapping open and head swivelling in every direction.

Unlike in the memory flooding my brain, it is not me holding the gun, but rather my brother. The chamber of the weapon acts as a tunnel of death and promises aimed toward a writhing Porter. Jude appears crazed: his arms shake, eyes possessed, and forehead gleams with perspiration under the construction lights.

Crow, Hayes, and Trenton are all surrounding me. Crow is the closest, his hand still on my cheek from when he was pleading for me to snap out of my daze.

When I try standing to approach Jude, Trenton's hands move to my shoulders, firmly keeping me on the ground with his fingers digging into my flesh. Crow's careful touch brushes over the side of my forehead, and a throb pings to life under the slight pressure. "She'll have a goose egg for a couple days," he states.

I jerk my head away from his touch to peer around him at Porter and Jude. A pool of red blooms around Porter. He gasps and squirms, hands cupping the upper inside of his thigh.

Fingers meet my jaw and yank my attention away from the scene. Chrome eyes flit over my face before landing on the swollen, puffy spot on my head again. "Goddammit, Remi!" Crow whisper-yells. "Never try to be a hero again. You're lucky he was aiming at Porter and not one of us." I wrench my head out of his grip again and shuffle backward, my mind a mess of confusion.

Jude begins moving backward toward us, his eyes and gun still locked on Porter. Once close enough, he spins around, falls to his haunches in front of me, and curls my hair behind my ear. "I fucking told him not to move, but h-he fucking moved, Remi. I told him not to. H-he made me do it. M-made me shoot him."

Swallowing hard, I will my throat and tongue to form words. When that fails, I just nod at him, hoping it comes across as reassuring in his moment of unhinged panic.

His hand leaves my hair and slams to the top of his own head where he clenches a handful of black locks — all the while, his opposite hand is still shaking with the gun aimed loosely behind him at a wounded Porter.

I lean forward, lift my hand, and run it along his bicep and forearm until my fingers wrap around the top of the gun. He lets go so quickly that I almost don't have a proper grip as it exchanges custody. When I do have a solid hold, though, I click on the safety and plop the weapon into my lap with a heavy exhale.

Both hands now free, I cup his face and focus on his wild eyes. "You loved him... it's not the same as other jobs. I get that. But he was never your 80 percent. Never. No matter how much he made you believe he was. Got it?" Jude's lips purse under the strain of my pressed palms but he nods in my hold.

Trenton lets go of my shoulders, stalks toward Porter, and kicks him square in the ribs. "He had that and more coming to him—"

A flicker of recognition alights in Jude's already deranged gaze, then a growling wail screeches from his vocal cords. He heaves away from me, lunging toward Trenton. "You fucking knew! You fucking knew and didn't do anything about it!"

I scurry backward, stand, and shove the gun into the back of my jeans. "Jude… Jude, stop," I plead, stepping closer. Crow wraps an arm around my chest and shoulders, pulling me back.

"At least it wasn't happening under our roof. Your sister was raped and beaten while you slept like a damn baby in the room right below," Trenton hisses, hunching over, ready to pounce. "At least she had someone to run to and talk to about it — a safety net, when under the surface of your roof was nothing but a sea of fucking danger."

Jude chokes and staggers, the previous derangement in his dark gaze morphing into painful recognition. He stops prowling forward, and his gaze darts to me. "You told them?" he asks with a strained whisper.

I shake my head emphatically. "No… it… it wasn't like that."

"You ran to *them*?" he bellows, fists clenching at his sides.

"You… you had your own problems. Work. Grief."

13

Jude shakes his head. "You chose which side of the stands to sit in, Remi."

"No… Jude… no. Y-you're not thinking right. This isn't you."

He's in shock.

High on adrenaline.

His judgement is clouded.

That must be it.

"I… I wanted to tell you," I explain in a rush. "More than anything. And I was about to—" I cut off the comment, focus darting to Hayes.

Hayes stopped me from telling Jude earlier tonight, just like he tried to stop Crow.

Why?

Hayes swallows hard and slides the papers that have been sitting on the nearby crate behind him and out of sight with a quick flick of his wrist.

Lost in the maniacal whirl of his unraveling mind, Jude doesn't catch the quick blur of motion; the papers go unseen. Hayes gives me two quick, almost unnoticeable, shakes of his head. Just like in the woods at the meet tonight, he is suggesting I continue to keep quiet on the matter.

"How long, Remi?" Jude repeats his question.

I shake my head repeatedly. "Jude…"

A phlegmy cough comes from nearby, and all attention turns to Porter. "Five years," he croaks.

"Shut the fuck up, Porter!" Jude screams. The wail comes out strangled, but the next statement drops to a whisper. "Five years." Spinning toward me again, a menacing growl coats his words. "You have been sleeping with Porter since you were eighteen?!" It's not really a question. Not entirely.

My eyelashes flutter and the muscles in my throat lock tight. Being on the witness stand is so much harder than I anticipated. Jude begins to pace, hand squeezing into the hair at the crown of his head. He then stops, pulls out his phone, dials a number, and holds it up to his ear with a deep, steady breath. "Someone needs medical attention in the bulk storage warehouse at the West Terminal of the PC Port."

"Shit," Crow grinds.

Jude ends the call without saying anything more, turns, walks to his car, opens the door, and slips one foot inside. "This isn't just about business anymore. Now, it's personal." He falls into his seat, shuts the door, and cranks the engine.

Before, the attempt to take over another crew was a strut — a show for attention.

…Now, the entire thing has turned into a grudge match.

CHAPTER THREE

Jude

My intention is not to stick around, but I find myself sitting in the entrance of the warehouse, idling long enough for Remi to make a choice. Even in the swarm of my unstable mind right now, I understand that I never gave her reason to choose me — not tonight and clearly not during the past five years. Ever since Dad died, I have been lost, detached, and self-serving when she needed me most. But for the five years prior? Guess I just had this convoluted idea that, no matter what, I would be the one person she leaned on through thick and thin.

This is one of those thick moments.

The guy with glasses grabs her wrist and tugs her backward. She stumbles a bit, head swiveling between me and his Bimmer. Our eyes meet through the windshield, but something one of the Revelry crew says has her attention snapping over her shoulder again. In this moment, I make the choice for her and throw the car into reverse. Our eyes meet once more and stay locked while I maneuver into a two-point turn and shift to first. There is so much dejection in her features and posture — curved shoulders, trembling bottom lip, red and watery eyes.

Before I can change my mind and make an even bigger mess of tonight, I launch forward and get the hell out of there. If these guys are protecting her — helping her — then she needs to be with them. I might be bordering on insanity, but one fact is clear: I'm the toxic one in this scenario, and I refuse to continue contaminating her.

I need to get my shit together.

For the first time since I started getting that weird feeling in my gut — the one undoubtedly trying to tell me about Porter all along — I know removing myself from her life is the right thing to do.

I will carry on alone, making Lance Industries thrive, moving forward with the plans to put these boys in their place and keep her free and clear of that drama like Dad always wanted. Whether she would admit to it or not, Remi is drawn to the lifestyle like a moth to a flame. By making a name for myself in the area, it assures my influence should keep her removed — just like Dad intended.

Damn, I was a fucking idiot to go along with Porter's plan to bring her into the fold.

He will no longer work with my family or our business.

Most importantly, he will never again touch Remi.

That is a damn guarantee.

CHAPTER FOUR

Remi

As soon as Jude is out of sight, I tug myself out of Hayes's grip, rush up to Porter, and squat to his level. With the amount of blood puddling on and staining the concrete, it's a miracle he was even able to speak a moment ago. Right now, his head lolls to the side, chest heaves, forehead is covered in sweat, and his eyelids are heavy.

I swing a glance over my shoulder and lock eyes with the first guy I see — Trenton. "Grab the shell casing and come help me!" I yell. The three men shift uncomfortably, but Trenton finds the shell, shoves it into his pocket, and jogs over after only a heartbeat of hesitation. Crow and Hayes share a look then jog up behind him, refusing to let Trenton come alone. I get that this is not their scene, and the more involved it becomes the more their uncertainty grows; they might street race, but none of them are warmongers.

Neither am I, but the lingering memory of that night at the LA Port is enough experience for me to understand the implications of Jude's emotional reaction. In a panicked rush, I explain: "Hold him down. I… I need to remove the bullet. Porter likely won't throw us under the bus to the authorities in order to save his own ass from incrimination, but… but… We can't leave any evidence just in case."

I've never done anything like this. I need to save Jude. Save myself. I refuse to give Porter more influence than he already has; the bullet is proof — yet another thing he can use as blackmail.

Trenton takes his shoulders, wedging his already bound hands between the concrete and his lower back. Crow restrains his feet. I grip his jaw, flinging his head upright and bringing us nose to nose. "Embezzlement across states and rape — those are at least two of the wrongs you've done that I can think of right off the line. I am sure there are more, and I intend on doing whatever I can to pin you with everything." His dazed eyes blink rapidly, but he still manages to fix me with an indignant glower.

When I let go of his jaw, his head lolls to the side again. I swallow hard and work my knees between his. The guys remain silently detached while I attempt to tear Porter's jeans at the spot where the bullet hit. My breathing turns choppy and manic and my arms weaken, refusing me the strength to tear the thick fabric. Panic and uncertainty bleeds into my whimper of budding defeat: "I-I don't know what I'm doing."

A hand lands gently on my shoulder and squeezes. "There are too many factors for you to know if this will work or not. If the bullet is in deep, you will need tools. There are too many ways this could go wrong and be fatal." The advice comes from Hayes as he reaches down and rips the fabric for me. Again, a memory of a similar scene tries to pervade my thoughts and strip me from the present, but blaring sirens echoing across the bay kick me back into gear.

"If something does go wrong and he dies on the spot, would that be so terrible?"

My hand launches to my mouth to cover the barrel from which those words were projected.

Oh my God, what am I saying?

"If you're going to do something, do it now. We really need to get out of here," Trenton grinds out, darting a glance through the black windows of the warehouse.

The tips of my fingers and thumb are damp and sticky against my skin; Porter's blood streaks against my cheeks as I slowly uncup my mouth and drop my hand back to his thigh. I give Hayes puppy-dog eyes, my confidence teetering on the edge. He bobs his head in a single, firm nod. I will my breathing to even out with a deep inhale and exhale then push my finger into the bullet hole.

Porter comes to life, every part of him seeming to animate at once: his eyes pop wide, voice screeches, and limbs thrash. Hayes slams his hand over Porter's mouth, preventing the harrowing wail from ringing through the steel structure. Trenton and Crow tighten their grips.

The squish and meaty warmth clenching around the tip of my finger has my breathing returning to erratic and eyes slamming shut. But a small lump snaps me back into focus; I fling my eyes open, suck in a gasp of determination, press my lips together, and curve my finger inward to loop the pad of my index under the lump and wiggle it gently in an upward motion.

Well… gently is entirely subjective, I imagine; Porter might disagree. Our gazes lock. His eyes bug, he blinks, and a tear pops free. The bullet *tinks* against the concrete, echoing through the suddenly overly-quiet warehouse. Porter's glazed attention bounces from my face down toward the bullet and back again. Then, everything stops: his muffled wail, the attempted thrashing, the tension in his muscles.

He passes out cold.

My breathing chugs like a train in my ears.

Muffled voices surround me.

Fingers grip.

Hands tug.

I fall back and am lifted at the whim of whoever is collecting me.

The surrounding din of port activity, the blazing overhead lights, the dead silence from Porter, and the sharp aroma of blood and still-lingering acrid smoke slams back into me — and they all blend with the piercing sound of sirens and red-blue flash of lights.

"D-DID I KILL HIM? Is… is he dead?" I whisper, staring at my blood-soaked hands. Fear, dread, euphoria, relief, sadness, mania — every emotion humans experience amalgamates, twisting my psyche, maddening me to the point where I can scarcely see straight.

The Bimmer drifts hard, and I tip over into…

Blinking repeatedly, I try to make sense of what's happening around me. I had gone so deep in my mind that reality kept fading in and out.

My head tilts back, shoulder smushing into a warm body. Crow. Crow is who I now find myself pressed against. He is worrying at his lip ring, eyes locked on the windshield while Hayes drives. His mind is preoccupied, too — processing the turn of events tonight much like mine keeps doing on repeat. But it doesn't take him long to recognize the contact — that always inappropriate buzz of recognition hums between our bodies.

The worrying of his teeth against his bottom lip turns into a dampening of his tongue as his chrome gaze drops slowly to mine, eyes crazy and wild… similar to the moment before he took me on the hood of his car.

The spiral — his unraveling — is my fault. The guys never asked for me to show up that night at the bar, much less to ultimately be dragged behind the scenes of grey-market dealings.

Just like on the side of Steel Field Road, I grab his face between my palms. "Crow… Hey…" I hush out, brushing my thumbs against his skin.

Only then do I realize the red. So much red. An arch of it transfers from my thumb over the defined line of his cheek. "Oh my God," I heave, dropping my hands back into my lap. Bile creeps up my throat. The buzz between us zaps off like an antique television, giving one final spark before humming into blackness.

"My… Hayes… I have blood all over me. Oh no… Your car!" Even in my lunatic state, I still worry about the condition of their vehicles — a practice that has been ingrained into me since birth. Born and bred. A shaky, psychotic chuckle bubbles between my lips at the realization.

When I seek out Hayes in the rearview mirror, I discover Trenton is actually the one driving; his sepia eyes crinkle in the corners, and he shakes his head in delirious amusement. None of us are in our right minds right now; a diabolical, drunken psychosis, fed by fear and the high of rebellion, figure eights through the car.

Guy by guy, my surrounding spins into focus: The steering wheel practically vibrates under Trenton's white-knuckled grip; Crow's fingers dig into his knees and his chest rapidly rises and falls, his system bordering on hyperventilation; Hayes is in the passenger seat, seemingly oblivious to everything around him as his wide eyes dart through the bundle of papers.

Papers. The stack he has been harboring all evening. In another wave of clarity, I realize that those papers were the catalyst for some of tonight's events. Hayes had mentioned the reasons why they didn't want any information delivered to my brother were in those papers.

What did he find?

Hayes freezes under my scrutiny, the muscles in his shoulders cording and bunching. He gently lays the papers in his lap and smooths them with shaky fingers before angling his chin over his shoulder and looking at me through his glasses. "I need more time," he responds to my unspoken question. I squint at him.

How did he know what I was thinking?

Trenton chuckles, and my attention whips back to the rearview mirror. "Your eyes speak louder than you do sometimes," he explains.

Ah… so Trenton passed the message onto Hayes in that uncannily wordless way that they do. Apparently it works outside of the bedroom, too.

"More… time?" I ask, returning my attention to Hayes.

Hayes swallows hard and his eyebrows curve inward.

My heart plummets.

They don't trust me.

I lost that trust when I submerged these amazing guys too deep into a version of the automotive world in which they don't belong. Whatever Hayes hoped to share, he changed his mind; the truth is in the set of his shoulders, the glassiness of his eyes, and the hard swallows he tries to mask.

I gulp down my shame and disappointment and change my focus to Crow. His elbow is propped on the plastic beneath the rear passenger window, hand splayed over his mouth and jaw. He senses my adjustment, and his eyes slant sideways for a heartbeat but quickly return to the window to watch cars, lights, and signs pass.

With each mile farther away from the port, another blast of clarity hits me — the dreamlike experience quickly fading to my real-life nightmare. The realization of my awaiting situation slams to the forefront; I have nowhere to go. The game of tug of war has abruptly ended with the rope snapping, leaving me alone in the center and grasping for either frayed end. Not because the guys would refuse me shelter — even despite the situation, I know in my heart that none of them would put me out on the streets — but because I can no longer be the reason for the tension force in the rope that caused resistance in the rope to begin with.

I need to distance myself and do what I should have done the first day Porter and Jude forced me into the job. Walk away.

Or, in my case, ride.

"Trenton? Take me to my bike."

CHAPTER FIVE

"A lready on it," Trenton responds, flicking on the blinker and coasting into a smooth stop at the intersection light where I made Porter crash. Now that we've crossed the bridge and are a good enough distance away from the port, he relaxes into the seat.

Trenton had pushed Hayes aside and took it upon himself to drive so Hayes — lost in the distraction of hypotheses and conspiracy — could study those mysterious papers. Seeing Trenton drive the Bimmer makes my thoughts relapse to the night we met. My heart twists at the memory of our conversation about imports versus domestics.

Driving an import doesn't suit Trenton. His very build and mannerisms scream domestic — the hint of his anger earlier an even better partnership for the muscle of his Monte Carlo. I have only been inside his car once — the night we slept together for the first time. The twisting of my heart kinks so tight I fear all the blood will be squeezed out until there's nothing left but lingering drips.

As though Trenton can sense my thoughts, his focus leaves the road occasionally to meet my gaze in the rearview mirror. Every glance holds a question. An uncertainty. An accusation.

The entire car ride, messages are spoken with our eyes.

Please forgive me.

You've given me no reason to trust you.

My feelings are separate from the drama.

So are mine.

I'm sorry.

Me, too.

The car jerking into park so soon comes as an unexpected surprise. My attention finally leaves him and travels out the window. My bike, an ink of black in the navy-blue night, sits parked under the stilted deck. I skip asking how he figured out where I lived, how Porter's car got back into the driveway after the meet, and at what point Crow drove here and parked that V Coupe across the street — the unfamiliar vehicle I saw in the woods off of Steel Field Road just hours ago.

My heart judders as I curl my fingers over the top edge of the driver seat. Trenton avoids my gaze as he steps out and pops it forward so I can exit. His eyes wander the opposite direction of my house — through the line of commercial buildings toward the beach where he had picked me up, noticed the bruise, and helped remove the sand spurs from my shoes.

With one foot out the door, I hesitate.

"Trenton—"

"No." He responds so quickly his word nearly engulfs mine.

My second foot joins the first, and I climb out. He immediately clicks the seat into the upright position and climbs back in. Before he can close the door and close me out completely, I quickly dip down and place my hand over his. Brushes of fabric and the creak of movement paints a vivid picture of Hayes and Crow reacting, finding the interaction interesting enough to adjust in their seats and pay attention. That… or to come to his aid.

I might be walking away, but not like this. Not with that wordless conversation left unfinished. If he drives away right now, our shared emotions going unchecked, there will be no recovery — no closure.

This is my window.

Tonight, while his mind is muddled and confused.

Right now.

The blood on my hands transfers as I push my fingers between his over the steering wheel, giving me a sick sort of fascination. His head falls back against the headrest, and he closes his eyes and takes controlled breaths.

I gently pry his hand off the wheel and pull it toward me, slowly encouraging him out of the car. When his body tips slightly, his eyes shoot open. He tries to yank away, but I tighten my grip. The words,

"Trust me," almost fall from my lips, but I catch the faux pas before it taints the quiet night. "I just want to show you something," I say instead. My eyes dart to Hayes and Crow. As expected, they're both watching. Crow's features are pinched in a scowl of frustration. Hayes is a bit dazed, his opinion of the matter blotted out by the imprint of the papers in his hand and the queue of hypotheses in his head.

One thing they both agree on, albeit without an actual discussion, is that Trenton has to choose; neither of them is going to step in on his behalf. They have their own demons to work through, after all.

Even still, when Trenton's foot slings outside, Crow curses in frustration and throws his head back against the seat.

Turning his head to the side, Trenton addresses Hayes: "She has ten minutes. You two go ahead," he states.

Hayes snaps to full attention. "What? No. We're not leaving you here."

The strain woven into that insistence has nothing to do with me; Hayes is worried about what will happen after my promised ten minutes are over — how Trenton will react when left alone. Where he will go. What he will do.

They share an undecodable look. Hayes's jaw moves over clenched teeth, but he unbuckles his harness nonetheless, slings the passenger door open, tosses the papers onto the dashboard, slams the door shut behind him, and stomps to the driver side. By the time he makes his way around to the driver side, Trenton is completely out of the car, too, his fingers still woven with mine.

Hayes and Trenton stare at each other while Crow remains both physically and emotionally distanced in the backseat, breathing through his stress.

"I will text you in ten minutes and every ten minutes after that. But... I'm good, I promise," Trenton explains.

Hayes adjusts his glasses with the knuckle of his index finger and shifts from foot to foot before giving Trenton a sharp nod.

The two switch places.

Before Hayes shuts the door, though, Trenton's fingers grip the frame, halting it from closing. He then bends down, grasps Hayes's shoulder, fingers biting into his shirt. "But you're required to text me every eight."

The earlier twist in my heart squeezes out those last drops, stealing the rest of my heartbreak. Their devotion to each other is terrifyingly fierce — thicker than blood.

Definitely thicker than anything they built with me.

CHAPTER SIX

Honeyed words have already been spilled and lies amended. Now, I intend to attempt what he and Hayes do best: communicate using cues and actions instead.

With a shaky sigh, I tighten my fingers. Trenton swallows hard and tightly grips my hand. The motion isn't sweet, though; it's a warning.

This is it for you. For us.

We both know tonight is goodbye.

His simple, yet profound, squeeze encourages me to make these minutes count.

I will my heart to untwist and pump again before I end up dropping at his feet and wrapping my arms around his ankles, shaking, crying, and utterly helpless. Turning inward, I seek out that steady *thump, thump* and tug him toward the house, focusing on every beat and matching it to each step up the stairs, onto the deck, and through the sliding glass door.

Under normal circumstances, I might have stopped to give him a quick tour of the fireplace room, kitchen, and office. But we race past everything en route to my bedroom. I have been given ten minutes, and this plan will take every second.

When we do get to my room, I pause and take a slow, recovery breath. I fight with the images — the memories — stepping across the threshold into this space always brings. Most of the time this room is not a sanctuary. It is a cell — a locked car when you want to be riding uncaged and wide open.

The walls and surfaces are bare.

No decorations.

No pictures.

Nothing that gives the space my personality.

That day I dropped the box of photographs of my father all over the closet floor and Porter came in to "help" mend my broken heart, I decided not to let him muck up anything wonderful and special to me.

What if I accidentally opened my eyes while he was ramming his cock inside me and my gaze fell on a smiling image of my father and Jude? What if the purple-blacklight glow of my favorite neon sign was the color stamped through my eyelids while they were tightly shut? Porter was ruining me, but I wouldn't let him ruin the few things in my life that brought me happiness and a sense of love. For that reason, all the important stuff remained in boxes, carefully stacked in my closet.

Time dwindling, I don't make an effort to explain any of these musings to Trenton. If I can feel the claustrophobia just by stepping across the threshold, he surely senses that debilitating energy, too. When I finally find the courage to look up at him, my worry as to whether or not he would feel it like I do, drains away. His eyes scan the emptiness and unmade bed, throat bobbing tightly around an excruciatingly slow swallow.

Together, our eyes fall to the digital clock on my bedside table. Usually, I seek solace in its numbers and the passing of time. Tonight, the numbers threaten to change far too quickly.

Still barefoot — having lost my heels in the woods before running to stop Jude from doing something unforgivable to Crow — I rush to my closet and slip on my Converses.

Trenton watches curiously as I begin my reenactment of the night we met. Just like that first night, I propel myself out of the window and onto the shed's roof and work my way down the side of the wooden privacy fence. I arch my head back to seek out Trenton. As hoped, he is bent out of the window, looking down at me. I wave a hand in a beckoning motion, turn away, and start walking slowly along the fenceline.

Curiosity is a difficult desire to refuse. Tonight, I use it in my favor. Instead of waiting on Trenton, I focus on my breathing and the sinking of my shoes in the sandy ground so that I am not tempted to dart a glance over my shoulder.

Soon enough, I hear a whispered curse on a wisp of gulf breeze immediately followed by the clang of his feet hitting the metal roof, the scuffs of him going down the fence, and the light *plunk* of him landing on the soft ground.

I navigate around the perimeter until we are back at the front of the house and approaching the street, my heartbeat thudding in my head like bass hitting in a compact car.

The Bimmer is no longer here.

Not too long after my shoes switch from sandy ground to solid asphalt, the steps behind me grow louder as they pick up speed. Trenton chooses to keep a short distance between us, not stepping up to my side and grabbing my hand or any chivalrous action of that sort. But he is still with me, and that is what matters most.

Knowing my time is still being tracked, what with his promise to Hayes and vice versa, I pick up the pace. At the first stop sign, I take a right. Then, I come to a full stop at the next one.

When we get to the main street a block over, at the corner store where Hayes dropped me off the day he gave me a grand tour of the area, a lone car — some late-night bar patron likely leaving at closing — halts our ability to cross. This time, Trenton does stop beside me.

I dare a glance up at his face. His eyes are trained on the hotel ahead of us, gaze tracing the letters of the sign. The Regency. He blinks a couple times, his recognition of my silent pantomime slowly budding.

As soon as the car passes, I take his hand and rush us across the road to the lot where he parked the Monte Carlo the night we met. Also just like that night, his car is sitting in the lot. Seeing his car gives me pause, and I stop midstep. Obviously, I didn't anticipate that part.

My attention flashes to him. The movement of my head draws his gaze down to mine. We still don't exchange words, though. His face loses all its color, and his palm becomes damp against mine.

Later. If I miraculously manage to earn an extension, I will ask why his car is parked here, why he blanched, and about all his feelings. But right now, the minutes are still ticking. My time is running short, and I still need to drive this charade home.

Pretending his Monte Carlo isn't here — that he doesn't have an easy escape — I continue, dragging him forward with the slight tug of my hand and brush of my thumb against the knuckles that are now cutting off the circulation to my fingers. He is low-key losing his mind right now. Silently. Excruciatingly. Part of me wonders if his death grip on my hand is also keeping him upright.

Perhaps my physical monologue is already working. Perhaps my wordless performance is getting through to him better than my spoken words ever could.

Not taking any chances, I continue using every last millisecond of this borrowed time to my advantage. When we stop at the end of the small path leading to the beach, he wiggles our fingers apart, removes his shoes, and rolls up the legs of his jeans. While I know he would take off his shoes so as not to later track sand into his car, this time, I can tell the action is because he is on to my plan.

Instead of being an audience member, he has decided to become a supporting lead, helping me recreate the scene.

Keeping my shoes on, we continue forward, walking toward the shore.

I tug Trenton down onto the sand, and he settles beside me.

His phone dings with a message notification — what I assume must be eight minutes on the dot. He immediately takes it out, checks the message, and returns it to his pocket.

Two minutes left. Heart rate taking the opposite course it took earlier, it speeds up to an almost unbearable pace now. With as much steady calmness as I can manage, I push off the ground and dust my hands off. Once he is standing, too, our hands reconnect. I appreciated his touch the first night, but tonight, I hold on a little tighter and appreciate it a little more. Because if this doesn't work, as soon as we get to the end of the walkway, he will leave. These moments are the final act before the curtain drops.

I rush us through the clingy sand, mentally counting down from one-hundred-twenty, if only to keep me from going mad. Plus, maybe if I count extra slow, my time will extend.

We make it to the edge in record time, collecting his shoes along the way. There, I sit, but instead of taking off my own shoes to painstakingly remove the collected sand spurs, I reach over and slowly remove one of his shoes from his hooked fingers.

The first reactive sound of the entire experience meets my ears — a quiet exhalation of breath. A restricted gasp.

One-by-one, I begin removing the sand spurs that he'd collected following me around the perimeter of my unlandscaped back yard.

For now, he continues playing my game, sitting beside me and beginning to work through the spurs on the other shoe.

When he drops his shoe and pulls his phone out to text Hayes, I'm not done. The scene isn't over. My fingers work furiously to remove all of the spurs before he finishes sending the text. But it doesn't work. I'm too late. I took too long.

When he sets the phone down in his lap, I can no longer see. Hot, salty, aggressive tears blur my vision. Spurs stick into my thumb and finger, little drops of blood mixing with Porter's dried blood. Tears drip down my nose. A sob shakes my chest. I clench my hand, curling my fingers over the collar of his unsalvaged shoe.

When I open my eyes to toss my failed attempt aside, he is no longer sitting beside me.

Instead, he is kneeling in front of me, his head bent over my feet, fingers deftly removing the spurs from my Converses.

I open my mouth and a quiet squeak slips, but he continues without so much as a quick glance up at me.

The play that was mine, turns into his.

I finish pulling the last few spurs from his shoe and nudge it aside. Then, I bring my hands down to his to help finish tidying my laces.

"Damn. Were you swimming in the dunes or something?" he whispers, repeating word-for-word what he asked me that first night.

That night, I manipulated the truth. Tonight, I refuse. "Ah, not quite," I respond. "I snuck out to protect myself from getting caught spending time with this amazing guy I met. The perimeter of my back yard is riddled with them."

His sepia eyes flick up to mine. I swallow hard, knowing what question comes next as though I wrote the script — not just memorized the lines.

"What happened to your cheek?" he asks low. My heart does a triple flip upon learning he memorized the lines, too.

"My brother's best friend, family business partner... and my ex-boyfriend... hit me," I admit aloud for the first time — to anyone.

Trenton sucks in a breath, his gaze lifting to mine. My eyes widen. Neither of us anticipated this part — the part where I don't actually lie. That first night, I jokingly blamed it on a foolish mix of drinking and bicycle riding. The admission tonight is freeing, but that doesn't stop a rush of adrenaline from shaking through my limbs on account of such an outward revelation.

Questions swim in his sepia eyes, but he fights against asking them, having reached a limit of luck that he doesn't want to press. For that, I am grateful.

When we're done cleaning our shoes, his fingers brush against mine as he stands. Trenton extends his hand out toward me, offering me the first lifeline all night. I accept, and he pulls me up. He doesn't stop the trip down memory lane there, though. Eyes locked with mine, he reaches forward, lightly brushes his thumb against the ghost of that bruise, and says, "You look different than you did that night at the bar."

Just like the first time he said that, my stomach flips uncomfortably. "Better or worse?" I ask breathlessly.

"There still isn't anything better," he whispers, eyes dropping to my mouth.

My head and mind sway with the dizzying déjà vu.

Not too long after the original rendition of that comment, I told him to put his flowery words into a vase — to take me home with him. And he did.

This time, though, he rewrites the script: "The flowers died, Remi. You forgot to water them."

CHAPTER SEVEN

Dizziness consumes me and I sway on the spot, blinking wildly to reset my equilibrium and clear the building tears in my eyes. We stand there in silence while I try to recover and come to terms with what his analogy means: my lack of judgement and responsibility cost me something beautiful.

I have no idea which version of myself I should be right now: The cowering, frightened, often distraught one? Or the confident, strong one?

The latter, I decide. The weak, messy Remi was reserved for Porter, and I had packed up her stuff and moved her out already.

With a final blink, I lock my gaze on his and give a curt nod.

Okay. I understand.

Does that mean I give up?

Nope.

I open my mouth to tell him there's an entire gulf of water behind us — that I'll collect buckets full of fertile saltwater and bring the flowers back to life or grow some new ones — but his voice beats mine. "Stop," he whispers, his forehead dropping to mine.

No more apologies.

No more trips down memory lane.

Our replay is over; this is now an improv.

Eyes closed, I inhale deeply, breathing in as much of him as possible.

He pulls his head away, and my lashes flutter open, eyes meeting his light-brown ones as they flick between mine. His fingers slip through the length of my hair, lift it, and his gaze drops to study the strands. While his body moves on autopilot, his mind is on everything other than the color or the feel of my hair — thinking, assessing, debating. What, exactly, I am unsure.

The shoes he is holding drop to the ground, and his hand grasps one of mine. "My car has been parked here since before we caught up with Crow in the woods near the meet," he states, clearing the emotion from his voice and returning to the matter of the clusterfuck of events in the past twenty-four hours or so. "Tonight… you need an alibi in case Porter tries to throw you under the bus." His eyes scan my body before lifting my hand and studying my blood-coated fingers. "And you need to get cleaned up."

Part of me is thankful for the change of subject. Yet a different part of me is envious at his ability to so easily drop this thing between us and get back to business.

He tugs me onto the walkway again and keeps tugging until we hit the sandy path. "You were with me. All night. From the moment I parked here," he instructs, fabricating an alibi while continuing toward the shore. "We'll both clean up here, but you should probably burn your clothes in case any of his blood got on them. As it stands, you touched the doors and window in your house. If he dies from blood loss, Jude never touched him — you did. You have his blood on your clothes. I have his blood on my clothes. Hayes and Crow..." His words are rushed and somewhat manic, but they trail. Once we hit the more compact, damp sand, he stops — the still and quiet surface of the endless gulf spread before us. He pulls in a lungful of salty air, turns to me, and with a choked voice says, "Remi... I'm not ready to forget you yet."

How do I respond?

Words didn't fix anything.

Begging won't change things.

My tears were enough to prove I don't want this to end either — my reenactment enough of a show. But I won't seduce, manipulate, or guilt him just to appease my own desires.

I want to say a number of things: I understand. Give me another chance. Sorry.

The words get stuck, however, and I say nothing while his hands move to the collar of my leather jacket. Gently, he slips each side off my shoulders.

His phone dings, nearly blending with the crash of a small wave and effervescence of bubbles lapping at the shore near our feet. He finishes removing my jacket and tosses it to the side before digging out the device and reading Hayes's check-in text. Unlike the last check-in, he responds immediately. Composing the message takes time. Occasionally, his eyes dart up to mine, face illuminated by the screen.

When he is done and the phone is returned to his pocket, I don't question why my nice leather jacket is on the sandy ground. What happens next is up to him — the reason, if harsh, inconsequential. Trenton might not trust me, but I trust him.

He steps back, crosses his arms, and stares down at the sand, toes curling into the fluff. "Undress," he states quietly.

My eyebrows rise sky-high, but his attention is too focused on the moonlight-illuminated sand to notice. I toe off my shoes, kick them to the side, unbutton and unzip my jeans, and untuck my black camisole. I opt to wriggle out of my jeans instead of my cami first, unsure what exactly is going on beyond executing our false alibi. The built-in bra and length of the tank offers my otherwise braless chest and bare ass a modicum of modesty.

Once my jeans have joined my jacket and shoes in the sand, I meet his gaze again, standing before him in nothing but my camisole and g-string.

His arms unwrap, hands drop to his sides, and fingers curl loosely into his palms. I resist the urge to mimic his earlier action by crossing my own arms over my torso to give myself more cover. The silent hesitation only lasts a couple more seconds before his hands whip to the hem of his shirt, rip it over his head in one quick motion, and he strips off his jeans and boxers — an act that took half the time it took me, yet leaves him completely unclothed.

I'm still unsure why we are taking these extra steps, but one thing I do know for certain is that seeing him this way is difficult — naked with shadows and reflective light highlighting and shading every part of him just right. Our connection was physical from the moment we laid eyes on each other, and that dynamic hasn't changed; he hasn't suddenly become a hideous creature just because he won't forgive me.

For that reason and so many more, when his eyes lock on mine and he offers me a hand, I accept it, slotting my fingers between his. And when he pads toward the water, thumb dragging lightly across the ghost of my lost string ring, I know without any doubt that if he pushes me under... I'll sink willingly.

CHAPTER EIGHT

Trenton doesn't pressure me to undress further, and I choose to keep what remaining clothes I have on to act like a bathing suit. If this is still only about alibis, the proof is mostly on my top layers anyway. Considering the repercussions of such a thing, I find my voice and whisper, "Leave your shirt and jeans here. I'll take care of them. Last thing you want to do is put them in your car."

He nods but otherwise doesn't say anything as the water kisses our toes.

The gulf is way cooler than my body temperature, causing goosebumps to cover me from head to toe and my jaw to clamp down at the contact. Part of the reaction is from the chill, but most is from nerves. When we get to about hip deep, Trenton tugs me to face him. I keep my eyes on the undulating water between us.

My body trembles slightly, and I lift my arm from the water to wrap it around my torso for protection — both from Trenton and the cold — but he slips his thumb under my palm and raises my hand to about shoulder level, displaying my bloodied skin to the moonlight like a sacrifice. He then lines up the pads of each of our fingers, creating a steepled triangle for a breath before pressing our palms together and entwining his fingers between mine.

Generally, I enjoy how he and Hayes silently communicate, but I prefer his jokester persona over this mysterious and intimidating one. Maybe Porter has something to do with that: The unknowing. The multiple personalities. How he could be sweet with the gentlest touch one minute, then extend his claws the next.

Fear and a resulting need to react — to survive — doesn't kick in with Trenton, though. A fear exists but only within my overactive thoughts. My body disagrees. Entirely. Even the simplicity of how delicately he squeezes my hand in his and studies the size difference and how they fit together, makes my center coil tightly.

Trenton twists our palms so the back of my hand is now facing him. His light-brown eyes eclipse, darkening as he adjusts and removes his fingers from mine to cup my hand instead. He runs his thumb over my knuckles and eyebrows curve inward.

Only then do I realize where his thoughts led.

My string ring.

If the moonlight wasn't already paling my skin, the new, reactive pallidness would be visible. This must be the first time he has realized it is gone, all of us too distracted by the events at the port.

My eyes lock on his.

Ask me, I wordlessly beg.

The deepening curve of his eyebrows tells me he already came to his own conclusion, though.

I shake my head and, no longer able to keep quiet, squeak out, "I-it broke."

"Yeah…" He sighs. "I never expected it to last as long as it did."

I-is he speaking in analogy still? Or literally?

The thought of the former has acid creeping up through my insides into my throat.

"Trenton…"

Goddammit.

I have no idea what to say or do or think.

How to behave.

What move to make.

Nothing.

His eyes move back to our cupped hands, and he dips them below the surface. His thumb begins rubbing along my palm, over each digit, to the back of my hand, then between each finger. Each circular stroke becomes more and more aggressive. After a time, he lifts my hand again and reassesses. No more blood. He then lets go and takes my other hand in both of his, dips it into the water between us and begins cleaning that one, too. This hand has more blood on it as it's the hand with which I dug out the bullet and the fingers the sand spurs pricked.

Watching the red bleed and swirl into the dark water between us, I find it difficult to ignore the bobbing of his cock against the surface, partially erect as though even his primal instinct can't decide if the animal in front of him is something he should avoid or dominate.

The unknowing in this moment is maddening. I still ache to do and say a number of things but am frozen with uncertainty that anything I do or say will only make matters worse.

Unable to cope, I close my eyes and give myself over. Submit. I stop worrying. Kinda like when Porter tosses me on the bed and I shut down. My breaths go from slightly increased to shallow and long. I focus on the lap of the water as it rhythmically ripples against my stomach. I will the goosebumps on my skin to subside, using the imagery of each one retreating to redirect my whirlpool of thoughts.

When Trenton finally speaks, his voice is a mere whisper: "Goddammit, Remi."

All the thoughts and worries I tried to overcome rush back over me like an unexpected, billowing wave. On the cusp of drowning, my breath catches.

A mix of cool and warm meets my face. The tickle of saltwater dribbles down the column of my neck while the pressure of his thumb and fingers depress on and around my chin to tilt my head back. His hot body comes next. That semi-erect cock from a moment ago has hardened more and now nudges against my lower belly. My throat trembles around a swallow, and my closed eyes leak a couple rogue tears.

"It wasn't supposed to be this way. You were never supposed to be more than a quick lay." His voice steadily turns into a soft growl. "I want you, dammit. Quick, slow, sometimes, all the time, hard, gentle, daytime, nighttime."

Weak of mind and heart, I keep my eyes closed, unable to engage. I become a sieve — his to pour in whatever he wishes, but only willing to collect the good bits, allowing the rest to sift through and disappear into a sea of loneliness.

After the first shake, though, the sieve empties, and nothing good remains: "But my loyalties aren't with you — they never were."

Despite understanding, the words still sting. No… not sting… stab. Ache. Debilitate. For the first time since he led me into the water, I give him something: a single, tight nod.

I hear and respect you.

I understand.

Do what you must.

Finish breaking my heart, but do it quickly.

Should I stand here much longer, I just might float away and never return.

And he does exactly that… with the press of his lips against mine.

One of finality.

Of completion.

His tongue slips between my lips and locks itself into my memories in an instant.

Him letting me go and wading away would have been so much easier.

CHAPTER NINE

Trenton sidesteps a few times, maneuvering us slightly closer to the shore — just enough to where his cock is no longer drowned in the salty current.

With a quick dip he bends, pushes my g-string over, slips between my thighs, and slides inside me. Then he wades us deeper and deeper until the salty water sways around my shoulders and splays my hair. "Open your eyes," he whispers.

I shake my head faster than I can process the demand; I can't look at him. Not like this. "Do it, Remi." He lifts and descends me on his cock.

"Please…"

Not *no*.

Not *why*.

But *please*.

A plea for leniency.

He keeps one hand tucked under my butt for support, letting the buoyancy of the water help suspend me. With the other hand, he drags a wet thumb across my eyebrow. "One more time. That's all I can give — all I can handle. Don't break my heart even more by shutting me out."

Water trickles down my temple until it meets with one of the very tears I had tried to barricade behind my closed eyes. My eyelashes, clinging with the salty mix, flutter open. Dark-brown locks with light-brown. With that comes another thrust — and another crank of the vice tightening around my heart. Our foreheads meet with the next thrust. On the one after, I roll my hips, engaging in the partnership — turning it from one to two.

Trenton groans. One hand squeezes my ass, the other peels the hair clinging to my shoulders away so he can access the back of my neck with his chilled fingers.

The word "why" plays on the tips of our tongues. I can taste his need to inquire about my betrayal. My secrets. And I counter it with a wordless why of my own:

Why won't you forgive me?
Take me... yes...
But keep me.
As-is.
Secrets and all.

But the answers dance in our kiss, too; this is how it has to be. He has shit to work through. I have even more shit to work through. Our interests, other than the one in which we're presently involved, don't align. He needs space. And I do, too.

But for tonight, we need this.

This temporary life raft.

A taste of forgetfulness.

Right now, we both need a one-night stand to take our minds off the things plaguing our real life grind. We need the temporary promise of happiness and pleasure, just like we did the night we met.

A small wave rises and falls over my shoulders. With the current, all our *what ifs* and *what nexts* drift away. As though he came to the same conclusion, his lips drop to my mouth and tongue slithers around mine like a lick of water creeping onto the shore.

My black camisole sticks to my body, adhered by the salty epoxy. The shirt that was, only moments ago, offering me protection, now feels too restrictive. I break our kiss and slip my hands between us to peel off my cami. Trenton helps by keeping us from sliding apart. Uncaring about the fate of said top, I simply toss it into the deep.

When my focus returns to him, his eyes are absorbing what extra skin is now revealed. He adjusts again, taking us a bit shallower, just enough to expose my breasts to the night instead of keeping them hidden beneath the surface of the water. Taking each of my hands, he drapes them over his shoulders before slipping a hand between my breasts and up to my neck, encouraging my head back into the black water and my torso to bend into an incline. Positioned just so, his mouth drops to my breasts, teeth immediately clamping onto the puckered flesh.

My fingernails dig into the muscles where his neck and shoulders meet. His fingertips press against the soft flesh of my neck, and his tongue flicks at my saltwater-dampened nipples. My eyes flutter closed, and a vibrating moan cycles through me as I raise my hips to accept him more, chasing the friction. His mouth leaves my breast as he wraps his hand around to the back of my neck, and he lifts me forward to bring our foreheads together and plunge at a new angle, submersing himself completely.

I circle my hips and buck, pursuing my release, so I can give him his. We'd finished together every time before, but this time he won't let go in that way — not without protection. His breathing hitches and chest heaves around attempted, but failed, controlled breaths. The corners of his eyes crinkle and nose scrunches up, his face contorting in a pleasure he wants... but refuses. I orgasm in silence, like the whisper of a retreating wave as it skitters away from the bank and back into the gulf so it can build again later.

Trenton's fingers squeeze the back of my neck. His breath hitches against my mouth. I bring my hands to his chest, push off him, and balance on my toes in order to keep my shoulders above water. Then, I dip my hands down into the water, trailing my palms along every groove and ridge of his build until my fingers can wrap around him. He immediately grinds into my grip, and his head falls back, the moonlight blazing against his features. With lips slightly parted, a low, rumbling groan escapes from deep in his chest as I grasp harder and stroke faster.

Even the build of his own release doesn't stop him from being able to keep his hands off me. They drift and cling everywhere possible, seeking a handhold, memorizing all of me by touch.

With one more partnered downward stroke and upward thrust, his cock trembles under my fingers, his groan of release whispers in my ears. When there's no more fluid left to add to the unending gulf, he caves forward, his forehead landing on my shoulder and arm wrapping around my waist so I no longer have to support myself on my toes.

Just like every experience with Trenton, he gave this one his all. There was no cutting corners. No rushing. Together we built a memory that will not soon — if ever — be forgotten.

Except in this memory, I didn't fall asleep in his bed. And I didn't wake up to Hayes's pour over coffee.

When we are done, I sneak away.

This time, he watches me go.

CHAPTER TEN

Trenton

Watching her walk away and not offering her a ride or even to walk her home goes against my personal policies. Sure, I bring women into my bed, but I'm still a gentleman enough to see them out of it, too.

Damn, I wanted to pull out a blanket, sit on the shore, and tell her everything — explain why that was it for us. The same reflection in her eyes ended me, though.

Shoulders straight and chin raised, she left just as much as I let her go.

The separation was equal parts mutual and dreaded.

Like a coward, I watch from neck deep in the gulf as she swims to the shore, the moonlight hitting all the right places and revealing inch by inch as she slowly steps out. She then wrenches into her jeans, slides her jacket on over bare breasts, and… just walks away without a single glance over her shoulder. Her strength and determination as she takes every bit of it in stride is what tears me up inside the most. No tears. No begging. No cattiness. I would say there was absolutely no fight in her, but there was. "Fight" is the very definition of this woman who ripped me open, gripped my heart, and manually pumped it back to life. Pumped a shit ton of blood to my cock, too, but that is always an easy feat.

I wait until she's completely out of sight before returning to the beach myself. Water dripping off me and onto the sand, I bend for my jeans first to dry my hands and text Hayes. I told him everything was fine and that I needed more than ten minutes, but I still expected a text from him every eight minutes to be waiting for me when I checked in again.

Crow, Hayes, and I have a lot in common; our depression and anxiety being a chronic illness due to shitty pasts is the highlight of our shared qualities. Not just any type of depression, though. The dangerous type. We depend on each other to make sure none of us spiral. Remi swindled her way into our hearts, and the club — the only other 'girl' who owns us — was put at risk.

Damn, we have all the feels for her, but that in no way trumps what this club means to us. It is literally our lifeline and the lifeline of so many other members, too. An escape. A way to "feel" when all we want is to do anything but — trading one dangerous thing for another.

Depression for adrenaline.

A few check-ins from Hayes shine bright on my phone in the surrounding blackness. I scrub some of the wetness out of my hair, toss the phone onto my shirt, and wrangle my boxers over my damp legs. Then, I pick up the phone and send him a quick response so he knows everything is okay.

I receive an immediate response back:

:Hayes: Get her pregnant, and we're really going to have issues.

Yeah... he knows me better than I know myself most days.

:Me: She doesn't have anything to worry about, but the fish might. Watch out ladies, they're swimming toward ya.

:Hayes: Seriously, bro? I was kidding. You couldn't keep it reeled in at least this once?

:Me: Hey, what can I say? I'm a man of my word. Promised her a Sex on the Beach, and I delivered. Now she can't say I owe her anything. Catch and release, my man. Catch and release.

Damn. The truth of that burns the lining in my throat and down into my stomach.

I clench my phone, having nowhere else to carry it since I'm leaving my clothes here, trusting her enough to at least follow through with the task of making them disappear — but not enough to not come back here in an hour or so and make sure she followed through.

The feel of my boxers sticking to my skin is uncomfortably similar to how her slick body clung against mine in the gulf. Those sensations still linger against every one of my nerve endings, heightened by the weight of the material.

When I get back to the lot, the Bimmer is parked beside my Monte Carlo. Hayes — the damn voyeur — probably used binoculars or something to watch everything go down between Remi and me.

I take my time making my way over to our vehicles, first stopping at the edge of the walkway to dust off my feet and get my socks and shoes on. As I hop on one foot to slip the opposite one into the sock, a sharp prick resonates through the ball of my bare foot and shoots up my leg. I immediately crumple over, hand darting out to the railing for support. I lift my foot and rest it across my bent knee. A sand spur. Goddamn I hate those things.

My eyes travel from my foot to the spot where I was standing. There sits the pile of them — the ones we had just removed from our shoes. I pinch a spine between my too-short nails and yank hard. After flicking it into the dunes on the other side of the railing, I plop down onto my ass on the last step and finish putting on my socks and shoes.

Another bout of déjà vu hits, and I squeeze my eyes shut tight, only to have her image flash behind my closed eyelids, too.

Sonuvabitch.

My eyes pitch open. I push up to stand and meander over to the Bimmer. Problem is, looking at Hayes these days tends to conjure images of her between us. Looking at Crow sure as shit doesn't help either.

Speaking of, I wrongfully assumed that Hayes was dropping Crow off a bit ago, since the V Coupe was parked across from Remi's driveway. But that's not the case; I spot the outline of his profile through the backseat window. Hayes probably diagnosed him as unfit to drive and was likely now at the receiving end of his gloominess.

My head pounds just thinking about where everything turned — how the three of us ultimately ended up convening here, in the beach access parking by the Regency across from where she lives. I still don't know what the fuck happened that brought Crow to her house or how he ended up riding with Jude and Porter after having stalked Remi to their meet.

Similar to a scene played out right here a couple hours ago, I wrench the Bimmer's passenger door open and plop down into the bucket seat. The loose clips of the harness dig into my bare back. Hayes takes in my attire — nothing more than the odd combination of boxers, socks, and shoes — and he fights against a tight-lipped smile.

"She steal your clothes like she stole your heart?" A lovely ray of sunshine bursts through the dark cloud in the backseat.

When I parked here earlier, before all hell broke loose, I knew nothing more except that Remi lived over here somewhere — but not exactly where. Parking in our original rendezvous location was my only hope considering my text messages to her were going unread.

Desperate to prove to Crow that Remi was home and not betraying us, I sat here for a while, listening for the rattle of her Duc and watching for the single headlight to appear—leaving it to Hayes to manage the rest of the Dine & Dash.

I would have waited here all night and on into the morning until I saw her if it wasn't for Crow's video chat ringing through.

Crow proved me wrong.

While I waited here, high on hope, he was there, catching her red-handed.

Does that mean I am ready to give him the game point? To outwardly admit he was right all along? Hell no. He can sit in here and fill the car with all the smugness he wants. Whatever.

I didn't know it at the time, but Hayes left the Golden Ticket event immediately, too, and was pulling the same stunt I was but from the store catty-corner from here, where she insisted they meet the first day they hung out together. As soon as he realized where I was, he crossed the street. I ditched the Carlo, hopped into the Bimmer, and watched the night unfold like a real-life horror movie right before my very eyes.

As soon as we found her in the woods, hostage to both sides of a club war, Crow insisted we pull a deeper search on her and proceeded to do so right there on the spot from his phone while we waited for Remi to finish talking to Jude. Hayes stepped out to encourage her into the car, leaving me to attempt finding the information Crow wanted: her actual address.

Hayes had been trying not to pull too many personal details about Remi while attempting to study up on Jude and Porter, so for a long time he refused to pry in that way. Last night, after she betrayed us, Crow insisted.

"You know what isn't lining up for me?" I adjust to my hip and look at him over the shoulder of the seat. "Why you went to her house to begin with, and why the hell you showed up at the port in the Skyline. You sure Remi is the one we should be wary of? That cloud of yours is throwing a lot of damn shade, Crow."

He leans forward, elbows on his knees. "I was looking for her cell phone. Noticed the one she was using in the woods was different. Jude was there for the same reason. I got to it before him and used it as blackmail to keep an eye on the two of them. He ended up needing a little help with Porter, and I was happy to oblige." Crow's eyes spark and his hands clench between his knees.

That explains the beating Porter took.

There is a ton of heat, dredged from our past, piping between Crow and me that promises to explode before the sun rises. But for now, I hold up a fist to bump his in appreciation. He accepts the gesture, and our knuckles meet briefly.

Unlike Crow, I am able to keep my smugness contained. I read between all those lines. He is just as stupid for her as I am. Going out of his way to find her cell phone? Crow was grasping at straws, looking for anything to back up her claims so he could find it in his cold, black heart to forgive her.

I readjust in the seat, facing forward again, but mid-motion a piercing glare from Hayes shocks me frozen. His gaze drags from me to Crow and back again. He clears his throat and adjusts his glasses. "While you were fucking around in the gulf and Crow was being all detached and morose, I made an executive decision: her involvement with us ended the moment she left the lot. All of us. She's too damn reckless; we need to stay out of her lane."

CHAPTER ELEVEN

W hile Trenton was screwing around with Remi — saying his goodbyes — and Crow was lost in his own world in the backseat of my car, I shoved the papers into my glovebox. Nobody is ready for the extra digging or the revelations it will take to understand and piece together what I found — or *thought* I found. Not even me.

Imports. Signatures. Company officers. The details are all archived in digital files. Everything is black and white. But even so, all the facts together don't make sense. Big chunks of information are missing.

When Trenton pops the box to get out a few napkins to wipe off with, the blood in my veins congeals. It takes a shit ton of effort not to react by reaching over and slamming the compartment shut. Of course, if I did that, Trenton's curiosity would be triggered, and he'd start digging in there. Thankfully, he simply pushes under the papers, grabs what he needs, and closes it.

I release a slow exhale, resting my head against my window. Unfortunately, I don't catch the drag of my palm against the back of my neck in time. Trenton shoots me a look, hand suddenly locked on the latch of the glovebox. I sit up straight again, curve my hands over the wheel, and work through the twitch of my fingers as I refuse the itch to tap them.

"Need a ride, Crow? Hayes can follow while I drive you and the V Coupe home," Trenton says, side-eyeing me closely.

Crow snaps out of his silent daze. "Fuck no. You're not getting in her car."

Ah shit.

Here we go.

The moment Trenton sat in the passenger seat, mostly naked, and Crow just had to open his damn mouth, the tight space filled with flames like the burner being lit under my gooseneck kettle.

Trenton whips around in the seat and grips the headrest so tight his knuckles turn white; I fear he will tear the damn thing off its poles. "How many fucking times do I have to tell you that I'm not my brother!"

Crow nods over and over again, madly. "You're fucking her. Tell me how that's not your brother."

Trenton's face turns so red it borderlines the abstract purple of my paint. He lets go of the headrest and slams his fist against his bare chest. "Me! I fucked her first! If anyone should get pissy about lies and cheating, it should be me. Because you fucking knew, Burke. You knew how I felt about her. So what was that night on Steel Field with Remi really about? Getting back at Travis? Is that it? I. Am. Fucking. Tired. Of. Apologizing. For. Something. I. Didn't. Fucking. Do!"

I sit in silence, hands still wrapped around the wheel despite the fact we've simply been idling for the past thirty minutes or so, waiting to make sure Remi left her house before driving back over there to get the V Coupe.

The entire time, that kettle heated.

Now, it hisses and whistles.

I watch Crow in the rearview mirror. Both his hands push through his hair, fingers twisting and pulling deep near the root, eyes squeezed shut tight.

My attention darts to Trenton. His chest heaves, but he takes in Crow's nervous breakdown and wavers… just a little. He drops his voice. "Listen to me, Crow. Listen good. Because this is the last time I'm going to say it. I'm sorry. I'm sorry my brother fucked up. I'm sorry I'm related to him. I'm sorry I look like him. I'm sorry she—I'm… sorry. I am so fucking sorry. For all of it. But you know what I am *more* than sorry?" Crow opens his eyes and glares at him. "Tired. Tired of serving his goddamn purgatory. Tired of walking on eggshells around you. I am so damn tired. Consider your crew two instead of three. I'm out. You never fully accepted me anyway. Not after what happened."

That's where my passive presence ends. "Wait, what? Trent—" The passenger door opens and closes so fast I can't even finish what I was going to say.

"Good fucking riddance," Crow scoffs.

"Get out. Get the fuck out, Crow." My patience has reached its max. With both of them.

"My pleasure," he responds, yanking up the passenger seat lever, slinging the door open, and hauling himself out.

Hands still gripping the wheel, I watch Trenton peel out in his Monte Carlo and Crow slink off across the main road. At this point, I hope and pray Remi already left and somehow we missed seeing her leave.

I give Crow enough time to get over there before putting the Bimmer in gear and heading in that direction, too. Cocky bastard can drive himself home — but not without an escort.

As soon as I turn onto her road, I flick on my brights and spot his outline just as he's finagling the door handle of the car that served as the fuel for the explosive argument between my two closest friends. He freezes under the blinding gleam, looks straight at me with squinty eyes, and gives me the middle finger.

Chuckling, I turn off the brights and wait. He can't exactly stop me, so he defaults to acting like he just got his license yesterday: flinging the dirt from the ditch as he skids out of there, rear end fishtailing on the asphalt once the dirt releases his tires, only for him to have to come to an almost immediate stop at a stop sign.

Much to his exasperation, I'm sure. I patiently wait for the squeal of another burnout. But surprisingly, he stays. Instead, he turns his lights off entirely for a few seconds before turning them back on and rolling through the stop sign, instead of turning left.

Unsure the reason for this strange behavior, I follow suit, turning my lights off and inching forward to the stop sign. Leaning over the wheel, I check out the intersecting road. The culprit is revealed right away: Remi lifts her feet and leans into the turn at the next stop sign.

I roll through in pursuit of Crow, but the sneaky bastard is gone, having taken advantage of the lack of backroad lights and my distraction. With his lights off, the black of the car blends in the night.

CHAPTER TWELVE

Remi

I curtail my thoughts with each task: Carefully changing my clothes without touching any bloodied items on anything; Wiping down any surfaces I may have touched in the house earlier; Bundling everything into a used grocery bag.

A fly on the wall might think I am cleaning up after a murder.

Hell, would it be surprising if Porter somehow faked his death and pinned it on me? A smart damsel should never underestimate the element of surprise after all. Surprise is dangerous. The best move would be for me to start seeing things in a range of colors. Every shade of grey imaginable, too. With that thought, for all intents and purposes, as far as I am concerned, Porter is dead to me regardless.

When every task is done and all I can do is hope for the best, I grab my backup backpack — a worn and torn one dating back to high school — and stuff as much as possible in there. Since my primary essentials are in my bag at Hayes and Trenton's, I scrounge for anything left: little hotel samples from our cross-country trip and what remaining clothes I have that would benefit me most for… for whatever comes next.

Backpack stuffed, I sling it over my shoulder and make my way through the dark and quiet upper level.

Stepping across my bedroom threshold and not being afraid of who would be in the kitchen or fireplace room — worried what I might be expected to do or say — is strange. There is both a lightness of freedom and a debilitating and burdensome weight of loneliness. Should I stick around? Wait for Jude? Beg him to understand?

No.

I mean... I could.

But his struggles go beyond our brother-sister relationship.

He has grievances to work through... among other things.

Sometimes being someone's 80 percent means leaving them alone.

So I leave. Then, I wait until I'm parking my bike in the lot beside the Regency before allowing myself half a second to think about Trenton. And Hayes. And Crow.

The Monte Carlo is gone.

That V Coupe was still across the driveway when I rode away, but not for long, I imagine.

Those chapters of my life are over.

Maybe one day I'll work up the courage to swing by their house and at least reclaim my belongings. One day. For now, though, I hop off my bike, jog down to the shore, and collect Trenton's clothes, following through with my promise.

From there, I ride down the street to the only other section of beach I have visited since arriving in this new town. The goal is to keep my bonfire efforts nowhere near the same area where Trenton parked and where we were potentially on cameras walking down the public access path.

After parking in the darkest corner of the large entertainment club's lot, I make my way along the side of the building. I then toss my bag onto the sand and begin a search for fire-starting materials. As a last ditch collection, I pluck a few handfuls of sea oats, pad back to my chosen spot, dig a decent hole in the sand, and strategically place all the items inside.

It takes a good thirty minutes for me to hand-spark my very first fire, but I manage — seconds before I am about to throw my friction-stick into the damn gulf and give the sand a few good kicks. Proudest moment of my life. Both because I didn't throw a tantrum... and because I created my own damn fire. Hell yeah.

As soon as the flames are big enough to where dumping in a pile of heavy clothes won't smother them, I begin tossing in one article at a time. Before long, I'm sitting cross-legged, doing nothing more than... relaxing. The flickers from the blaze and screen of heat mixed with an occasional cool breeze from the gulf is a heady mix that soon causes my eyelids to weigh a ton. Far more than the weight of my problems. So much so, in fact, that they close entirely.

But not for long. The wild events of the last few weeks are enough to set my subconscious on guard. A quiet squeak of feet against sand seeps through my floaty haze. My eyes spring open and head twists to the side, facing the direction from which the sound came. Between the orange sparks and glow of the fire and the white bounce of the moonlight from the water, there's enough light to outline a curvy human form.

A woman.

A naked one.

I quickly flick my gaze back to the blaze and feign nonchalance.

She circles around the fire and disappears behind the dunes only to return again several moments later, wrapped in a towel and carrying a bag. The unrecognizable woman sits beside me. Like… right in my personal bubble. "Do you believe that sometimes the Universe gives you exactly what you need, right when you need it?"

My eyebrows lift, and I blink repeatedly. "Um…"

"Hey, all good… You don't know me. No need to actually answer. But, I believe it. And, damn, I just really fuckin' wanted a bonfire tonight."

She has a Southern accent, something I hear occasionally with the guys but never strong enough for it to be the defining feature of their tones. The lilt immediately makes her sound super sweet, in spite of the foul language; there's just not as much punch to the swear. Amused, I press my lips together and nod.

Sure would be hella nice to receive any pleasant gift right now — from the Universe, whomever, or whatever. Bring it.

Hell, I have a fire; maybe I can scrounge up a sacrifice, too.

I clear my throat and dart a sideways glance at her. "Glad I could provide."

Oh, wait. There *is* a sacrifice there. Porter's blood.

Well, would ya look at that.

Huh.

Maybe the Universe will provide after all.

A hand is shoved in my sightline — the very sightline that was unfocused on the flames while I entertained all sorts of ways the Universe could provide.

"Name's Lacinda. Nice to meet you."

I blink a few extra times, bringing my focus back to the present, accept her hand, and give it a friendly shake. "Remi."

"Figured since you're breaking at least four laws out here tonight, you might could use some company."

At that, I whip my head toward her and really give her a good look for the first time. Blonde hair — unnatural, if the dark roots peeking through near her scalp are any indicator. The rich tan of a beach girl — unless that is unnatural too, considering there doesn't appear to be any tan lines on her shoulders or around her neck. Eyes a lot like mine, lightened only because of the flicker of firelight. If she was flaunting her natural hair color, we could almost pass as sisters.

"Oh?"

"I can read people pretty well," she explains. "Law number one: you don't look like the type who would have a fire permit for an impromptu, early-morning bonfire."

"Permit. Right. Okay. Point."

"Law number two: said fire is within 200 feet of a marked sea turtle nest." She inclines her head just over her shoulder, and I follow the direction of her nod to a nearby area taped off by yellow tape with a very obvious sign. "Law number three:" — she uses her toe to nudge a piece of oat straw that somehow escaped the fire — "Pulling, cutting, and even walking through the sea oats is a violation of the law."

With a hard swallow, the two of us return our gazes to the fire, and she continues, "So… even if you did have a permit, you would be up shit's creek — or in this case the gulf — without a paddle."

I catch the inside of my cheek between my teeth and nod, eyes once again unfocusing on the flames. Oh the irony that would be. Get arrested for building a fire without a permit with sea oats near a sea turtle nest… only to discover the perp should actually be charged with homicide.

Jokes on you, Universe.

I take a deep breath and let it out in a vibrated, exaggerated way through my lips. "Zero and three. You said there were four? Hit me."

Our eyes meet, and her lips curve into an amused grin. "Sleeping on the beach is prohibited."

I grimace. "I wasn't sleeping."

"Not yet."

"Right."

Her sparkling attitude and contagious smile straightens, and she clears her throat. "I would offer you a place to stay… but I live in my car."

That iconic grimace almost appears again, but I catch it in time. Do I react like people probably tend to when she decides to share that information with them? Or do I keep the conversation … chill?

Chill, I decide, figuring she probably gets enough flack as it stands. "Heh, well, I would live in my car, but I ride a motorcycle."

Her smile returns and eyes light up almost faster than I can get out the last syllable. "Oh yeah? Bet you're looking forward to the autumn rally here next month then, hm?"

Her sudden swap in behavior pulls the first chuckle from me since all the terrible things happened hours ago. "Ah, I just moved here. Not too sure what this rally is you speak of."

"Oh, you are definitely new to the area then. Every fall and spring we have a huge motorcycle rally."

I internally groan. "Motorcycle rally. Ah, okay. Probably a lot of bobbers, choppers, and touring bikes. I ride a sportbike. I mean she cruises well, but not rally-well, you know?" A memory of the night I met Trenton and he made a comment about the tourist season flashes into my mind.

"Yeah. During Bike Week sportbikes and supersports are definitely the one-percenters of the event, but they still play around. I know a few guys who never miss a rally." Her demeanor transforms a bit at this mention — the bold straight features loosening, turning a bit more demure and coy as her gaze drops from the fire to her toes and she wiggles them into the sand.

"Anyway" — she sighs deeply and clears her throat — "I can recommend a couple places for you to check out if you're looking for a place to kick your feet up for the night."

With a mimicking deep sigh, I lift my gaze to hers. "Yeah, thanks; I would appreciate that."

She gives me a warm, knowing smile. "Well, depends on your tastes, I suppose. There's a fancier place just down on the opposite end of this street. Keep straight at the curve. If you need something a little less… demanding… check out the trailer park on the West End. Both have an amazin' view of the gulf, regardless of price. Either place, just let them know Lace sent you."

She pushes off the sand and dusts her hands off on the towel. "Mind if I get dressed now?" she asks.

"Oh… no… not at all!" I stammer a bit and avert my eyes toward the gulf to make her more comfortable, the awkwardness poofing over me like a plume of agitated sand.

"Thanks," she responds, chuckling. The pitch of her voice sounds a bit farther away, indicating that she likely turned her back to me. "In case you're curious as to why I'm here at four in the morning, it's because I work at the club across the street. Ya already know I sleep in my car. But I like to bathe in the gulf sometimes. The club has a shower… but, eh. Not enough bumps in the world could make me shower in there."

"Club?" I direct the question toward the gulf, unsure if she is done dressing yet. I'm parked and sitting behind a closed club, but something about her explanation indicates she might be referring to somewhere else.

"The gentlemen's club at the far end of that shopping center across the street?" She pauses, and the squeak of sand meets my ears. I take the sound as a hint that she's done and I can turn back around. "Hey, stop by sometime? I can hook you up with a lap dance, if that is your thing. Or a pizza. The place next door to the club makes the best dough."

A memory of Hayes strikes — of the day he took me here at sunset and paid for the pizzas I ordered. The memory of Jude and I joking about working there instead of sticking with the automotive industry follows.

I push that thought to the back burner, bringing forward the one of Hayes. Both recollections hurt, though. Unfairly. The reminder that he knew the pizza delivery driver flares to life, and I instantly wonder if any of the guys know Lacinda — Lace? — too. Might shed some light on their favored extracurricular activities when not running engines.

"Think too hard and you'll burst that vessel in your forehead," Lacinda chuckles.

Controlled by the psychosis of a crazy few months, a lack of sleep, and too many errant thoughts, I spew out the words clinging to the tip of my tongue. "Do you know Hayes, Trenton, and Crow?"

Lace stills, hands no longer drying her hair with the towel. Her eyes dart to mine. "Yes, I do. Crow mostly." Well… that doesn't surprise me for some reason. Jealousy churns in my gut. She sighs and drops her towel hand to her side. "Not for the reason why you're likely thinking," she elaborates, probably accustomed to having to do damage control where her clients are concerned.

I push off the ground, dust off, and start nudging sand toward the flames to help smother them. "Ah, no need to defend him. Crow is a grown man and certainly not tied down. Definitely not by me."

Lace remains quiet, studying me. Only a second passes before her lip quirks up at the side. "Girl. I know that look. Trust me, I deal with it every night. Look… ya don't have anything to worry about with him. I haven't seen him at the club since…" her eyes flit over my face. "…since Rachal died."

CHAPTER THIRTEEN

"Rachal?" I ask.

"Yeah." Her mouth curves into a small frown. "His wife?"

All the blood drains from my face, and I stagger a bit. "W-wife?"

"Ah, shit, hun…" she whispers in that sweet Southern drawl of hers. "Look, I don't know you. I'm real sorry. I just assumed since you know Revelry, you know about Rachal. Anyone in the local street scene knows that story." She pads backward a couple steps.

With a sudden rush of common sense and adrenaline, I snap out of my dizzying surprise and dart a hand out toward her. "No. Wait. Don't leave yet."

She stops.

I maniacally start hand-shoveling sand onto the burning clothes and sticks.

Movement in my peripheral draws my focus back toward her. She bends down and begins to help. "Hey… what's a little story around the bonfire, hm? Nothing you can't find on your own online in news articles," she says with a soft smile, scooping some sand into her hand and tossing it onto the blaze. "Crow was married to one of the girls at the club. They had a baby girl. Bree."

She pauses, eyes locked on me, awaiting a reaction.

Boy is it hard not to react to that news. Nearly impossible. Bile creeps up my throat, but I swallow the acidic mixture down.

A wife.

A daughter.

I simply give her a tight nod.

She continues.

"Trenton ever mention his brother to you?"

Goddamn if this woman doesn't stop with the hits. Words still stolen, I simply shake my head and continue covering the fire with sand.

"Travis. Always had a thing for Rachal. He wasn't quite right in the head, that one. He lost his shit one night. Followed her away from the club. What he didn't know that night at the time, was that Crow and Rachal had swapped parenting duties. Rachal had just stopped by the club, Bree in the backseat in her carseat, while she ran in and made sure her shift was covered for the night.

"They got into an altercation inside; the owner had to escort him out. Rachal stuck around for a bit to make sure he was good and gone. Far as we could all tell, he was. Last thing out of her mouth before she walked out of the door was that she was headed to Steel Field to watch Crow race. Smitten, those two. Anyway" — she waves a sandy hand — "long story, short, Travis chased her all the way to Steel Field. The rest of Revelry was already there just shootin' the shit. Rachal called Crow mid pursuit. He told her to keep to the speed limit. Travis waited until she was at a curve to pull up beside her. The rest is kinda guessing. Crow thinks it spooked her. Whatever went through her mind, we'll never know. She accelerated. Travis's car got squirrely and clipped her. She swerved, flipped several times, and hit a tree. The car went up in flames.

"Revelry watched the entire thing go down. Since they were racing before then, Hayes had a fire extinguisher in his car. He put the fire out while Crow tried to remove Rachal and Bree from the vehicle. The doors wouldn't budge. They ended up having to get the jaws of life out there. It was too late, though. Coroner report said they died on impact. Trenton had to detain Travis until the cops arrived — his own brother."

The fire snuffed out about mid story.

Tears poured hot and salty down my cheeks.

Even so, I still managed to sniffle out the question hanging on the tip of my tongue. "Why did he start The Gulf Coasters?" I know the answer, though. Waiting, I draw my knees against my chest, warding off a chill that has nothing to do with the early-morning temperature.

When she answers, it only serves as reaffirmation. But the twist of my heart happens nonetheless. "Rachal hated street racing. She cheered him from the sidelines regardless, but was always telling Crow he should do something to make it safer — use his sway and influence. Everyone loved him. No one could beat him. He did it — built the community — in memory of his wife and daughter. He stopped racing in their memory, too. Since she didn't like it and all. Street racing related deaths have gone down significantly in this county ever since."

I turn my head toward the gulf and stare off into the distance through blurry eyes, pressing my cheek against my knee. A warm, gritty hand cups my bicep, and her soft voice swoops into my ear. "He saved the street racing community, but in doing so, destroyed himself. That club is the only thing keeping him from the temptation of joining his family. There's more… things the articles didn't get into. The aftermath. But that's information you'll need to get from another source."

News about last night's events mustn't have made their way to her yet. Probably because she was working and still hasn't settled into her car and turned on the radio.

"My advice?" she asks. I shrug. "Challenge him. Get him talking. Someone needs to return the favor — to save him when he has saved so many others at the cost of his own wellbeing."

I turn my attention away from the gulf back toward her. "You're nudging the wrong person," I state on a hitched breath. "My involvement would do nothing but drive him further into desolation."

I drop my arms, encouraging her to let go, and stand. She follows suit. Instead of lingering or pressing any further, she simply steps away. A few paces toward the dark dunes, though, the wind carries with it one last comment: "Crow deserves a stipend from the Universe."

Yeah, well…

Whatever — whoever — is the Universe's adversary, that's who sent me.

Crow was right: I am poison.

CHAPTER FOURTEEN

F*uck her.*
Fuck him.
Fuck it.
Fuck everything.
Fuck everyone.
I'm done, too.
Let Midnight Runners have what they want.
What-the-fuck-ever.
The girl.
The crew.
The club.

My brain goes into autopilot, driving a route I haven't driven in years. Only when I stop and put the V Coupe into park, do I realize where I am. My head falls back against the seat. One hand slams against the wheel. The other grips the gearshift, vibrating with the need to put her in reverse and get the fuck out of this dreamscape. The muscles in my legs and forearm refuse to work, and my fingers twitch; I can't seem to get the car into gear and moving no matter how hard I try.

If I'm stuck here, I refuse to look — to open my eyes and face my past. Instead, I recline the seat and commit to keeping them shut until I can bring myself to leave. Seems my body and mind are quite conflicted on the matter, though.

A steady *tap*, *tap*, *tap* jolts me on the spot, and my eyes pop open, landing immediately on the time. I actually fell asleep. For an hour. I blink a few times to adjust to the pure black, then turn my head toward the visitor lingering at my window. My hands drop from the wheel to the window button, and I slide it down.

"Huh. Fancy seein' you here tonight."

"Hey, Lace."

"Club's closed. Missed us by about forty-five minutes." She snaps her fingers, gives me a friendly smile, and leans her elbows on the window track. I move my gaze back to the windshield, despite there being nothing more than a fence to look at — a dumpster if I want to get extra desperate.

"Been a while," she whispers, voice dropping to that sympathetic tone I absolutely despise... from anyone. Even Lace. Hell, especially Lace.

The only thing visible behind her is the shine of the moonlight bouncing off the roof of her wagon. "I see not much has changed." I tilt my head toward her living situation and throw a quick glance at the club, too.

"What can I say? I'm a creature of comfort."

It's hard to not bite my tongue. I wanted Rachal out of this type of club scene about as much as she wanted me out of the car club scene.

Comfort.

For fuck's sake.

Spare me.

Guess there's a fine enough line between the written definition of comfort and money.

"What brings you over here at, oh" — she drops her gaze to her bare wrist — "five in the morning?"

Damn good question. I pull the lever on my seat to an upright position. "Wrong turn."

She straightens, stepping back from the window, and chuckles. "So that biker chick I met on the beach tonight has nothin' to do with your sudden and unexpected appearance? You know I have a knack for seeing through lies, Crow. Even with that talent, it doesn't take a rocket scientist to put one and one together."

No. Apparently, in this case, all it takes is a stripper.

I tuck my lip ring behind my top teeth, silently cursing my fucking luck. Or lack thereof. Stay here long enough, and she'll start spouting that shit about the Universe.

"Sorry, Lace. Guess you're losing your touch. The biker community is more your taste, not mine." I turn the engine over, flick the lights on, and shift into reverse.

"Seems she didn't know anything about you having a wife and daughter. Funny thing, that."

My fingers pinch the key, and I accidentally turn the engine over a second time, sending a grating squeal throughout the quiet back lot.

All sensations disappear from my fingers, lips, feet. Everywhere. Sweat covers my forehead, my vision blurs, and heart pumps wildly. "What did you tell her?" I manage to get out without throwing up. The vomit is there, thick and heavy, lining my throat. I swallow repeatedly to prevent it from creeping any higher.

"Nothing more than what she would've discovered with a simple web search."

Too much. She told her too much.

I know Lace wouldn't have said something if her "intuition" or what-the-hell ever wasn't telling her to. So, instead of lashing out — because Lace is good people, she really is — despite wanting to fucking throttle something right now, I whisper through gritted teeth, "Why? Why, Lace? Why tell a complete stranger my business?"

Lace steps back a few more paces toward the direction of her camper wagon, a soft smile pulling across her face. "You already know why, Crow. A lot of people are rootin' for you. It's high time you root for yourself, too."

"Fuck you." Okay, so maybe I don't have as much restraint as I thought.

"No thanks. You're not my type. You said it yourself... Bikers are more my taste." Her smile isn't gone; she knows there isn't any backbone in my verbal threat. "And woo-wee, that woman I met tonight has me questioning all sorts of things — preferences and such."

I roll my eyes and toss my head to the side to narrow a glare at her. "She must have waved a Benjamin under your nose; those tend to change your 'preferences' quite easily."

She flashes her teeth and gives me a wink. "Tune up, Burke."

CHAPTER FIFTEEN

Remi

O nce Lace disappears, I look up the lesser-expensive place she mentioned. In part out of spite of the posh life I grew up living — as a middle finger to both Jude and Porter for sending me that dirty money. As it stands, unfortunately, I need to spend some of it if I want a roof over my head. But the less of those funds I need to fall back on, the better, though.

A second reason for choosing this place over its fancier counterpart, is because it's near Crow's house. Not that I would admit that to anyone. Hell, admitting it to myself is hard enough. I'm not planning on going over there, but… I don't know… being close at least feels safer. As strange as that seems, considering I fell out of his good graces before I could truly fall into them.

As soon as I get on my bike and leave the parking lot, I instantly feel the relief of discarded baggage. A new generation of vehicles are starting to appear on the roads; all the late-night, weekend bar and club-goers, now tucked away in their homes or the homes of their temporary partners, are soon-to-be-replaced by the early-morning businessmen and women and families with school-aged kids.

The sun won't likely rise for another hour or so this time of year, so I revel in the remaining darkness and sparse traffic. When I pull up to the entrance and park in front of the desolate office, my new reality drapes heavy over my shoulders, mimicking the nearly unbearable weight of my previous backpack. Despite the fact that my current bag is much, much lighter in comparison to the one I packed all my shit in and walked away with the first time. Seems I traded the contents for problems, instead.

A smothering sense of loneliness washes over me as I dismount and remove my helmet. The relief from the stinging pressure due to the puffy lump on my forehead is welcome, though; it got worse over the hours, as impact wounds tend to do. With nothing better to do than wait, I plop down onto one of the mobile office's rickety, wooden steps, lean my head against the railing, and stare out across the road toward the gulf on the opposite side.

Lace was right — if nothing else, this place has quite the view. Dare I say it must be one of the only places in the entire county that doesn't have the obstruction of a high-rise condo or beach-front restaurant muddling the scenery. To both the left and right, tall signs highlighted by street lights mark public access points.

Millions. This land is probably worth millions. I dart a studious glance over my shoulder at the dilapidated manufactured homes and broken down vehicles — such a contrast aesthetically to the monetary value of prime real estate. My eyes become increasingly heavier as I study the area, and before long too heavy to keep open. Hugging my helmet and old backpack as snug to my chest as possible, I listen to the waves crash in the distance and the occasional car zoom by, allowing those soothing sounds to eventually lull me to sleep.

The nap doesn't last long, though. Before I know it, the sky is growing brighter, the pale blue causing the veins in my eyelids to appear. I blink, adjusting my eyes open, just in time to see the sun peep above the shoreline. Just a sliver. I missed the proper bold colors of the first stages of the sunrise, but the sight is gorgeous nonetheless.

A beautiful sight — and sound of waves and gulls — that is suddenly blocked by the powerful, unmistakable rumble and sight of a chopper leaning into the court entrance.

Well... clearly some of the lots' inhabitants are well-off. This one in particular. His bike is easily three times the cost of mine. The man's head swivels when he passes my Duc and me, never once letting his eyes off us as he pulls into a motorcycle-sized gravel spot to the left of the office and methodically takes all the steps one must take before dismounting.

He makes his way toward the steps, giving my girl the barest of sneers. "What can I do you for, ma'am?"

I launch to a stand, dart my hand out, and plaster on a grin. "Hello, Sir. Name's Remi. I'm looking for a place to shack up for a few days. Your establishment came highly recommended by Lacin—Lace."

He raises a grey eyebrow at me over his shoulder while unlocking the front door. "You friends with Kal and his brigade?" Again the man steals a glance at my bike.

"Uh, nope. The name doesn't ring a bell." I nearly spout that I know the Revelry crew, but I catch the slip before it falls from my tongue. Because, while I do know them, I am not a member. Never was, really. Certainly never will be.

"Huh. Well, alright then, come on in." For whatever reason, he doesn't seem convinced of my answer.

The two of us cross over the threshold. Unfamiliar with the area and residents — and certainly unaccustomed to the lifestyle — I work my way through my backpack straps and tuck my helmet against my side. If I could hold my bike, I would. Alas, that's a bit unmanageable.

Only when he's on the other side of the desk-turned-counter does he nod at me in acknowledgment and introduce himself. "Foster. Now, what are we working with?"

Friendly fella, this one. "I…" A grimace pulls at my features and I give him a puppy dog look. "I'm afraid I'm not sure what you're asking exactly."

A little ding chimes behind me, and I twist to the side to glance at this incoming guest over my shoulder. The little ding is quite the contrast compared to the slam of the door as it finishes its aggressive inward swing and hits the plaster wall.

My eyes widen, meeting Hayes's midnight blue ones behind his glasses. His eyes dart over my shoulder toward Foster. My head swivels back that direction. He had pushed out of his seat, ready to defend his turf no doubt at Hayes's aggressive entrance.

"W-what are you doing here?" I squeak out.

"Ah…" His hand whips up to his neck, and he rubs it aggressively. "Lace called me. Suggested I should check on you."

Foster mumbles behind me, followed by the squeak of him plopping back into his chair.

"Okay…"

What else am I supposed to say?

"You have a place to stay," he whispers, but there's no backbone in the offer. He's being a gentleman, nothing more.

With a deep, steadying breath, I steel my shoulders and lift my chin. "I know." I lean my hip against the desk, ease my helmet onto a stack of papers, and clasp my hands in front of my lap. "Foster here was just about to give me the keys."

Tilting my head down, I meet the older man's eyes from under my lashes. He grumbles and clears his throat, but reaches behind him, snatches something from a box, and a set of keys lands with a jangle near my hip.

I swipe them off the desk and narrow my attention at the torn and stained white sticker dot barely hanging onto the circular portion of the small, bronze key. Leaning over the desk again, I drag a finger along the map of the court in search of my assigned lot. As payment, I dig my key remote out of my pocket and slide it over to him, offering my baby as collateral. It hurts. Pushing off the desk and walking away becomes that much more difficult. Being strong-willed and independent sure is a bitch sometimes.

I push past Hayes and jog down the steps.

"Remi… wait."

Hayes's steps pursue me and so does a grumbling owner's. I stop at my bike and run my palm over the seat and up and over the tank, hitching up my shoulder to rebalance my backpack. When I spin to face Hayes, Foster steps between us, arms crossed, back to me, an imposing form directed at Hayes.

Hayes shuffles and attempts leaning over to look past him. My lips curve up to the side. I clear my throat to hide my amusement, step past Foster, and stand beside Hayes instead. "Thanks for the place," I direct at Foster.

"Thanks for the bike," Foster smirks. I shoot him an eyebrow raise. He shrugs and walks away. I immediately turn to Hayes. He opens his mouth to finish whatever he started, but my response is quicker. "Let me do this."

His mouth slams shut, and he swallows hard.

Once again, before he can respond, I continue: "I'm not out to take advantage of you guys. Nev—" I'm a heartbeat away from saying that I "never was," but that's not entirely the truth. I renege my comment and reword. "I lost your trust. I get it. If I go to your house again, it'll be because I've earned that trust back. Let me earn it back. Or at least try."

Staying here is symbolic of more than just that, but admitting as much exceeds my present level of pride. When he doesn't respond, my plea becomes a little more desperate. Mixed with a lack of sleep, I fear if he doesn't accept what I'm saying, if he pushes me over the edge, I very well might have a breakdown right here on the gravel. "Hayes… I need this."

Now it's his turn to steel his shoulders. "Fine," he says, fingers twitching at his sides. "But I'm telling Foster about Porter. Guys like that always find a way back, Remi — they have an uncanny way of doing that."

My throat tightens, and I give him a tight nod. I can only assume that based on that comment, they have received an update. One that I am way too damn tired to hear. Coming to my own conclusion is enough — he's still alive. The rest can come later. "He will find me faster if I'm at home or at your place. At least staying somewhere unexpected bides me more time."

Hayes returns a tight nod but then shuffles from one foot to the other before stating in a whisper, "Want me to bring you your stuff tomorrow?"

The question damn near debilitates me. I dig my fingers into the seat of my bike to aid in holding myself up.

Be strong, Remi.

I blink a few times and clear my throat. "Um… I'll leave that up to you."

Seems my response has a similar effect on him. At least that's how I choose to translate the bob of his Adam's apple and fluttering eyelashes.

Unfortunately, his reaction affects me far more than his words did, and my eyes and nose begin to burn. His entire profile goes blurry as my eyes fill with tears. But I don't bother to blink them away when I take a couple slow steps forward, wrap my arms around his neck, and bury my face into his shoulder.

"Thank you," I whisper, hating the sniffle that comes after. "For everything." Hayes doesn't return the hug — his arms remain tense and hands hang fisted at his sides. I put distance between us and grip his biceps gently for one more comment: "I am so damn sorry. I truly am."

I hadn't said either of those things yet. No offering of thanks, no apology. Maybe they come across as empty to him, but they are honest. Wholeheartedly. Instead of his blue eyes meeting mine, they dart up toward the sky, lips pressed firmly together.

Taking the hint and having said what I set out to say, I step back toward my bike and dig the key to my new, temporary home out of my pocket to give my hands something to do so I'm not tempted to reach out for him again.

The crunch of his shoes hitting the gravel, and then quieting as he walks away from me makes my heart crumble, mimicking the broken rocks. But then the steps stop and my name immediately floats to my ears. "Remi?"

I spin around. "Yeah?"

His eyes finally lock with mine. "I am proud of you. For leaving him… for not going back. Doing that is hard."

Not as hard as it was losing you, Trenton, and Crow... and Jude.

"Thanks," I whisper.

Hayes is not done, though: "And I understand your loyalty to Jude. We all do. More than you know. Loyalty is all we have left. Crow, Trenton, and me." And that's why this thing between us can never turn into what we thought it might. He doesn't verbalize that truth, but the strain in his voice and the curve of his eyebrows are enough proof.

CHAPTER SIXTEEN

Hayes doesn't look back on the way to his Bimmer. He doesn't look ahead at me through the windshield, either, when he plops down into the seat and buckles. His attention remains locked on his tasks: eyes dropping to the clips, lifting to the ignition, head cranking to the side and focus turning to his blind spot as he reverses into the street. Not even when he shifts into first gear and rolls forward do I get a quick head turn or side glance as his attention adjusts forward again.

I grip the key Foster gave me a little tighter, reveling in the pinch of the metal serrated edge against my sensitive palm. The bite only partially overrides the ache in my heart — that particular ache much too strong considering the only person at fault in this horrible situation… is myself.

Hayes might not have been willing to steal a final glance, but I can't tear my eyes away. The only thing that prevents me from running into the street to chase his taillights is the phlegmy clearing of a throat. Teeth clenching, lips pressing into a thin line, I take a deep recovery breath in and out through my nose before loosening my features and facing the owner of this establishment.

Foster still has his arms crossed firmly over his broad chest. Whatever he planned on saying is interrupted just as quickly as his throat clearing pierced my desperation a moment ago; a jaunty jingle chimes, muffled from his pocket.

He drops his arms, digs the phone out, swipes the screen, and presses the device to his ear. He never speaks to the caller, though — simply listens, eyes narrowed at me.

A single grunt is his response, and a couple seconds later, he disconnects the call and shoves the phone back into his jeans. "Lot numbers are all sorts of fucked due to the emergency system the county has in place. I put you in the far back. Last lot on the left. Take the Duc with you. I want payment. Cash. You have two days."

Fuck.

Cash?

Who the hell carries cash on them anymore?

I sure as shit don't.

My lips pull back, and I bare my teeth in a combined grimace and smile. "Two days. Yep."

He bends and picks up something behind him then tosses it in my direction.

My helmet becomes a blur in the air. In a panic, I drop the key and pitch forward. The black globe lands in my curved arms just shy of hitting the ground, key remote nestled inside.

I glare at the old man.

He gives me a sloppy grin. "How fast a biker catches their helmet unaware is a sign of how much they respect their bike. But it also indicates their willingness to lay it down when things get squirrely. Pick your priorities, girl."

I pocket the remote, fit the helmet over my head, and pluck the key off the ground. "Can't say I've heard that one," I respond, mounting my bike.

He chortles. "That's because I just made it up." His wrinkling hands cup his chin and he looks up sideways into the sky. "That was some poetic shit, though. Damn."

I pop the kickstand, start her up, wave the key at him, then shove it into my front pocket. "Thanks," I offer, revving the throttle and wheeling forward toward my new abode.

Over a mix of wind and rumble of my engine, Foster yells, "First night's free!"

I lift my arm and give him a high thumbs up and a rear tire wiggle in thanks.

THE DEEPER INTO THE PROPERTY I RIDE, the more conflicted I become. Being in the far back has its perks but also its downfalls. Like… who's gonna hear me scream? But, also, at least my bike can't be seen from the road, right?

The unit is a small trailer. I pull around to the side and park out of view of neighbors, shut down, and dismount. After taking off my helmet and tucking it under my arm, I remove the key from my pocket, double check the lot number, and step up the planked stairs to the front door.

As Foster mentioned, each lot has two numbers: one for the actual property lot number, as designated by the owner, and one for emergency services, I presume—displayed on a crude piece of bright-green metal similar to the mile markers found on freeways.

I fit the grooved key inside the lock. Turning the key and opening the door takes a bit of effort, though. Not because it's physically difficult to do but because of the mental and emotional challenge.

My heart rate speeds up and my hands become clammy against the metal. Clearing my throat of the oncoming acid and straightening my ever-increasing curved posture, I twist the lock open and barge in. Rev the throttle. Punch the gas.

With equal fervor I slam the door shut, not trusting myself to not back right out of here and simply curl up on the small, wooden entrance deck instead.

A musty stuffiness attacks my senses first. A hazy, dusty orange glow next. I blink rapidly, trying to both take in the details of my new place and snap back into cognitive thinking and move. Act. Do something other than stand here with my back adhered to the closed door.

I loop my backpack off my shoulders, place it on the ground by my feet, and put my helmet down beside it. If I simply stick a foot out, the tip of my shoe touches a washing machine. The main living area is to the left. I bend at the waist, still using the door for unrealistic protection by keeping my butt pressed firmly against it, leaning my torso forward and angling my head to the side to peer into the conjoining dining area and living room. I adjust and peer the opposite way. To the right of the washing center is the bathroom and the bedroom.

Okay. It is a house.

Small, but seemingly functional.

A cough racks my chest, and I'm reminded that the stuffiness in here is godawful. I clap my hands together and watch as a plume of golden dust agitates in a stream of dim lighting that streams in from the bedroom.

One tentative step at a time, I push off the door, and walk toward the dining table. Just past the washing and drying machine and around the wall separating rooms, is a quaint little kitchen.

I reach over the sink and open the small window, then turn around and open the larger window behind the table.

One window at a time, I make my way through the entire place. A pleasant breeze rushes through, and I inhale, sucking in the fresh gulf scents, even if in this instance they are mixed with old memories that have since turned to dust and mildew.

Like a proper home owner — well, squatter, if I can't figure out a way to get Foster some cash — I toss the key onto the table, plop down onto the slipcovered couch, and prop my feet on top of the old coffee table, arms outstretched, head nodding in approval.

But just like that, my heart does one heavy, reverberating thud, and all the air rushes from my lungs, smothering me. I clutch at my chest and lean forward until my head is resting on my knees. An overwhelming, overpowering sob racks my body and steals my senses and sensibility. All I can hear is the manic, erratic beating of my pulse in my ears and the soppy snivel of my snot and tears. All I can feel is the shake in my shoulders and the splintering of my heart.

For the first time in my life, I am all alone...

CHAPTER SEVENTEEN

I cried myself to sleep — curled up in a ball on the musty couch and passed out mid salty waterfall. A sticky tightness remains in my eyes and clumps of buildup adhere to my eyelashes.

A quick glance at the clock hanging above the small entertainment setup across from the couch tells me that I was only out for about an hour. But based on the slight dimness in the room, it seems longer. To double check, I shuffle to my backpack and dig out my phone.

Sure enough, the clock is incorrect, but not entirely. I pad over, reach above the television, and remove it from the wiggly nail it's hanging precariously on. On further inspection, I learn there's not even a battery inside.

Time is inconsequential right now anyway. I have no agenda: Nowhere to clock in. No dates. No assignments due. I blow a raspberry from my lips, toss the clock onto the couch, and pick up where I left off prior to my little breakdown — a tour of the place. After a full walk-through, I note that there is definitely an immediate need for groceries in the least.

Much to my delight, however, there's a few sample-size detergent boxes in the cabinets above the washer. I immediately strip the linens off the bed and the slipcover off the couch and start a wash. No telling who has been in here and how long it has been since the place was cleaned.

Each action keeps me busy and helps distract my mind from every side street it would prefer to explore. To bide time while the wash cycle completes, I dump the contents of my backpack on the table, shoulder it, and head out to the closest grocery store for a few basics — whatever I can fit on my back, at least.

It's not often I curse having a bike instead of a car, but this is certainly one of those instances. I quickly come to realize just how dependent strictly being a bike owner makes me. Other types of vehicles are clearly the better option for shopping. I love my bike, but I sure as shit don't like feeling incapable.

The ride is just long enough to keep my mind working through the steps I'm going to take with this new living arrangement and short enough to prevent it from wandering too far as longer-distance rides tend to do.

Grocery basket in hand, I work through how the hell I'm going to get cash. As I approach the counter, spoils collected, it dawns on me that this will be the first time I will be using my credit card or tapping into the funds Porter and Jude transferred to me.

It takes all of a couple breaths to decide I don't much like that. The digital paper trail, mostly. Cash is sounding more and more beneficial. Gaze alternating from the basket to the conveyor belt and back again, I make a knee-jerk decision to ditch it and come back. I tuck the basket under the conveyor belt area, give the cashier a heads up, and leave, knowing exactly where I want to go to solve my dilemma.

Strippers deal with cash. A lot of it. Maybe if I transfer Lace some electronic funds, she might be willing to exchange it for cash.

Plus, that way, the money is going to a person instead of a business linked to a certain geographical location where I could be tracked down. Maybe Lace was right after all: the Universe is giving handouts, and I intend to cash in.

Heh.

Cash in.

This ride takes a little longer than the one before, going from one end of the beach to the other. The weight of my predicament begins to take root, settling heavily in my limbs. In part, being wholly independent is freeing. Encouraging. But it still comes with that unfair, weighted loneliness.

Perhaps because Jude and I have always been so close. I never intended on staying home too long after graduating high school, but… things happened. Dad convinced me to stick around until I finished at least my first degree — said I could reassess after that point. I did and decided to stay while working on my four-year degree. Of course, that's when life turned to shit. Jude lived on his own already, but as soon as everything happened with Dad, he sold his studio apartment and moved back in with me. If only to begin taking care of everything… and to both provide and receive sibling companionship during the tumultuous grieving period.

The period that seems never ending.

God what the hell is even happening right now?

I'm all for leaving the nest. But like this? I don't know. Everything feels so…

…unfinished.

My wayward and self-pitying thoughts carry me all the way to the shopping center and around to the back employee parking area of the club Lace mentioned. The herbaceous smell of dough and spices float through the air, taunting me since I haven't eaten in well over twenty-four hours at this point if my math serves me. But an unfavorable mix of rotten garbage from the large dumpster I pass by has the opposite effect, causing what little I do have in my stomach to churn.

Lace said she lives in her car, and since she was washing in the gulf, I assume she sleeps back here somewhere. Or at least nearby. There are several cars, though, and we never chatted long enough to get into the specifics of what type of vehicle she called home.

Thankfully, two of the four don a magnetic pizza delivery sign on the roof. The other two are bare, and parked farther back toward the opposite end of the building.

Of the two remaining, one is a wagon that I notice, upon closer inspection, has sunshades inside all the windows, blocking any light — and peeping toms, no doubt.

The hatchback is old — an Electra Estate, practically the size of a hurst. Definitely sleep worthy, that's for sure. Well, as sleep worthy as vehicles can get, I suppose.

I pull up beside it, engage the kickstand, turn off my bike, dismount, remove my helmet, and tuck it under my arm — grimacing a bit at the pressure against my lovely goose egg.

Blowing out a preparatory raspberry, I rap my knuckles against the passenger window. Not three seconds later, a dainty finger slips beneath one of the screens in the back seat and a brown iris peeks through a small opening. The screen pops closed and the door inches open, a bare foot following.

Lace steps out. The daylight allows for a much better visual of her than the wee morning hours did. She is still wearing the lace sundress she put on after the fire, but this time I notice tattoos — faux, lacy stocking patterns that peek out under her short dress and line down the sides of her thighs and legs.

She clears her throat, and my traveling gaze snaps upward. "Not every day I have to remind a woman where my face is."

My lips quirk up sideways, and I shrug. "I like them. Um… your tattoos, I mean. Not… women."

Wow. Holy shit.

"All good." She giggles. "That's what they all say at first anyway."

"Oh, okay."

"So, how can I do you?" she asks, propping against her vehicle.

Yes, right. Here for a reason. "Right. Um… do you take online fund transfers?" Oh, my God. "Okay, hold the phone." I renege a bit, "Sorry, that did not sound good. Guess a lack of sleep and food will do that to a person." …and a broken heart and the uprooting of your life. But hey, who's keeping track? Me. I am. "Let me try this again. I am in a pickle. I have plenty of money, but no cash."

"Ah ha," she grins wide and bites down on the corner of her lip before letting it go slowly. "Ya went to Foster."

"You got it. I am also really trying to lie low right now… and there's a chance that my accounts are being tracked."

Lace holds her hands up, palms out. "Now, I'm not totally opposed to helping, but I don't need any trouble finding me, ya know?"

"Right. Yeah, hey I get it. Honestly, I have no idea to what extent you'd be at risk. All I would really like to do is transfer you some money in exchange for cash. Worst case scenario, you get a visitor and tell him I… purchased some services… for my friends?"

With each added suggestion, my confidence in the plan weakens.

With each added word, her eyebrow rises higher.

She brushes away the awkwardness with a wave of her hand, though. "You know what? Yeah. Hell yeah. I'll give you a boost. Got any info on who I should be watching out for?"

My phone is out and the photo app open in a heartbeat. I step beside her and flick through my pictures. Every single one of them from several months ago. Before Dad died.

"This one is my brother."

"Damn, girl."

"Yeah." I give her a small smile. "He's a bit unhinged — especially right now — but otherwise a pretty great guy. This one" — I flip to one of Porter and me. One that Jude took, not thirty minutes after Porter convinced me into a quickie in the bathroom — "is the one you need to be wary of. Don't let him in the club at all if you can help it."

"Mind texting the picture to me?" she asks. "I'll show it to the bouncers and make sure he doesn't get inside any of the clubs around here."

My eyebrows shoot sky-high. "Y-you have that sort of sway?"

"A veteran stripper, yes girl. A guy so much as touches my big toe during a dance, and he'll be put out on his ass. If I warn 'em in advance, he won't even make it into the lobby."

A fluttery warmth fills my belly, overpowering the dull, vibrating hunger. Porter is probably still in the hospital still right now, but knowing that word here, in addition to the street racing community, is already getting out and tarnishing his reputation, elates me to no end.

Lace and I exchange numbers and money-transfer details. I send her the picture and a bit of money to get me started, and she hands me the cash. After chatting about it for a few more minutes we decide that too much money would likely put up a red flag, so we keep the transaction simple. Just a few hundred dollars to give me a one up.

I'm not remiss to realize that I am sharing quite a lot of information with someone I know very little about — who engages in a scene I am also quite unfamiliar with — but sometimes, when you know, you know. Lace's alignment is good.

…But then she has to go and bring up Crow again. "You know, Crow showed up here this morning not too long after you left."

Hearing his name hurts. Hella bad. But not in a way damaging to this new, blooming friendship. My heart pistons but grinds to a stop all at once learning that he stayed in this area of the beach all morning.

"Seems ya have a knack for dredging up his past and dangling it in front of him, hm?" she chortles.

I shake my head emphatically. "No... well, that was never my intention. I knew nothing about his past until you said something."

She sucks in the corner of her bottom lip, crosses her ankles, and tilts her head down to look up at me through her eyelashes, her eyebrows drawn in slightly. "Ya should," she states. "That boy needs a jump start, if ya catch my drift."

I inhale deeply, nostrils flaring, and straighten my posture. "Look, I... appreciate... whatever it is you see in me where Crow is concerned. But that ship has sailed. Thanks for the cash." I wave the bills in the air, turn my back to her, and put them and my phone into the clutch I have shoved in my overly small, built-in storage compartment.

With my back turned to her, the compressed breath of a sigh reaches my ears just before my helmet covers them. "Sorry," Lace states. "Hey... come back anytime, okay? I'm used to slinging cash." There's humor in the words, and the banter nearly cracks through to me. Nearly.

But the manic pounding of my head and the continued splintering of my heart still overpowers any remote sense of happiness.

CHAPTER EIGHTEEN

"**W**hat the hell am I even doing?" I mutter under my breath, the sound of my own voice humming inside my helmet as I ride on autopilot back toward the store. Everything is such a sludge of shit right now.

I have already learned the hard way that secrets and lies always come back to haunt you — to ruin you and everyone around you, depending on their severity.

Sure, I removed myself from those who were the most affected by my wrongdoings, and now I have a place of my own, but what next?

Settle in and simply live detached from my past?

What progress will that make?

The precarious situations will still exist: Dad will still be dead; Jude will still be pursuing his long-term goal to monopolize the East Coast, and Revelry will still be blindly at the receiving end of those plans. Porter will still be hustling.

The lower speed and my knack for hitting every red light on the scenic beachfront road makes my wayward and spiraling thoughts worse. When my wheels aren't spinning, my thoughts are. Eager to get to the store, finish my adult task of filling my refrigerator, and get out of my damn head — to somehow be productive by maybe formulating a plan to clean the slate and start fresh — I cut over and turn onto the higher-speed road that runs parallel with The Strip but still leads straight to the store.

Only when the throttle is open and the wind and engine drowns everything out does my head begin to feel a bit clearer. I hit a red light, though, and those spinning thoughts return. Well, almost. Instead of my thoughts carrying me away and snapping my concentration like a twig, the rev of an engine beside me does.

My heart does a damn quadruple jump. For a moment in time, I freeze completely, unable to even bring myself to check who my challenger is. If it is a challenger. I have no idea, because… I just can't. I turn inward, sucking in a shaky breath, eyes lifting to the traffic light. The vehicle revs again. I quickly surmise the easiest conclusions of all: the sound isn't distinctive of a bike nor the incredibly loud *brap*, *brap*, *brap* of the Skyline — two quite unmistakable sounds that are not easy to confuse with anything else.

In a panic, I pull on my memories of hearing the Mustang. My heart nearly stops entirely at the thought. The blood rushes to my fingers and toes. I release the handles and open and close my clenched hands to bring back sensation. The car impatiently revs again. My breath hitches.

Not the low rumble of a Mustang.

Not the prattle of a Supra or Bimmer.

Not the raw power of a Monte Carlo Super Sport.

After ticking off all the vehicles in my inner circle, it becomes a game; my panic flips to curiosity. But the traffic light beats me to a conclusion. Without thought, I open the throttle and *squrrrt* away from the intersection, keeping my focus ahead and choosing to listen instead of fully engage. When the car revs, peaks, and shifts, I open the throttle wider, eager to make an early statement and end this stupidity before it truly begins.

Sound wise, it most resembles a domestic muscle car. Muted, though — not as formidable as the Monte Carlo.

My mind flicks through images of cars in the area, and only one comes to mind: the kid who drives that Trans Am.

With an eye roll, a slight speed drop, and the flick of my flashers to claim the win just as Jude had done that one night, I finally allow my gaze to flick to the mirror.

Nailed it.

Well, for a half a second.

The proof is in nothing more than a blur of red.

Boyd speeds up even more.

The next traffic light comes fast.

My eyes flick from the light to him and back again.

A three horn blare pierces the air.

This kid's out of his damn mind; he is going to get himself killed.

My heart rate ratchets.

The light is super stale green as we approach.

One light. Maybe if I give him one light, he'll calm the fuck down and stop this nonsense.

He absolutely cannot win anyway. Surely he knows that?

The light turns yellow, and Boyd is all in. At this point, neither of us can stop in time anyway. No more time for thinking, I twist the throttle wide open and just fucking… go. If only to encourage him to hurry the hell up and get through the intersection as quickly as possible.

I curl my fingers around the clutch lever to switch into that final gear, but the clutch slips; my engine over-revs, rear tire locks, and the bike gets loose.

Of all the things possible to flash through my mind, Foster's poetic advice from this morning flashes in bold letters: "Choose your priorities, girl."

Dying wasn't my priority of choice…

…but it was a hell of a lot easier to do than living had been lately.

Fast.

Painless.

No white light.

No flashes of memory from a life well lived.

No regrets or unfinished business.

Everything was color as I leaned to the asphalt, but in the next heartbeat, I had laid her down, and all that existed was black.

CHAPTER NINETEEN

Jude

The night of our first Midnight Runners' meet, Crow and I exchanged numbers after working together to disable Porter. I never in a million lifetimes would have expected to receive a call from him. Especially one telling me that my sister had been in an accident.

"She's alive. Just get here safely."

He doesn't say anything more. I know that the vague update means her life is in the balance, but he doesn't want to risk me driving stupid just to get there and find out. In that one sentence, he attempted to give me hope.

By the time I get there, she's in emergency surgery. Several hours are filled with paperwork and dozing in and out in a chair in the waiting room. The Revelry guys and I make up the four corners of the otherwise empty room. Nobody sits beside each other — everyone attempting to stay as far apart as possible; clearly, something happened between their crew, and they're all at odds.

The longer I sit here, still knowing nothing about how Remi got into a wreck, the more my own conclusions begin to form. And I don't much like how those conclusions are looking. Fear and anxiety slowly simmering into rage and vengeance, my focus turns from dazed to razor sharp as I alternate glances at each member of their crew. My knee starts a slow bounce. My fingers curl tighter and tighter into my palms.

I shoot out of my seat, finger pointing accusingly at none of them in particular. "I want you guys out of here." They had something to do with this; their features are riddled with guilt.

The one in the glasses and nerdy shirt matches my motion, immediately launching into a defensive position, meeting me in the center of the room, separated only by the long coffee table at our shins.

I'm two seconds away from darting my hand out and wrapping my fingers around his neck, when he reaches behind him, picks up the laptop he was using for the past several hours, and sets it up on the table between us, screen facing my direction.

A video pops up, displaying what looks to be street cam feeds. Remi comes to a stop at a light, and a very familiar red Trans Am pulls up beside her — the same Trans Am that raced me not too long ago. I watch in horror as the kid challenges her, and she does everything to try to classily let him down. "He challenged her to a Pottstown race in the middle of the day? I mean, I get that he's an overenthusiastic kid, but he should know better."

The video feeds had been edited; multiple feeds were combined from various traffic cams in order to get all the different angles, zoom in certain spots, and span in others. It is messy, but in the end, the entire thing can be played in a loop with only the occasional glitch in stitching.

As soon as the other two guys realize what we're watching, they jump up and bracket me. In a manner of minutes, we move from being as distanced as possible to hovering around the small screen as a unit, watching as Remi lays down her bike and slides along the ground in what feels like extra slow motion.

"Wait…" The one who owns the Monte Carlo speaks up, finger pointing at the screen. "Did you catch that? Play it aga—"

"Mr. Delancey?"

The guy in glasses slams the laptop screen shut, and the four of us jolt our attention toward the nurse. I fell into a squat to watch the footage but quickly scramble upward. "Yes. That's me." I make my way toward the lady, entire body shaking.

"The surgery went well; we took some of the skin from her thigh in order to graft it to her arm. Remi-Sue is hanging in there, but she has a long road of recovery in her future."

The nurse's eyes flash upward and widen a little on catching the faux pas of her choice of wording. *A long road, indeed.*

She leaves, and I turn back to the crew. "Anyone seen or heard anything about the kid since he left the scene?"

Crow steps up to me, shakes his head, and holds out a closed hand. "No, but rumor has it Porter is on the mend and his room has been quite active with visitors."

Visitors? Who the hell does he even know here that would visit him? I hold my hand out to accept whatever Crow is trying to give me. His fingers uncurl, and a small bullet drops into my palm. "None of us want to hold onto the evidence of your lapse in judgement."

My eyes stay locked on the small piece of metal, a bundle of disjointed thoughts and memories twisting in my mind. "Where did you get this?"

"Remi dug it out herself that night at the port. Wanted to make sure no incriminating evidence led to you."

The words he uses hit far too close to home… to a different port and a different bullet. I shove my hand and the bullet into my pocket and plop into the closest chair, mumbling a quiet "Thanks." Crow pulls a face, shrugs, and returns to his original seat.

The four of us make a home of that waiting room for the night. No one sleeps. No one speaks. Everyone just… waits. Studying the video. Thinking. Processing. I never stop rolling the bullet between the pads of my fingers, thoughts mulling and rolling right along with every swap.

CHAPTER TWENTY

Remi

*B*eep.
Beep.
Beep.

Beep.

Beep.

The sound plagues my dreams forever it seems.

Beep.

Beep.

Beep.

No matter how fast I try to pursue it, I can never catch up.

Beep.

Beep.

Beep.

Beep.

At times, a moving truck backing up materializes in my mind, always reversing.

Beep.

Beep.

Beep.

Beep.

Occasionally, the sound presents as several three-horn blares back to back.

Beep.

Beep.

Beep.

Beep.

Worst, the sound I often imagined was what remaining life my dad had prior to Jude and me arriving at the hospital that unforgettable night — nothing but a steady hum. A flatline, echoing in my ears ever since.

Beep.

Beep.

Beep.

Beep.

Exhausted, weak, and totally over hearing the incessant noise, I am ready for silence. But my mind and body seem to be attached to a rubber-band like noose that just keeps rebounding backward anytime I try to pull. To rise.

Beep.

Beep.

Beep.

Beep.

That sound. Damn that sound. Over time — so much time — it became increasingly louder to the point where it was all-consuming. Each beep matched my pulse. Each beat thrummed a rhythm in my head. Loud. Excruciating.

Too much.

Too noisy.

I clench my teeth together and pull that rubber band noose so hard it snaps. My eyes pop wide, and I gasp, shooting upward.

The beeping continued but took on a new pace.

Fast.

Faster.

A flash of movement catches in my bleary, peripheral vision.

I know exactly where I am and why. My head pounds even harder. The sound, lights, motion, and the rapid beating of my heart is all too much. I plop backward, panting, gasping for breath — eyes squeezed tight against the pain, fingers clutching into something cool and pliable.

A voice lulls to me. A familiar one. I try hard to open my eyes against the bright lights, but it's so damn hard. When my eyelashes part, it is only minusculely. The outline of a person hovers above me.

My tongue tries to form Jude's name.

My hand tries to reach out for him.

But my efforts are all for naught.

His hand moves to my face and fingers brush against my forehead and behind my ear. "Remi?" his whispery voice calls to me.

After another failed attempt to speak, I swallow hard. Since my eyes seem to be the only part of my body willing to even hint at functioning, I work through that first, blinking repeatedly. The beeping is still incessant. The light is overwhelming. I am unable to talk, but I can press my lips together and furrow my brows.

Jude pulls away, and a moment later, a whoosh sounds and a dimness shrouds the room. That human outline returns. I want so badly to reach out and touch him — to speak his name. I feel his pain, his unbalanced emotions; they vibrate around and through me like light caught in a bulb.

Again, I swallow hard, my throat working out the idea of vocalizing his name. All I can get out is the first syllable, the "ooo" sound painful and challenging to form with my unused lips. The fingers still resting lightly near my cheek curl behind my ear and clench through my hair slightly. The last syllable of his name is a bit easier, though, so I stick with that approach, managing to get out something that sounds more like "Judd" than Jude.

"J-Jd?" I repeat, attempting the inflection of a question.

His hand drops slowly from my ear, fingers falling to my jaw instead, and his blurry profile turns to the side briefly then back toward me. "He… he stepped out."

My entire body seizes. The beeping increases yet again. I blink repeatedly, over and over and over again.

Instead of black-brown eyes looking down at me, steely-gray ones are. His teeth worry at a labret piercing. My eyes sting from more than the act of becoming adjusted. Now that I can see Crow clearly, I regret my efforts. The last time we spoke was at the meet, when he found me betraying Revelry. Betraying him. I turn my head to the side and squeeze my eyes shut hard. His fingers spread wide over my jaw and cheek, and my face nuzzles into it.

Tears seep from the corner of my eyes. Half of them drip over and down my nose; the other half drown his thumb in a salty sea of emotion.

A coolness washes over me when his hand leaves my face. The creak of him plopping down into a seat next to me follows. His hand never leaves me, though. It trails from my face to my shoulder and down my arm as he changes from standing to sitting.

Then, his fingers curve over my palm and lock there. A moment later, there's a slight depression beside our interlocked hands. Only then do I reopen my eyes, being too much of a coward to open them before, on the off chance he was looking at me.

The curtains behind him are pulled shut. I quickly surmise that was where most of the light from earlier must've been coming from and he closed the curtains, understanding that I was struggling to open my eyes because of the amount of light in the room.

My gaze travels over his black clothes and hair and lands on our hands. At the number tattoos on each knuckle. I lift my thumb and drag it lightly over each number. Crow's head jerks up, and his gaze pierces mine. His hand twitches, but I tighten my fingers around it before he can jerk it away. "Th-thank..." Damn, talking is a bitch. Instead of saying "Thank you for being here," like I want to, I stick with the first and last word, hoping he can fill in the blanks. "H-ere."

His hand returns the squeeze, and he gives me a sharp nod.

For the first time, I study the room a bit more.

The seat along the window has a pillow and blanket haphazardly placed there. Again, my eyes return to Crow. He was following my traveling gaze, and at my silent question, he clears his throat. "Ah... someone had to. You know... in case you woke up."

I raise an eyebrow.

Visitors are certainly not a requirement in hospitals.

He keeps going...

"I... I don't sleep well most nights anyway."

For the first time since waking up, a small smile quirks on my lips. Crow doesn't catch it. He shrugs and refuses to make eye contact, happy enough with his deathtrap on my hand.

He rambles on...

"After the first week, Trenton had to go back to work."

"Hayes… he is in the cafeteria right now."

"Jude… is… busy."

After the first week? H-how long have I been here? How long has Jude been busy? Did he even ever come?

My slight smile drops and eyebrows curve inward. He catches the change, having looked at me while delivering the news. I try asking the last question my thoughts led to: "H-has… here?"

Goddammit.

Somehow, Crow understands. His voice drops, and his other hand comes up to my cheek. "Yeah. Jude has been here. None of us have seen him for a while, though."

CHAPTER TWENTY-ONE

T wo weeks is about how long I was admitted for before they finally released me. I remembered everything about the race and the wreck. But not about my hospital stay — not until I came fully to that second week and Crow was in the room with me. He explained that I traded my goose egg for a loss of several layers of skin and muscle in my arm, then came down with a terrible infection in the wound. They had to place me into a medically induced coma because the infection took hold so fast that my body struggled to fight it — to heal.

I waited until he was out of earshot and a nurse was in the room to ask her how often Crow came and stayed the night.

Her answer? He never left.

Not once.

Not even to eat. He apparently would insist they bring me food in case I woke up and was hungry but would eat it himself every time. They knew. The staff was apparently all quite smitten with this behavior and let it slide.

Crow explained that Jude showed up the night they brought me in. He stayed the night every night during the worst of it. But as soon as he signed off on the papers agreeing to the medically induced coma and

I started showing immediate signs of improvement, he left to "take care of business." In the underground scene, we all know what that is code for. As soon as I could sit up and function, I ached to call or text him, but my phone had become roadkill.

I asked Crow to pass on a few messages using his phone and he agreed, even despite never receiving a response back after each attempt. Having been familiar with him leaving for "jobs" in the past and often not hearing from him for quite a while, I tried not to let it bother me.

:Me: I'm feeling better today.

:Me: I can move and walk and all the things now.

:Me: They're letting me out of this place!

I slide into the passenger seat of Crow's car… but it's not the Supra. Instead, it's that V Coupe he was in the night all went to shit. "Nice ride," I state. "Never really pegged you as a Caddy guy."

Crow swipes his tongue along his bottom lip, giving the lip ring a quick flick. "That's because I'm not a Caddy guy."

Even after I started interacting with the nurses, Crow still never left the hospital; he spent time with me, joked, shot the shit... like we had been friends for a lifetime.

Being in a vehicle with him and out of the confines of the hospital, the feeling is different, though. There was an uneasiness that bloomed as soon as we stepped foot through the exit doors.

And now? Being in his passenger seat? That uneasiness easily morphs into the spark we could never run from. The sterileness of the hospital seemed to overpower it for a while. Crow would hold his breath every time they took my vitals as though the news of the results were going to be terrible. As though my recovery was a dream and everything would turn into a nightmare again.

There was an unsteadiness of danger lingering... versus the freedom of safety we have now. Crow waits until we're in forward motion to break the buzzing silence: "This was my wife's car," he states with a steady voice. "Rachal." He chuckles darkly. "She tried to like it but ended up wanting nothing to do with performance vehicles. So, we got her the non-sporty, sedan version, too." There's a long pause, and his throat moves unsteadily. I scarcely breathe for fear he will stop. But... he continues. "The regular CTS was better for a family anyway — fit the carseat and all." His gaze floats sideways and fingers grip the wheel a bit harder. "Lace told me she met you."

I simply nod, tongue and throat locked tight.

"You didn't just infiltrate a normal club, Remi. There's nothing normal about the mess you stumbled on. We are tight, but not without issues... without history. There's a reason Trenton went back to work instead of staying at the hospital with you — he didn't want to leave your side."

My heart stutters and flips, and I speak for the first time. "Crow..."

His eyes remain steadfast on the road. "The hospital wouldn't let more than one of us stay. Trenton stepped aside..."

Again a long pause. When his voice returns, it's low and whispery. Pained. A struggle. "I fought to stay at your side. He left for my benefit. With Rachal and Bree... the opportunity didn't exist. They never made it that far. Because I have the worst fucking luck, I saw your wreck. I was there, driving back home after fucking wandering all morning and afternoon. I was the first one on the scene. Just like I was when Rachal and Bree died."

Crow converts to taking these short, excruciating pauses, never long enough to ruin the flow or for him to back out of the confession. "After their crash, I learned Rachal had been fucking Travis — Trenton's brother. The same fucking guy that got her killed. But see... that's the thing about people who lie — who keep secrets — they are really damn good at it. I couldn't grieve properly, because then I hated her as

137

much as I missed her. But one thing I could do was make sure no one ever fucked me over again. Trust no one. Love no one."

And the truth of those words — the poison I had administered — fills every empty space and crevice in the car.

* * *

WE PULL INTO THE JUNKYARD where my bike was rumored to have been taken. Neither of us said another word after his confession. I had nothing to say in response. I was that person — the one who had fucked him over when he was still vulnerable. He saw everything firsthand, witnessed the repercussions. He knew there was a good reason behind my secrets. He had accepted the unraveling and outcome of it all. I had accepted my punishment — and still was.

What was done could not be undone.

I lied and kept harmful secrets.

Ones that directly impacted him.

Saying sorry is… empty.

Rubbing salt in his wounds is unideal.

There is nothing more to say or do.

So we carry on, wordlessly, with our agenda.

With today. The present moment.

That is the best we can do.

That is all either of us want to do.

He puts the V Coupe into park, unbuckles, and exits.

I follow.

We walk in silence through the rows of broken down and mangled vehicles. My heart turns into a gigantic magnet, guiding me straight to my bike as if I somehow, intrinsically, know exactly where she is. And when I see her, I cling to her just like a magnet would.

My eyes blur. I dart a quick glance over my shoulder at Crow — seeking support? Strength where I had none?

He stopped when my walking turned into a sprint, though, and now lingers in the background, his black clothes and rough-edged personality blending with the rusty and damaged scenery.

Crow leans against an old beater, crosses his feet at the ankles, and shoves his hands into his pockets. His chrome eyes tell me everything I need in that moment:

This is about me. Not him.

I don't need his strength… because I have my own.

But he is here, should anything change.

I sink to my butt, wrap my arms around my knees, and lean my shoulder against the rear wheel.

Then, I cry. For a long, long while. Shoulders shaking, vocal cords wailing, snot running — my entire body involved in the purge. Crow never approaches, and I am grateful for that — for his distanced support despite all the shit I put him through since the moment I walked into The Crow Bar and Grill.

Eventually, my eyes dry. Painfully so. They are overused and aching. Swollen. Stinging. Raw.

With a deep, shaky, breath I finally push off the ground and dust off my body and hands. I attempt to pry away the seat in order to get my clutch out from inside the storage compartment, but no luck. So, I go on the hunt for a crowbar or something to pry it loose. For a split second, Crow twitches, tempted to leave his resting spot. But he changes his mind and settles again. Our eyes lock for a moment when I bend down to dig through a scrap pile.

With that one look, I can tell his thoughts are speeding faster than his Supra with a squeeze of nitrous; his chrome eyes are slightly manic and teeth are worrying nonstop at his piercing. He keeps quiet, though, still seemingly content to let me do my thing.

His presence is enough; I am exceedingly grateful that someone is here with me regardless of baggage. I manage to wrench free one of those long pieces that connects a steering system together — a drag link, if my mind serves me — and make my way back to the bike, makeshift tool in hand. With a bit of effort, I work the seat off. Wrecks, it seems, are similar to natural disasters in the selective way they tear into one thing but leave something else untouched. As is the case with my clutch inside. I pull it out and pop the snap. All the cash, my license, and little odds and ends things are all still there… including my undamaged cell phone. I'm about to set the seat loosely back on top when a hint of white catches my attention.

I gently place the seat pad back down on the ground near my feet and finger out the item. Whatever it is had somehow been tucked under some of the metal framework. The crash must've jarred the piece loose. Likely something that had fallen out of my clutch or that I had put in there a long time ago and got buried, seeing as my Duc is—was—going on seven years old at this point. I yank out the tightly-folded piece of paper and open it. But this is something I most certainly have never seen before. I recognize Dad's handwriting immediately, though. My heart pangs at the reminder of his death, and again as my eyes flick from the paper to my bike. Aside from pictures and a floundering company, she was the only thing I had left of him. The only damn thing. And he only gave me one rule: "Don't drive stupid, Remi."

That exact rule stares back at me in his bold scrawl. "Don't drive stupid, Remi," I whisper, reading it aloud, eyes tracking over the itty-bitty paper. I stumble, knees nearly giving out on the spot. My hands catch the mangled metal of my bike, preventing me from falling back to the ground and doing a second lap.

"Dad, I tried." My eyes blink rapidly, and I sniffle. "Dammit, I tried." I wipe my eyes with the back of my hand.

A faint smudge of ink in the bottom corner has me brushing my damp thumb over the crinkled fibers. Eyes tracking the movement, I realize it isn't a smudge, but more writing. I squint and bring the paper close to my eyes.

Three small alphanumeric characters: CR2.

"Think fast," Crow's voice snaps me back into the moment, and I spin on my heels. A black blur flies through the air directly at me.

Ah shit… again?

Despite Foster's sound advice, I still react — still attempt to cradle-catch my helmet.

This time, I manage to do so without dropping the item in my hold. The note from my dad remains clutched tightly in my grip.

Crow had closed the distance at some point during my monolog with the man I miss more than anything and heard my whispered speech. My focus drops to my helmet. "You rode smart," Crow says. He flips the helmet over in my arms. The air rushes from my lungs, and I heave to recapture it at the sight before me: Half my helmet is gone. All the layers of protection visible like the center of a stump from a cut

142

tree — all except for the final one that had lain flat against my head.

"I watched you lay her down." His gaze drops to my arm and back up again, reminding us both about the horrific, still tender, scar just beneath the material of my long-sleeved shirt. "It was fucking terrifying... and really damn amazing. I've never witnessed someone ride as smart as you did."

"I should've pulled over instead of encouraging him."

"You flashed your emergencies. He should've taken the hint."

"I didn't pull the clutch fast enough."

"We checked. It wasn't your fault. We watched the traffic cams — over and over again — took your bike apart and inspected it. You did everything right," he insists. "Your clutch was in great condition..." His focus flicks briefly to my bike. "It was your transmission."

Neither my clutch nor my transmission should have been messed up, though. We did a full inspection on her before leaving California. That would explain why everything sounded a lot louder than usual before I went down, though. Even considering my Duc's natural rattle.

Crow drops the topic. He slips his hand through the lip of my helmet's visor, takes it from my arms, and places it in the gape of my storage compartment.

Then, he steps forward, standing so that our feet are zigzagging — one of his between both of mine. "Sorry I showed up at the Midnight Runners' meet that night and treated you the way I did," he says.

He lifts his hand and drags a thumb along that long-gone bruise on my cheek where Porter had marked me and all this mess began.

I steel my shoulders and lock my gaze with his. "You don't have to apologize because you've suffered a loss and want to make amends through me. I'm not deserving of your apology, Burke." He flinches at my casual use of his real name. But we're here, talking about real things, in a real moment, and doing so just feels like the right thing to do. "You were right not to trust me. I proved as much."

"Remi…"

"Burke…"

This… this showdown is what feels comfortable with him.

Except for when he grips my face between his hot fingers and pulls my mouth to his. The move is hardly fair, and one that I can't counter. He knows that. I know that.

Our hot, wet tongues battle, and his labret piercing scrapes against my bottom lip, causing a delicious sort of pain — a welcome sort of pain compared to all the pain I've had over the course of several months now. Both physical and emotional.

Except that his tongue cuts even deeper. Right into my soul. As soon as I sense my body giving in — melting — a surge of adrenaline hits me, and I shove him backward, shaky fingers immediately coming up to drag across my tender mouth.

Crow gets in my face, finger lifted and pointing at me accusingly. "Snake bites? Scorpion stings? Where do you think they get the cures from, hm? From the fucking source." He stops, chest heaving. Then his voice lowers, but his eyes remain locked and hard on mine. The lowered voice isn't menacing, though; it's riddled with pain. "You're my fucking antivenin, Remi." Crow closes the distance between us again and pushes his fingers through the hair against the base of my neck. "Heal me."

"I still have secrets," I whisper, sharing an equal amount of pain in the whispered confession all the while I clench that little paper in my fist with all my might.

"So do I," he states, dragging his piercing along my bottom lip.

CHAPTER TWENTY-TWO

C row drags the conclusion of our kiss out, sucking in my bottom lip, depressing his teeth into my soft flesh, and ending with small kisses over the throb. His hands drop from my face and move down my arms, until one is cupped in mine and he can tug me toward the V Coupe. He opens the driver door, pops the seat, and digs one of those large, hole-riddled hospital blankets out of the trunk. I take advantage of the opening and toss my clutch inside, choosing to shove the note into my pocket. Finding the collection of a hospital blanket a bit odd, I lift a brow at him, and he shrugs, closing the door with a gental bump of his outer thigh.

"The entire time I was there, I joked about how comfortable the blanket was. They gifted it to me on my way out when I was loading everything up."

I can't help the small chuckle that escapes me. "Breaking hearts everywhere you go."

Crow doesn't respond; he simply leads me through a maze of vehicles, blanket draped over his shoulder. This gesture clearly means one thing. Our very silence is riddled with the foreplay: The twitch of his thumb against the back of my hand. The slow, forward progress. Occasional side glances.

Each behavior — every step — drags everything out, leaving our imagination to create an exciting scene.

By the time we reach his intended destination — a late-forties, b-series truck — the rise and fall of my chest is exaggerated with every breath, and my eyes are having difficulty focusing on anything other than the precursory lust. Crow's hand squeezes mine, warm and damp from the same anticipation.

He lets go and floats open the large blanket, spreading it out evenly on the wooden, planked flatbed, and folds it in half to create a little cushion.

Attempting to be mindful of my breathing, lest my heart pound straight out of my chest, I inhale deep through my nose and exhale slowly from my mouth.

A large oak canopies over the truck, the midday sun streaming through the branches and leaves, dappling the off-white hospital blanket with light.

Crow's tattooed fingers steal the frame, popping into my view and snapping me out of my assessment of the area. I accept his proffered hand, and we work in tandem to get me inside the truck bed with him.

Once standing inside, the closely-slatted, wooden-caged frame comes up to about hip level, providing an ideal barricade for any potential passersby.

His hands curve around each side of my hips, and he spins me around, drawing my pelvis flush against

147

him. The hard length of his cock against my lower belly is a good indicator that his mind has been bogged down with intent, too.

He wraps his arms around my lower back and grinds against me, nuzzling his nose along my chin to encourage my head back before dragging it upward to my jaw and beyond until our mouths are parallel, and little wisps of our breath can be seen in a stream of light, hot against the rare, cool, early-October afternoon.

Instead of kissing me, though, his hands release my waist, fingers grip the hem of my shirt, and he lifts it off, baring me to the entire junkyard behind us. My nipples instantly pucker at both the exhibitionism and the blast of chilly air. He then guides me down to the blanket, rests me flat on my back, loops his fingers under the waistband of my sweatpants, and pulls those off.

Crow peels away all his clothes, as well: shirt, boots, jeans, and boxers. Despite the cold, he still juts out proudly. He settles between my spread legs, lifting up my ass to drape my thighs over his.

Starting at my knee and ending just below the crease where my bareness is open and revealed, he traces a line along the inside of my leg and thigh.

Once he stops, only then do I notice the slight tremble vibrating from his fingertip. Slowly, I engage my abs and carefully prop up on my elbows, testing my arm's ability to do so, in order to bring my face closer to his. But instead of offering him a kiss, my eyes flick to the spot on my inner thigh where he now circles. Crow is intent, studying the faint scar of the donor location for my skin graft.

When he's ready, his hand moves up to between my thighs and cups my sex, but he doesn't linger there. Instead, he moves on over to my hip then to my wrist, which he pins to the blanket. Using his other hand to brush his fingers along the much more unsightly scar on my forearm, he studies every indentation, every raised and dipped sinew, every thin and thick line where the grafting had struggled to take at first during my recovery. Thankfully, I ended up healing exceptionally well, but there will be lasting marks, both physically and emotionally.

He cups his hand over my flesh and lightly rubs some warmth along the thin skin turning extra purple from the lick of cold air around us. My heart doesn't have a chance to grieve the aesthetic loss, because Crow steals my grief and makes it his own. His touch slicks my wounds with a balm of adoration and respect.

That touch leaves my arm, moves back to my hip, and slips between my thighs again. I watch, eyes hooded, chest heaving, as his tattooed fingers disappear inside me.

Instead of my eyes fluttering shut, they meet his steely gaze and lock there as he twists inside me and rubs his thumb along my clit.

He slowly removes his fingers and splays them along my uppermost inner thigh, nudging my legs further apart while he knee-walks backward and gets adjusted. His mouth brushes against my knee first. The sensitive skin at the side next. Then on to the upper portion of my thigh. When he reaches the donor spot, his tongue flattens against my marred skin and swipes slowly, hot and wet. That heat is then quickly replaced by a ping of iciness from the air hitting my damp skin.

The hot-cold contrast continues; replacing the chill, his palms lay flat on the tops of my thighs, thumbs curving downward. The motion is planned. Intentional. Because in the next second his tongue is speared inside me, and those palms and thumbs are gripping me harder to defend against my body's knee-jerk reaction to coil tightly and squeeze my legs together. Arms shaking, I ease onto my back and squeeze my eyes shut as he spears and twists over and over again.

With every spear, my pussy walls tighten. With every twist they loosen and vibrate with need. When my hands dash to his head and fingers clutch into his messy, black strands, he drags his bottom lip along my clit, sending an electric wave through me and making my body convulse.

"Oh fuck…" I breathe out, heaving.

Crow chuckles and does it again, using that lip ring to drive me. His hands grip harder in opposition to the way my thighs threaten to close and bottle up that release, refusing to let it free before he is inside of me and we can do it together.

Even Crow knows the second time is nearly too much. He laves me with his tongue and delves inside me once more before pushing up, leaning back on his calves, and digging around in our pile of clothes for the condom stashed in his wallet.

When I reach forward to help, the motion fails, and my arm plops back to my side useless. The act is quick, though, and before long his body hovers over mine, hands gripping the blanket at each side of my head so he can dip down and swipe his tongue into my mouth with a similar thrust as he had done down below just moments ago.

Again, he pulls away and straightens — this time to line up with my entrance. He watches, eyes hooded, and tongue toying with his piercing, while he slips slowly inside me.

I moan, supping on every thick inch as he draws out the motion. Once his base is flush against my opening, he pulls out and drives inside me with a seductive, fluid thrust. His hands cup my hips with the next thrust, and together we merge deeper — him pulling, me bucking.

His long, dark lashes flutter downward, but just as quickly spring open. He freezes inside of me and head jerks to the side, eyes scanning the junkyard.

He then drops down, body flush with mine, chest heaving against my cheek. I wriggle beneath him. "Cr—"

His hand scoops over my mouth, muffling my attempted question. He curves his back and brings his mouth as close to my ear as possible. "Shhh. Someone is here."

My entire body tenses. I tilt my head back to look up at him. When our eyes lock, I give him a nod of understanding. He slowly releases my mouth, hand dropping down to my neck instead. His fingers wrap around my throat, and he groans against my ear while simultaneously thrusting deep and low inside me with a tight grind.

His fingers tighten around the column of my neck, and he thrusts and grinds again. The sound of conversation and metal being moved floats around us. But even still, my body throbs with need, muscles clenching around him. He twitches inside me and curves his hips, penetrating me deeper, harder. A low moan vibrates from my chest and trickles past my lips. Again he cups my mouth, barricading the sounds from the junkyard customers.

But it only serves to make me ache more. My lips open against his palm and tongue snakes out to taste him. He cups my mouth harder, and slams inside me, a moan of his own vibrating in his chest as he battles to keep his own sex noises contained.

When I lick him again, he releases my mouth and slips one finger inside, giving me something to toy with. "Keep testing me, and you may get more than you expect," he whispers low and hot. I buck my hips upward and grip his ass with my fingers. He arches, matching me motion for motion. Every deep thrust drives me closer to the finish line. He works in and out of me, antagonizing me, urging me to wail despite threatening me to keep quiet. He does it on purpose…

…and I don't fight it.

…I let them trickle out of me. I allow myself to rebel — to challenge him. He responds by adding a second finger and then a third into my mouth. Once the third is in, I can no longer lathe and flick. He shoves his cock inside me while pressing his tattooed fingers along my tongue and inching them backward, finger fucking my mouth while taking the rest of my body.

Together, we spiral. Together, our noises can no longer be contained.

He shudders inside me, and I hum around his fingers, head tossed back, pussy squeezing him dry. We also crash just as quickly as the customers stop conversation and everything falls eerily silent.

Their footsteps crunch away. Crow's tense body loosens as he rolls off me and falls to his back, panting, finally letting out all the pent-up breaths he was holding in all for the sake of trying to keep quiet.

New footsteps approach, distanced at first. However, they soon pick up pace. Crow reaches over me, slings a corner of the blanket over my body, scoops up all our clothes, and says, "Time to go. Better keep pace."

He then launches into action, and I join him. We jump out of the flatbed, him buck naked and me wrapped in the hospital blanket, and dash through the junkyard — me squealing with laughter while an irate junkyard owner hollers and shakes his fist behind us.

CHAPTER TWENTY-THREE

With a twinkle in his eyes and a devilish grin lighting up his face, Crow takes off like a bat outta hell.

While he drives, I plug my phone in to his charger and work on getting my clothes back on. Once I am fully dressed, he lets go of the wheel and tells me to take it. My eyes pop wide, but he doesn't give me any opportunity to refuse before sliding the seat all the way back and lifting his bare ass off the leather in order to attempt putting a long leg into his boxers while still pressing the gas.

When he lets his foot off the gas and the nose of the vehicle dips in response, I panic and tug the wheel a little too hard. A car passes us, horn blaring. "Crow!" I squeal.

He laughs. "Don't get us killed, Remi." There is absolutely zero fear in that statement. He does it all over again with his jeans. These take more time and effort, and his foot is off the gas long enough to where we're nearly moving at a snail's pace in the slow lane.

I have never been more thankful for an automatic transmission than when he proceeds to put on his boots. Once the right boot is on, he punches the gas again, and my knuckles and lungs tighten. After the second boot is on, he grabs his shirt, throws me a wink and a quick lip ring flick before tossing it over his head and slipping his arms into the sleeves.

Then, he finally settles back into the seat. One hand wraps around the wheel, the other wraps around my temporary driving hand, fingers slipping between mine before he removes our hands from the wheel and settles them, clasped, on the console between us.

In this moment, I equal parts love and hate him for the trust he offered me today. How he agreed to try — to give in a little — despite any lingering secrets between us.

Thing is… I believe him. Trust him. One day, the truth of what happened with Dad will be revealed. When that happens, I truly believe Crow's feelings for me won't buckle — not because of the secret, at least. The consequence of it coming to light, though. Perhaps.

"Thanks for bringing me to her," I say as we merge onto a side road. "I… I don't know if Hayes told you, but I was staying at that trailer park down the street from where you live."

"He did."

"I… don't know if Foster is willing to take me still — or if there is even a spot available any more. But I have the cash now." I wave my clutch in the air.

"You don't have to stay there."

My heart pangs, but I cover it up with a playful gasp. "Aww, are you saying I can move in with you?"

Crow's throat seizes, and he chokes over nothing at all. "Ah… nope. I was going to throw you on Hayes and Trenton's doorstep… bundled in that hospital blanket like an abandoned newborn."

I raise an eyebrow at him, and he raises one back at me.

I chuckle. "Chill out. I… actually… I meant what I said when Hayes stopped by that day. I need to do this. To cut the apron strings, you know? It's past time."

"Figured you'd say that."

"You know…" I nudge him playfully with my knuckles on his bicep. "You're welcome to stay the night. We can have a good 'ol fashioned sleepover."

The ensuing laugh is so genuine that crow's feet even form in the corner of his eyes. But then he opens his damn mouth and ruins everything: "Oh, we're definitely having a sleepover. You don't have a choice. Funny to think you thought you did. We're not leaving you alone."

The sentiment is sweet, I give them credit for that. "Oh… fun! Well, chauffeur, bring me to my house first, please? I… want to see if Jude is there. Maybe pick up a few things." Those are definitely a couple of the reasons I want to make the pit stop, but the main reason is that there's something to be said about that tiny writing at the bottom of my dad's note. And… I think I know exactly how to follow that trail.

Chrome eyes dart to mine at the suggestion, before returning to the road. Crow gives me a nod of approval. Since the wreck happened on the beach side of the county, my bike had been delivered to the closest junkyard, which, in turn, was somewhat near my house; he only needs to reroute slightly in order to get there.

Nothing more is said until we drive up to the house. I gape at the emptiness there. Not a single vehicle is parked in the driveway or under the deck. Not mine, of course. Not Godzilla… which was somewhat expected. But… not the Mustang either. My heart immediately hops like a fleeing rabbit.

I had been foolish to think Porter was still holed up in a hospital somewhere. But to see his vehicle gone and know he is out there somewhere with the unfinished business that has to do with me and my dad, terror freezes me and everything around me.

Crow's fingers wrapping loosely over my knee steal my focus right away, and everything returns to normal motion again. I blink repeatedly, willing my breathing to normalize. "Porter came back?" I ask shakily.

"Ah…" Crow gets weird, teeth worrying at his lip and knuckles whitening over the steering wheel. "Jude mentioned borrowing his car last time we spoke to him."

My eyebrows shoot sky high. "Jude… borrowing Porter's car? Hell must've frozen over while I was indisposed."

"Mm, something like that."

I hesitate still. This stilt house is a mansion of haunted memories.

"So… umm… he's not in there?"

Crow shakes his head. "I can go in with you, if you want."

"Yeah. Definitely. I want."

He squeezes my knee, lets go, unbuckles, and leads the way out, encouraging me to follow suit with a quick dip of his head back into the car when I don't immediately open the door.

Our eyes meet, and his gaze is soft. Such a rare sight for the black-hearted, cocky Crow I met. The softness works on me, though. I grab my phone, shove it in my clutch, unbuckle, and step out. He follows me up the stairs and inside the house, the two of us only pausing long enough for me to dig out my key and unlock the door.

As soon as I step into the kitchen and place my clutch on the bar top, I freeze again, unable to move. Crow's arm goes around my waist, his touch pulling me out of my stupor once more. I exhale a pent-up breath and give him a weak smile. "Sorry. I don't know what the hell is wrong with me. Let me just take care of a few things, and we'll get out of here. I'll try not to be long. Um… get comfortable?"

He gives me a sharp nod and moves toward Dad's leather recliner in the corner.

I walk past him, into the hallway, and steal away in the office room, closing the door and locking it behind me.

The desk is a bit disheveled, which is an unusual state for Jude to leave it in, but otherwise everything else seems to be in order. I plop down into the office chair, give it a little spin, and let the motion carry me until it stops. For a moment, I close my eyes and imagine the dizzy sensation is a vortex that can take me back in time so I can redo the past.

When the chair stops, my eyes open and land immediately on the large, panoramic print of Dad and me standing beside my motorcycle. That feather-light piece of paper in my pocket turns into a brick. I reach inside and pull it out to unfold it once more.

"Okay, Dad. Why was this in my bike storage?" Dad wasn't a sentimentalist, and he most certainly wasn't a handwritten-notes type of guy — give him electronics and a speedy digital workflow any day over sticky notes and ledger books.

I look down at the small writing. CR2 is an image file type — a raw version exclusive to fancier cameras like the one Jude used to have. That combination of alphanumeric characters is also less recognizable to people who aren't familiar with the type of image; in other words, less people who could decode whatever hidden message my dad hoped to relay.

The quote on the paper was spoken on my birthday right after Jude took the picture that now hangs on the wall. Coincidence?

I shake my head and press my lips together. Jude didn't print this until after Dad died. Even knowing that, I have no other trail to follow. So, I climb onto the desk, pull the large frame down, and carefully situate it flat on the floor, image side down.

After popping off the metal prongs that are holding the mat to the frame, I scan the back of the photo paper for any clues.

The path leads to a dead end.

I knew better. CR2 files have to be converted before print—

I quickly put the frame back together, carefully balance it between my forearm and bicep whilst climbing back on top of the desk. With a bit more effort than it took to get it down, I balance and hang it on the hook.

Dad always insisted Jude keep the raw images. Eventually, Jude insisted he set up a special cloud account for them so that the overly-large files would stop bogging down their shared computer. So, naturally, my next step was to access the cloud storage where he kept them all.

There's a chance Dad just meant for me to remember that day. Those words. But then why scrawl the format code?

I power on the computer and pace the room while it boots up. As soon as everything is powered on, I immediately access the account, adjust the "sort by" filter to "created," and scroll to the date of my sixteenth birthday. Easy peasy.

Holding my breath, I double click the file, thankful Jude still has the necessary conversion programs to do so. At first glance, the image is exactly the same as the print. It's simply a less-vibrant version.

I fall against the chair's backrest and rock myself. Then, I lean forward again and zoom in as much as possible without losing too much quality. Frame by frame, I scan the image. Frame by frame, I find nothing. Until an odd pattern catches my peripheral just as the screen scrolls to a new section of the image. I drag it back, squinting at the odd mark. White and black squiggly lines like something out of a Pac-Man game. The mark nearly blends seamlessly with the headlight. I climb the desk and bring my nose close to that spot on the panoramic. No black squiggles.

A heavy rapping nearly makes me almost fall off the desk. "Remi?" Crow's voice filters through the door, jump-starting me into action.

I hop down, sling all the drawers open, and begin digging through them for a thumb drive. "Yeah, sorry. I... I'm just going through a few things."

"Okay. Um... your purse thing keeps vibrating."

My head jerks up, eyes slamming on the closed door, heart going wild. Not having a cell phone for such a long time, the possibility of it still functioning never crossed my mind. I figured the service was paused or shut off. Does this mean Jude finally is responding to me? Does he know about this picture stuff? About the note?

"Okay, thanks! Be right out!" I respond a little over enthusiastically as my probing fingers land on the cool, metal thumb drive.

CHAPTER TWENTY-FOUR

I pop out of the office with far too much wide-eyed enthusiasm. When I claim to be through, Crow raises a single eyebrow but otherwise keeps his curiosity to himself. I mentioned wanting to search around for Jude and collect a few things, but neither task was actually accomplished. He extends an olive branch of trust regardless and keeps his pierced lip zipped.

Together, we gather as many food items out of the refrigerator and pantry as possible to take back to my, hopefully still available, place. I fully expect him to try changing my mind about going back to the trailer park, but he leaves the topic alone, and we load up and settle in for the drive.

Ever since Crow mentioned my phone vibrating, I've been eager to check my notifications, so I dig my phone out of my recovered clutch and read my most recent texts — all of which are from Trenton or Hayes. None from my brother.

:Trenton: Hey, Pet. Crow gave us the good news. Glad you're out of there. Sorry about your bike.

:Hayes: Any big plans for your first night back in the real world?

I start typing, imagining my little text bubbles are flashing on their end. But Trenton messages again, beating me to the send button.

:Trenton: So… a while back… this girl accidentally dropped a twenty on her way out of the bar. Next time you come by, I'll put it on a tab under your name.

A sting builds behind my eyes and a quiet, watery chuckle escapes me. Instead of clicking send on my composed message, I drop the phone in my lap, toss my head back against the seat, close my eyes, and sigh heavily.

A drink never sounded so damn good.

Just as I'm working up the mental energy to compose a message again, Crow turns into the trailer park. Instead of stopping at the front office, though, he drives straight through, around curves, past lots, until we near the end of the—

My eyes bug wide. The Monte Carlo and Bimmer are parked in my meager gravel yard. But the most shocking sight of all is the naked Duc parked between them, black helmet balanced on the seat.

My blurry eyes dart to Crow. He avoids my gaze, casually throwing the V Coupe into park and getting out. I scramble to collect all my things but end up, in a

165

flustered moment, pushing everything to the floorboard just to get it out of my lap so I can exit the car.

The motion is so fast, the seat belt tightens against my chest, the edge of the material rubbing against my neck. I fidget with the buckle and clip, cursing myself under my breath for breaking a damn world record for the longest time to get out of a vehicle.

I finally make it, stumbling out unceremoniously and slamming the door shut behind me. The *bang* instantly puts me in my place.

Fuck, I shut that way too hard.

My shoulders go ramrod straight, and I grimace the queen of all grimaces. With a deep breath, I move forward, one foot in front of the other. Hayes and Trenton have joined Crow outside of the trailer by the time I reach the Duc. Each man stands in various positions on the small deck and steps.

Hayes leans back against the front door, hands shoved into his pockets. Trenton rests a hip against the stairs, elbow propped on the railing. Crow sits on the second step, forearms draped over his thighs. None of them move to approach me.

My fingertips meet the raised passenger seat and trail all the way to the headlight. From there, I move on to inspecting my helmet, palming each side and picking it up. My eyes lock on the unexpected, small decal at the bottom edge of the visor: *Revelry*, it reads.

My hand launches to my mouth, eyebrows curve deeply inward, eyes fill and blur all over again as I shake my head side to side.

"Guys," I squeak, muffled behind my cupped hand. Instead of crying more, I sniff hard, drop my hand, and lift my chin. "We were not in a good place with each other when I got into that wreck. I… I love it. All of it. But I'm not deserving. Not at all."

Not even a little.

Hayes holds his hand up, cutting off what I plan to say next. "If it makes you feel any better, the bike is a gift from Jude. Not us. We just… made sure all the transactions were taken care of."

"But… We… we were strapped for money."

Hayes leaves his spot against the paneling and jogs down the stairs holding a piece of paper. He steps beside his car, slides the paper onto the hood, and places his palm on top so the beach breeze doesn't blow it away. He then turns around, snaps his fingers, and Trenton tosses him something. A pen. Hayes's mouth quirks to the side. "Jude sold the Mustang."

I gasp. "Porter signed off on that?"

"Sure he did…" Crow says, that mischievous twinkle back in his eyes.

A quiet scrape snaps my attention back to Hayes. He slides the pen in my direction. "Sign the title, and she is all yours."

"What about the decal?" I ask, shoulders curving inward. I do feel better that Jude was the one who put the purchase of my bike into motion. But, while the gesture of the decal is sweet, I am not a member of Revelry. And I mean to *earn* something like that, should they allow it.

"The decal is for your protection," Trenton speaks up from just behind Crow. "Something happens to you again, and Crow isn't around to see it go down, the sticker will make sure your information gets to the right people. If someone challenges you and they see the crew name, 90 percent of local street racers will back off."

That does make me feel a lot better. I appreciate them looking out for me. I really do. But… "If you let me, I will earn the decal one of these days. I promise." I bend over the title and scrawl my name: R. S. Delancey

CHAPTER TWENTY-FIVE

Trenton

R emi doesn't notice when Hayes slowly slips out the carbon paper from beneath the signed title and carefully shoves it into his back pocket.

He shoots both me and Crow quick glances as he moves back up the steps, wordlessly reminding us of the conversation we had about a week ago — the plan we made. Crow and I share a look, the memory of that meeting passing between us; when Hayes plopped down the papers he had harbored since the night of the meet, Crow and I scrabbled to snatch them up first. I was too slow; Crow beat me to it.

Much like how he studies Remi as she pores over the title for her new bike right now, the other day I studied Crow in silence as he scanned the documents, his tattooed knuckles tightening once he got to the last page.

At that point, I couldn't hold back any longer, yanking the papers from his grip and dodging his knee-jerk swipe at the stack. Until that meeting, our only communication had taken place in the waiting room the night she was admitted. Clearly, a couple weeks or so into our breakup, and both of us were still sour as hell.

I tried to put the entire meeting behind me after storming out of there, but with the four of us together again now and a plan in place regardless of whether or not I choose to play my part, the memory latches onto my mind and continues to play: Hayes, ever the mediator between us, slammed a palm against Crow's chest when he stalked around the table to get to me. I peered over the edge of the papers with a smug grin as Crow's hands fisted and tensed at his sides.

It took me a minute to understand what the hell I was reading: docket upon docket of shipments for car parts. It didn't take a damn genius to figure out that all those car parts were pieces to a bigger puzzle. Illegal imports. But the trigger line that threw us all for a loop and had gotten Crow so worked up was Remi's signature at the very bottom of the last page: R. S. Delancey. She signed off on an actual import.

Remi is way more involved in the vehicle industry than she ever let on. The night we had brought her to the marina to interrogate her, Hayes had only shown me part of those papers — the part where she was an officer on a board for some vehicle company. That night, she came clean about which company and who her father was, but never once admitted to her officer position. For whatever reason, Hayes dropped it… only to bring it up to us again as soon as she was on the upside of recovery.

Now, we don't give a shit if Lance Industries is meddling in the grey stuff. But, we do give a shit about how that behavior will impact the industry here. On our turf. Neither Jude nor Porter signed it. Remi did. The night before her father's obit said he died, nonetheless… and that shit doesn't sit right. None of it does.

So, Hayes proposed an idea, and we were all just this side of confused and fed up enough to agree. Crow played his part, getting her over here. Hayes played his part getting her signature. Now it's my turn, regardless of whether or not I like it.

And I don't fucking like it. Not one bit. Hypocrites, all of us. I find it incredibly ironic that we were so jaded by her secrets, yet here we are, engines swapped.

I push off the railing and walk down the few steps to the sandy gravel, the crunch of my work boots drowned out by the reverberating pulse in my ears.

I… I can't do this.

I freeze.

Hayes clears his throat.

The blood that began to drain to my feet spikes again, and I stumble back into motion. Trouble is, I don't see the scarred and recovered Remi in front of me. I see the one who gutted me that night on the beach in the water.

The night before the world almost lost her forever.

And just like that, my act becomes real.

I step in front of her, Hayes and Crow watching what we had rehearsed come to life.

"Hey, Pet," I whisper, lifting her chin with my finger when her gaze slinks downward. The nickname rolls like gravel off my tongue. "So... about that bar tab."

Her eyes spring wide, and a larger-than-life smile spreads across her face. I nearly collapse on the spot. That night on the beach I promised myself not to look back — not to engage in something that would demolish my family, whether it was truly her fault or not.

I promised to let her go.

My thumb lifts and drags across her bottom lip, and she sighs. But just as fast as she melts, she hardens, inching back enough to break the connection. "Maybe," she says.

I give her a winning grin. Fakest shit ever, but apparently she buys it because in the next breath she says, "Not tonight. I need to adjust. I need a night to myself, you know? One spent in a bed that belongs to me — kinda. A bed not tainted with memories of a self-serving bastard. Sleep not spent in a hospital… or under the influence."

Wait… she didn't buy it. She… she said no. Women don't tell me no.

Like a confused kid who isn't sure how he should address a stranger, I dart a glance over my shoulder at Hayes and Crow. Crow has a shit-eating smirk on his lips. Hayes's mouth is pressed into a tight line.

I want to yell out, "I'm fucking trying!" but I return my attention to Remi instead, and stutter out an "O-o-okay."

She blinks repeatedly, firms her shoulders… and she fucking sidesteps me. In fact, she leaves all of us. She takes her title and new helmet, floats up the steps, and enters the trailer.

Hayes, Crow, and I stand outside, gazes darting around our small circle for a frozen moment until Crow jumps up, heads toward the V Coupe, pops the trunk, and gathers armfuls of stuff.

He shoves several grocery items into my chest, then does the same to Hayes. But instead of his usual hard expression, something is different. Content.

Nostrils flaring, I narrow a glare at him, arms clutching canned goods. Fucker has the audacity to flick his lip ring with his tongue and wink at me.

And that is when I realize he'd come back to life. Somehow, Remi brought him back from the dead when she rose from it herself.

And he means to win the girl.

CHAPTER TWENTY-SIX

Remi

Something is so very, very wrong. The buzz of tension outside was thick and muggy amid the light and airy gulf winds.

Inside the trailer is similar — dusty and hot, just like it was during my first visit. I distract myself by opening all the windows, ending with the window behind the dining table, expecting to hear conversation flow in from the guys outside. But only the breeze wisps through.

Hayes enters soon after, shortly followed by Trenton and Crow. They all unload armloads of stuff onto the table. Crow takes the first look around, boots clomping against the torn linoleum as he makes his way through the kitchen and into the living area. Trenton doesn't seem as interested in a walkthrough; he and Hayes share a look but otherwise keep quiet.

"You two are welcome to take a look around." I attempt being a proper hostess, pretending like this life is for me — like I own the place. Fake it till you make it and all that.

"Already did," Hayes grunts, placing a case of water bottles onto the table. "Trenton made your bed."

My attention darts to Trenton. "You had started a load of laundry. As soon as I heard you were being discharged from the hospital, I ran the wash again and put everything into the dryer," he explains. "Then, I made your bed and put the slipcover back on the couch."

"The laundry stayed in the washer for the entire time I was gone? I figured surely Foster would rent the place to someone else."

Trenton and Hayes both dart wary glances over at Crow. Crow puts down the non-functioning clock I had pulled off the wall and placed on the entertainment center. "Uh… yeah. Courtesy of Lace."

"Lace? Lacinda? As in the stripper?" I gape.

Crow raises an eyebrow, leans against the entertainment center, and crosses his arms. "Exotic dancer. And, yes, her."

"So, she paid for, what, a month of rent?" I ask, stunned.

"Yeah. Guess she likes you or some shit."

Great… someone else I owe. Despite the kind act, anger and indignation course through me: Jude for the bike. The guys for the decal. Lace for the money.

Sure is pretty damn hard trying to be independent when a dozen mother hens are clucking around you.

I sigh and make a slow circle around the room, scanning each guy in passing. Crow remains by the entertainment center. Hayes wedges into the corner between the refrigerator and counter. Trenton has since taken a seat in one of the dining room chairs.

That same tension that smothered us outside makes an unwelcome presence in my new home. I take a seat opposite Trenton and complete the widespread circle.

My eyes land on the one who might cave easiest and give me some information. "Trenton?" His eyes flick to me, elbows propped on the table instead of him being relaxed and leaning into the chair. "Thanks for making my bed." I plaster on a soft smile. The tension eases from his shoulders slightly, and he nods once. Those shoulders instantly spring tight again with my next words: "How is Revelry doing?" Sweet and sour. Hot and cold. It was the best, easiest way to get a reaction that would answer my question without using words — something I once loved and adored about Hayes and Trenton.

Now, they're not speaking for entirely different reasons, having nothing to do with camaraderie but everything against it.

I shove out of my chair, stomp past all three of them, and lock myself in my new bedroom like a fitful child. When I get inside, I press my back against the door, slide down to the floor, tuck my knees up toward my chest, and wrap my arms around myself. The faintest of throbs zing up my arm, and I twist it once to peek at my scar.

Footsteps approach from behind the closed partition. A muffled voice follows: "We disbanded." Hayes reveals what I had already surmised. "The decals will stay for the community's sake, but we're no longer running together."

"Yeah," I whisper. "Midnight Runners?" I ask, wanting to know if my original deceit is why — if somehow while I was out of commission, Jude pulled out all the stops.

"No," he whispers. "Takes more than the rev of an engine to tear us apart."

We're silent long enough that he eventually starts to walk away. "Was it because of a girl?" I mumble under my breath.

The steps freeze. For one, horrifying, moment I worry my words somehow made it through the door — that I would actually have to hear the answer I already know to be true with every fiber of my being. But his footsteps resume.

There's history where men fighting over a woman is concerned — sword fights, gun showdowns... car races.

Instead of staging a dig, though, they all simply drove different directions. Because of me. At least in part, no doubt—

I bolt to my feet and sling the bedroom door open. "Hey..." My gaze seeks out Trenton. "About that drink..."

CHAPTER TWENTY-SEVEN

Since Trenton was the one who made the suggestion, he was the one who followed through later in the evening after I put all my pantry items away, showered, and changed. Naive little me had hoped they would all join us — like always. Not this time, though; there's no safety in the group dynamic as Trenton slides my first drink across the bar, comes around the counter, and sits in the stool beside me.

Our eyes meet, and he lifts his beer, tilting the rim of the mug toward me slightly in a wordless cheers. I lift my curvy glass and return the gesture before pushing the straw aside and taking a taste of the thick, icy liquid.

A daiquiri. A safe drink. So sweet, in fact, it's a shock to my taste buds after having consumed bland hospital food for such a long time.

I place the glass down and twirl my straw through the slush, eyes trained on how the little flecks of sugar on the rim shine under the bar lights. "Rare day off, hm?" I ask, breaking the conversational ice.

"They let me get away with it sometimes."

A female bartender takes residence at the opposite end of the bar, running down the clock with mindless tasks like drying glasses and checking the bottles.

"You mean you let yourself get away with it sometimes?" I scoff-chuckle and take another sip.

He tips his mug toward me, this time in his own cheers. "Truer words have never been spoken." His eyes glint with the first hint of amusement all night.

We rode separately. My pride insisted, still trying to be independent even though riding my new bike for the first time was pretty much a panic attack on the blacktop the entire ride.

Taking separate vehicles was easier, though. I can't even imagine having to sit in the cab of a vehicle with this shady version of Trenton — or any of them, for that matter.

When we got here, he took over the bar long enough to make our drinks, despite not being on the clock. Having him on that side, with me on this side of the bar felt good and right. The way it is now, feels awkward.

Not choosing something cooler to wear was a poor pairing for the stifling warmth inside the building, even despite my cool beverage. I place the glass down again, slip my fingertips under the cuff of my sleeve, and push it up.

When I start to push up the other sleeve, I hesitate, the first inch of my scar a self-conscious reminder. Instead, I switch sides and tug the first sleeve back down, pulling the cuff over my palm and gripping it with my fingertips, suddenly feeling overexposed.

A drink-chilled hand wraps around my wrist. Trenton angles me toward him and pushes my sleeve up gently, eyes tracking the scar from wrist to elbow.

He smooths his palm up the marred area then drags his thumb along the lines on the way back down. "You were a little wobbly tonight. Things spooking you easier?"

I lift my gaze from where he now has his palm flush against mine and thumb depressed at the pulse point of my wrist. "Yeah. A little." I take a shaky breath. "The wheels will feel like feet again before long, though. Being caged isn't really my thing."

Trenton chuckles, his palm steadily becoming warmer and damper against mine. "Spoken like a true biker."

A half grin pulls my mouth to the side.

Trenton lets go of my hand, wipes his palms on his jeans, clears his throat, and pushes my other sleeve up, tugging the tightly clasped material out of my grip.

We both lift our drinks at the same time. I bypass the straw again and chug half the glass, smacking my lips. "Wow, this is an 'I'm definitely not getting her drunk and taking her home' drink," I semi-mimic what I had said to him that night he gave me a Long Island.

He huffs out a chuckle, chugs his beer, and slams it down on the counter before raising a finger in the air.

The bartender flits over. "Shots of tequila, please. The works. Keep us busy."

The tender raises her eyebrow, Trenton returns the expression. I watch in bemusement.

She lines up several shot glasses and expertly fills them all with a smooth, slow, singular pour before gathering the lime wedges and salt and placing the plate in front of the glasses between us.

"Ah… a 'we're not even leaving the parking lot' drink." I grin, slipping a finger between two of the glasses and sliding one his way.

Trenton has absolutely nothing to say to that remark. His sepia gaze follows the movement, locked on the scar that runs up my arm, clearly conflicted with a number of thoughts and emotions.

While I do have moments of insecurity, I decide this won't be one such moment. I give my heart permission to do an extra fluttery thump, my throat permission to pull an extra, hard swallow, and my lungs to take in one more shaky breath. Then, I lift my scarred arm, bring the inside of my wrist to my mouth, and slowly lick along the sensitive skin while reaching for the salt shaker with my other hand.

Adequately damp, I douse it in salt crystals before resting that hand loosely on the bar top. Then, I place the salt back down, grab Trenton's hand, thumb depressed against his palm between thumb and forefinger, and lift it to my mouth to swipe my tongue along his wrist.

That smidgen of insecurity tries to peek through; I don't know what this is between us anymore — why we're here tonight. I lift my gaze upward to lock with his just prior to snaking my tongue out.

Regardless of what the purpose of all this is, I do know that connection we have is ever present. Those weeks spent in the hospital didn't make it go away. Our silent promises to end everything didn't work. So here we are.

He swallows tightly, and his eyes drop to my mouth, so I open my lips and press my tongue along his warm skin and swipe the width. Then, I drag his arm over to the counter, rest the back of his hand on top, and apply the salt.

After I put the salt down, the fingers of our free hands meet at the plate of limes. We each pluck one up and swap them to the fingers of our prepared wrists, careful not to bump off any salt. We then both reach over and pick up our designated shot glasses.

I tilt my glass toward him, and he tilts his glass toward me. "On three?" he asks.

"On three."

"One. Two. Three."

We both lift our wrists to our mouths, lick off the salt, toss back the liquid, and shove the lime between our teeth. I bite down hard, desperate for the sweet-sour zing to chase away the burn.

Somehow, Trenton keeps a straight face. My expression, on the other hand, clenches into a grimace: teeth bared, nose scrunched, eyebrows drawn inward. Trenton belly laughs, his torso shaking, as he pulls the peel off the lime and pops the fruit part inside his mouth. "Waste not, want not," he states when I pull a face at him.

I stick my tongue out with a blech motion and sound, then warily side-eye the line of remaining shots.

This promises to be a long, wild night.

CHAPTER TWENTY-EIGHT

I had a number of plans when I made the decision to take Trenton up on his offer for drinks. Getting wasted was not one of them.

Trenton shoves over a glass of water. "Drink up," he insists.

My stomach churns. "Oh, God. I... I can't fit in any more liquid. I'll burst." I throw a hand over my mouth and pop my cheeks out.

Trenton reels backward to avoid the mess. I drop my hand and burst into laughter. "I was kidding. You're safe. For now."

We fall silent. He pretended to keep drinking a while ago but had actually stopped entirely. I was not remiss to notice.

I use the moment of content quiet to attempt chasing my original plans. Everything is a bit duller, though: thoughts, movements — even the constriction of my heart when I remember the main reason I agreed to this.

To help bring Revelry back together.

If not the crew, at least their friendships.

I lean my head on Trenton's shoulder. He slips his arm around me — probably to make sure I don't fall off the barstool.

Plan number two: I lift my finger to my lips and tap on them. Oh… right. Electronics. Of which I have none. What I do have is a thumb drive with a super-shady code begging to be cracked. The memory of Dad flashes in my mind, but I allow it to swim away with the haze of alcohol. Thumb drive. Code… And the only person I know other than Jude who has a computer — the downfall of still being the new girl in town.

Earlier in the night — only a couple shots in — I quickly surmised that I didn't want to use the family-slash-business computer to open what I have concluded must be an itty-bitty QR code. Which led my thought-train to Hayes. I hate how the ideas — the plans — zip and dash through my mind stilted. But that's better than nothing, I suppose.

I plop my hand onto the bar and wiggle my fingers at the water glass just barely out of reach. Trenton chuckles and pushes it closer. I wrap my hand around the wet glass but still can't seem to engage my muscles and lift it to my mouth.

"You're quiet," I say, the chuckle he let out having been the first sound he has made since insisting I hydrate.

"So are you," he points out.

"Touché."

I tighten my hand around the glass, but then give up and let my fingers fall limp to the bar top.

Trenton's shoulder rises under my head, and a slow trickle of breath hits the top of my hair as he lets out a massive exhale. Movement draws my eyes upward, and I catch the motion of him plucking a straw out of a nearby container.

I had every intention of living in my new, humble, abode. Alone. Independent. But my budding plans won't work if I do that. I need access to the guys and to a computer — to Hayes's computer, specifically — for a much much bigger plan that my fuzzy brain can't handle organizing right now.

But, yeah, I need to somehow get — and keep — them in the same building? Room? Bedroom? I don't know… something. If I am the one who helped tear them apart, maybe I can be the one to bring them back together.

The only way to fix everything would be to fix that broken tug-of-war rope — fusing the many frayed edges and splicing those loose strands.

So. Many. Strands.

Ugh, my head hurts.

I lean away from Trenton's shoulder and drop my forehead against my forearm. "This is your fault," I grumble. I then drop my voice in an attempt to sound like him. "Are you wussing out on me?"

He laughs and swivels his chair to face me. "Hey, I was quite offended when you claimed you could drink me under the table. Had to prove you wrong."

I lift a finger to argue — to point out that he stopped drinking — but I change my mind.

His plan is his, my plan is mine.

Or something.

Whatever.

"Damn, I'm drunk." I had meant to gripe those words in my mind, but they came out aloud. I turn my head toward him, placing my cheek, instead of my forehead, on my forearm.

"Yeah... me too," he states, sinking the straw into my water. Liar, liar. The straw bobs up and down for a moment before he covers the hole with his finger and pulls it back out. "Open up."

"Are you straw-feeding me water?" A giggle escapes me. Giggling is where I draw the line to this embarrassing drunkenness.

Must. Not. Fucking. Giggle.

Clearing my throat of the offensive noise, I launch upward, toss my head back, and "open wide," tongue flat out, eyes aimed toward the ceiling.

The cool plastic hits my tongue, but the rush of water doesn't flow out. Instead, Trenton taps the plastic against my tongue again with a breathy laugh. "Goddamn, Remi. Close your mouth."

"But you just said—" I try speaking the words with my mouth still wide open, head back, and the straw depressed on my tongue, but I end up spluttering instead and have to clamp my lips over the thin plastic or else risk drooling.

Trenton releases the suction and the liquid trickles into my throat.

I straighten my head again and pop my lips open so he can remove the straw. He dips the straw back into the water and follows the same process. Stupefied by this coddling, I open my mouth like an eager hamster and allow it to happen again. And again. And again. Until it's very evident that he's no longer doing it to make sure I get hydrated but to watch me continuously, eagerly suck on something.

He was just as mesmerized as me but, unlike me, didn't notice when I came to this realization. The next time he places it in my mouth, I suck harder, hollowing out my cheeks and pursing my lips.

He groans.

I bite down on the plastic and steal it from between his fingers. He snaps out of his perverted haze, quickly swivels forward in his stool, and palms his lap.

Truth is, the reason why I finally started to chase those plans in my mind again was because it has been a couple hours now since I took my last alcoholic drink, and I am on the top of that inebriated mountain, about ready to roll down. I think.

In fact… I am fairly certain I might even be able to stand. So, I slap my hand on the counter and carefully scale down the stool like a mountain goat balancing expertly on a steep edge.

As soon as my feet hit the ground, I snatch up my clutch and start walking backward toward the exit. Trenton jumps into action, stumbling out of his chair, frantically digging in his pockets and pulling out a wad of cash and tossing it onto the bar top.

My back hits the door as I watch on in amusement while he shuffles toward me. Maybe I was wrong; maybe he had more to drink after all. This fumbling, awkward Trenton is an amazing sight to witness, though. Another giggle percolates in my throat, but I clasp my mouth with my free hand.

"And just what do you find so amusing?" he asks, pressing his hand on the glass above my head and leaning over me.

"You," I answer honestly, breathlessly, inching up on my tiptoes until our mouths are a hairsbreadth apart. Trenton's available hand loops around my waist, fingers splaying along my lower back. He presses firmly against me, drawing my pelvis forward until we're pressed together.

I tilt my chin up just enough to encourage him. He slips his hand into my back pocket. Then, his finger drags along my hip and to my bellybutton before he lifts his hand into my peripheral. My eyes dart sideways and focus adjusts to the item he is holding — my keyless remote fob. In a very bartender-like move, he wiggles it, and the door behind me slowly relinquishes its support as he palms it open.

I narrow a super serious evil glare at him, spin on my heels, and walk out of the now-open door into the night. Not that I was planning on riding my bike this tipsy anyway. Smart ass.

He jogs up behind me and slips his fingers between mine. We walk hand-in-hand to our — his — vehicle and stand next to the passenger door staring at each other for far too long. I'm moments away from asking him if I can just go to his place for the night. Because I don't want to be alone. Not really. Despite having said over and over to myself that I do.

I'll already be riding with him, might as well go east instead of west, right?

Plus…

Those plans.

He steps forward, eyes pinned on me. I step back until I bump into the side of his car. He shoves my fob into the pocket of his jeans. I wipe my palm on mine.

Trenton steps forward again, but there's nowhere for me to go. His fingers loop the hair behind my ear and his lips skate against mine.

"Trenton…" I breathe out in warning. I have never been able to refuse him. We said our goodbyes on the beach a few weeks ago. I can call a taxi. Plan be damned. I can reassess said plan tomorrow… when I am sober and Trenton isn't closing the distance between us with every beat of my heart.

His eyes fall closed, and he sucks in a shaky breath. "Come home with me," he whispers.

"Yes," I whisper back.

CHAPTER TWENTY-NINE

Trenton's hand slips behind me, and he lifts the handle. I move forward and to the side so he can swing open the heavy door before ducking and entering. The door closes with a steely thunk. I drop my clutch onto the floorboard and toss my head back against the top of the bench seat, heart pounding, breaths pacing quicker by the second.

Trenton takes his time joining me, though, stopping just outside his door and propping a hip against it. He rubs a hand over his face, digs something out of his pocket, then draws his arms to the front of his body. Surrounded by darkness, the flare of white light from his phone screen fans across the front of his body.

Once done, he simply returns the device to his pocket, enters the car, and drops into the seat like this has been the most exhausting night ever.

I blow out a raspberry and sigh. "Hey... thanks for easing me back into the real world tonight. I had a lot of fun. Might hold a grudge against you in the morning, but that bridge can be crossed when we get there."

In the morning.

Oh shit.

I had just far too easily assumed me coming home with him meant I would be waking up with him, too, and that he'd still be speaking with me tomorrow.

I wave a hand in the air, dismissing the last part of my comment.

He rests his head back and stares up at the roof. "I can't drive yet, either," he admits.

"Oh… well… I can order us a taxi. On the house. My house. Well, I mean your house… but I'll pay." Shut up, Remi. "I pay, we go to your house, in a taxi. That I'll pay for." Yeah, that made it better. Goddamn.

Trenton rolls his head toward me and presses his lips together to hide a grin. The amusement is still there, though, sparking in his eyes and in the twitch of his pressed lips. He steels his features and clears his throat. "Ah…" — he darts a look over his shoulder through the strip of dark glass behind the rear seats — "nah… I should be good in a bit. You okay with just hanging out for another hour? We can play Paper, Rock, Scissors or something?"

My eyebrows rise high. "You mean Rock, Paper, Scissors? That's… pretty random."

His stifled amusement cracks a little more, and I give a mental fist pump. "First thing that came to mind."

"Okay, yeah." I shrug. "I've got nowhere else to be."

For the first five minutes we sit in silence. Zero sound. Such little sound, in fact, that I can actually hear the sound of no sound — that strange buzz-like ringing.

Unable to handle it anymore, I hold my palm up between us and place my other hand into a fist-like position on top.

"On three?" I ask. A memory of him saying that right before I drank way too many shots of tequila has a sudden burst of nausea hitting me.

"I was kidding." He laughs.

Eyebrow lifted, I set the challenge, raising my fist above my hovering, open palm.

He angles toward me on his hip with a sly smirk. "Loser has to remove an article of clothing."

My second eyebrow mimics the first, bringing both hairline high. "You were so not kidding."

"Nope." He places his hand over my fist and leans closer. "But I'm not in grade school anymore, Remi. So we either play like adults or not at all."

An equally sly smirk lifts my lips. "I don't have to play 'Paper, Rock, Scissors' to take my clothes off for you," I point out. "As you very well know."

"Mm. I do. But it sounds fun anyway." He lets go of my fist and makes one of his own.

Our eyes meet.

My lungs threaten to burst from holding my breath.

Trenton calls the game: "Paper…" we bounce our fists the first time. "Rock…" we bounce them the second time. "Scissors…" we bounce them the third time. "Shoot."

Trenton pulls scissors, I keep my hand balled into a fist.

"Son of a bitch!" He bends down and takes the easy route by removing his shoes.

We go for another round and another and another and another and another until I begin to lose count. Halfway through our games, the parking lot lights shut off indicating the bar had closed and everyone went home. Of all the rounds he only wins once, and I choose to hide my bare feet from him by tucking them under my butt — just because I can.

Trenton is completely naked, bare ass on the supple dark-purple leather of his bench seat. Cock standing at attention. Poor guy.

"Okay!" He claps his hands together and rubs his palms. "Once more. I'm determined to at least get your shirt off."

This time I call it: "Rock…" we bounce our fists the first time. "Paper…" we bounce them the second time. "Scissors…" we bounce them the third time. "Shoot!"

Just like the first round, Trenton pulls scissors and I keep my hand balled into a fist. "Goddammit!"

he wails. "I don't have anything else to take off! You've stripped me bare!"

"Correction," I start. "You stripped yourself bare."

He changes his scissors to a single, pointed finger. "You" — he waggles said finger at me — "are not wrong."

He loses with a sigh of defeat, eyes looking down at his nakedness with a frown. His gaze then shoots up to me but nonchalantly reroutes as though I definitely didn't just catch the fact that he clearly came up with an idea. All he needs to do is start whistling, and the picture would be painted perfectly.

While he casually looks around the cab of his car, formulating whatever he's formulating, I casually sneak a peek at his twitching cock.

Been a while since I've eaten… and damn I'm hungry. Before he can catch me, I turn my gaze to his. Watching. Waiting. He then, quite unexpectedly, gets onto his knees and knee walks toward the middle of the bench seat, cock bobbing along with the adventure.

Damn that thing is distracting.

"My eyes are up here," he hums, straightening, cock now right in front of my face as he starts messing with the roof of his car.

Temporarily preoccupied by something other than his distracting cock, I lean back against the passenger door — lest I lick him — and watch as he deconstructs the T-top. He removes each panel, carefully angled, and places the large halves on his rear bench seat.

When that's accomplished, he overexaggerates dusting his hands off and plops back down.

Much closer to me now.

Still naked.

Cock still… there.

"There," he says, jolting my attention away from where my eyes have, once again, drifted.

Yep… there. Still there.

Takes me a minute to realize I'm conversing with him in my head. Because of his head. The one between his legs.

Anyway.

"There? There what?" I blink repeatedly and swallow hard.

"Since I can't take off any more clothes, I took off my T-top."

"Ahh… well played."

"Well, I sure as hell thought so. Now… what elementary school games are you realllllllly bad at?"

"Are you sober enough to drive yet?" I toss back, satisfied with my winnings and ready to cash in.

"Nuh-uh. Don't deflect my question."

A half grin cocks — I mean lifts — on my face. I raise a finger and tap my lips. "Spin the bottle."

Trenton snorts. "Don't play around. There's a dumpster right over there that has plenty of bottles we can use. Plus… I don't need to spin a bottle to kiss you," he points out. "As you very well know."

"Mm. I do. But it sounds fun anyway."

This replaying scenes between us thing seems to be becoming habitual. I kinda like it. I also purposefully try to forget about the first one — the one where I led him through the series of events the night we met.

Every time we fall silent — every time we're not distracted by playing silly games and sobering up — I know that night is where his mind goes, too. But, like right now, neither of us bring up the topic.

Neither of us leaves to get a bottle, either. Instead, we both adjust so our backs are against the bench seat, our heads rest at an angle, and we can gaze up at the stars.

The world around me no longer spins from too much alcohol, but the fuzziness is still present, fogging my mind a bit and rendering me still not fit to ride.

I suspect Trenton has been sober enough to drive for a good while now. However, content to stare at the sky without a care in the world in this moment, I decide not to press leaving too soon. "I've never had a T-top experience from inside an older, domestic, muscle car like this. Only electric sunroofs. This is way better."

"Yeah it is. The T-top is what I love most about this model."

Hearing the word "T-top" come from his mouth slams a memory into the forefront of my mind. The night we met, he said that term was something he likes to be addressed by, and I have since heard Crow and Hayes use it a couple times.

I flop my head to the side and study his profile as he looks up through the opening. "Is that how you got the nickname — your love for the T-top?"

His chest had been moving steadily with each breath, but after processing my question, his breathing stills and he blinks a couple times. "Uh…" The non-answer comes out as an exhale. "No."

I prop up on my side, elbow dug into the back of the seat, palm pressed into my cheek. "No? Well, there's something we can do to pass the time, then — you can explain."

His eyelashes slowly descend and his Adam's apple gives one, long bob. I follow his line of sight all the way to his cock — the one that had partially softened but now shifts upward with every passing second.

"That is… definitely something we can do to pass the time." Trenton licks his lips, then turns his sepia gaze on me. "But you'll have to take your clothes off."

CHAPTER THIRTY

"All you had to do was ask." I shoot him a wink, whip off my shirt, and toss it onto his stupidly distracting cock.

He groans and slams his eyes shut tight. "Never mind. Put your shirt back on."

I have just enough alcohol still in my system to not take that comment personally. I simply pluck my shirt off his cock and—his hand wraps around my wrist, halting me just as I'm lifting the shirt to put my head through.

With his other hand, Trenton pulls the material from my grip and flings it to the seat beside him. Keeping his eyes closed, he lifts my wrist to his mouth and brushes a light kiss against the thin skin.

He then drags his lips down the inside of my forearm as he raises it, until my arm is draped over the seat beside his head, his lips are skating along the inside of my elbow, and my legs are straddling him due to the gentle persuasion of his other hand on my hip.

The center of the T is directly above my head, so I need to keep curved a little, but the lack of space is inconsequential when Trenton cups each side of my face and pulls me down into a kiss. His tongue slides between my lips. I twist mine with his. He sucks, and I dip in even deeper.

The hands cupping my face were his protection — his control. Such a sweet gesture, but with such telling consequences. He uses this control to guide my head back, disconnecting our kiss. Eyes still closed, he whispers, "Tell me to stop, Remi."

"Never," I whisper back.

His hands drop to my hips, and his fingers dig into my bare flesh. He then lets go and pats the seat beside him. "Stand up."

"Stand?" My eyes dart upward. Oh…

With the T-top open, I can stand on his seat and my torso will be outside. I scramble out of his lap onto my knees beside him and use his shoulder and the passenger door as support to push upward. Once standing, my hands move to the center bar and outer frames respectively.

When I look back down, Trenton has his arm flung over his face, chest back to heaving. I nudge him with my bare toe — the bottoms of my pants long and tucked under my heels.

His arm remains flung over his face, but his free hand slips from his naked thigh to the top of my foot, and he squeezes. The contact is enough for me; I release my worries and let curiosity take over. Resting my ass against the back portion of the frame, I look around, studying the parking lot, the woods ahead, the building behind — the stars above.

Trenton's fingers twitch against the top of my foot and then slip under my baggy sweats to move up my calf until the tips reach the delicate, ticklish back bend of my knee. He draws a figure-eight there before pulling out his hand, removing his arm from over his face, adjusting onto his hip, then moving up to his knees between my feet.

That position is what gives everything away: T-Top must be Trenton's signature "move."

My knees slap together, nearly slamming into his nose. But he must anticipate the motion, because his hands come to my knees right at about the same time, and he pries them open… with little resistance on my part.

Trenton "T-Top" pushes his palms up my thighs and to my hips before his fingers dig under the waistband of my sweats and underwear. He inches them down slowly, baring me centimeter by centimeter.

By the time the band is around my knees, the drunken haze is back. This time, the heady sensation has nothing to do with alcohol and everything to do with the anticipation that lust brings.

Trenton pats the back of my thigh, and I have enough remaining sense to understand it as a command. I lift one foot then the other so he can pull my clothes off the rest of the way.

"Mm. Damn you are a piece of artwork," his voice, husky and vibrating with need, travels to me from the cab below. His palms work their way back up my thighs until his thumbs are resting in the little dips where my pelvis and hips meet.

My pussy throbs at both the sound of his voice and the nearness of his touch. The throb soon turns to an ache as he slowly drags his thumbs along the inside creases of my thighs over and over again, while his gaze brushes against everything else. At first, I scarcely can tell the difference between the touch of his gaze and the pressure of his thumb when applied flush against my clit.

He swipes a slow line downward until pressing the digit inside me and placing his opposite thumb on my clit to give it attention again.

While the pleasure-giving thumb rubs circles over my clit, he adds one finger and then another inside me to join his opposing thumb, spreading me open, challenging my size and shape in a new way. He eases in deeper and slowly twists his wrist until his fingers can curve forward, that thumb slipping out to take its turn along my clit while his fingers strum my insides.

My toes curl into the leather seat and knees unlock, unable to remain solid. My fingers dig into the framework of the T-top, and a low, long moan rolls from deep in my clenched belly all the way up my spine and past my lips.

Trenton's mouth comes to my belly button, and his tongue laves around it. The hand that had been flicking my clit first, scoops under my thigh, adjusts to the bend of my knee, and presses inward, encouraging my knee toward my chest. He then moves his hand down my calf until his fingers can wrap around my ankle. "Rest your foot on the top of the windshield," he instructs.

I do exactly that, thankful for the extra support. But with the awkward spread, my knee-jerk thought is to do the same with my other leg. Trenton answers my unspoken curiosity by pulling his fingers out and following the same path of guidance on my other leg.

In a moment of panic as my foot raises and I have to scramble to test my upper body strength by plank-pressing myself up using only the frame of his T-top, I squeal and dart a glance down. "A-am I allowed to sit my bare ass on the roof of your car?" I ask as respectfully as possible.

Trenton chuckles and his hands move to cup my ass and direct the edge of my cheeks to the edge of the T-top frame. Then, just like how I swiped my tongue along the inside of his wrist in the bar tonight, he swipes his over my pussy.

My body trembles, goosebumps rise everywhere all at once, my nipples pebble, and my head falls back, eyes springing open wide as I gasp in a lungful of air. "Oh fuck," I pant as his tongue slips inside me and he licks back up to my clit again.

Trenton hums and the sound vibrates against me. With a quick flick of his tongue, my insides explode. He shoves his fingers inside and twists. Each twist and thrust sends me into a higher rpm until my body is in the red and can no longer push any harder.

On the edge of his open T-top, I come to a full stop just as fast as I raced to get there, shaky, breathless...

...ruined.

* * *

"I THINK I CAN ACTUALLY HANDLE RIDING my bike now," I state, snaking my arms through the holes of my shirt.

"Nice try. You already said 'yes.'"

I pause for only a moment before responding. "You still want me to come home with you?"

He pauses for even longer. "Yeah." He buttons up his jeans, sticks the key in the ignition, and turns her over. All that hefty power rumbles to life.

"Okay. Swing by my place — my new place — so I can grab a few things?"

Trenton shakes his head adamantly. "We still have your bag... and I texted Hayes earlier to grab a few things from your — new — place before he headed home."

Much more clear-headed now, I understand what I missed before, and I slouch in the seat, feeling duped. "Y-you never intended on bringing me back to the trailer, did you?"

He bites on the inside corner of his lip, focuses on putting the car into reverse, and shakes his head.

"Why?" I ask calmly, fighting the fire burning inside. Even if I do need to go to their place anyway. Regardless.

"Not at liberty to say."

"Oh. Is that so?"

"Yep."

My nostrils tighten as I inhale through my nose sharply. Seeing that this particular topic is going nowhere useful, I double back to his comment about Hayes. "You texted Hayes, what, a little over an hour ago?"

He darts a glance in my direction while pulling onto the road. "Yeah?"

"Why was he still on the West End an hour ago? I thought he went home when we left for the bar."

Trenton freezes, focus hard straight ahead, fingers tightening around the wheel, thighs bunching in his jeans. "Ah… Um…"

"Ah, um? Really?" My jaw tenses, but I catch myself before my teeth start grinding and I wake up in the morning with an even worse headache than is already beginning to ping at my temples.

Trenton exhales sharply. "Damage control."

"Damage control?"

"Remi…"

"Trenton…"

He slaps his forehead and drags his hand down his face, groaning. "We had a Golden Ticket event planned — before the disband. He's working his ass off to cancel it. It's not as simple as throwing in the towel. Not with an annual anniversary event."

"Anniversary? Of The Gulf Coasters?"

Trenton looks at me, honest this time, and curves his eyebrows inward. "No, Remi… not of The Gulf Coasters."

Every drop of blood existing in my veins seems to rush downward. I nearly have to fold forward and put my head between my knees to keep from passing out. But then Trenton would see that. Instead, I lie my head back and look up into the sky, hair whipping over my face. Thanks to the white glow from the moon, I can blame it for the blanching of my face.

"Rachal and Bree?" I ask.

"Yeah… Rachal and Bree. Guess he told you, huh?"

"Lace did. But, yeah… He told me. Some of it." Trenton darts another glance at me, and I elaborate: "I know that Travis was the catalyst. Look… it's really not my business. I don't need to know. We can just drop it. Right here. Right now. Okay?"

Trenton nods. "They arrested Travis on the spot, but he is still awaiting trial. Two counts of murder. Hayes had to detain Crow — save him from going to jail for the same reason. Crow… it's hard for him, you know? Travis being alive and his fate still in limbo, while Rachal and Bree's fates were determined right then and there that night on the roadside."

"I can't even imagine," I whisper.

"Be glad you don't have to."

Damn, what a hurricane I got in the middle of. Problem is, there isn't even an eye — a calm center — it's all just spiraling madness.

This entire time, I've done nothing but add more heat to the system. Fed it. Churned it.

These guys need the eye.

I need the eye.

That inkling of an idea I had earlier about bringing them together again, pre-inebriation, churns and forms a tropical depression of its own.

CHAPTER THIRTY-ONE

Exhausted, both mentally and physically, and a little woozy from the rest of the alcohol still seeping out of me, I must've passed out on the ride to Trenton's place, because I wake up to the mixed scents of soap, stale restaurant food, and... the smell of coffee.

Hayes.

My eyes spring open wide, and I shoot upward, wrapped in Trenton's comforter. I immediately regret the fast movement and fall backward, clutching at my head with a groan.

Must. See. Hayes.

Get up.

Now.

My second attempt is slower. I roll sideways and off the bed, crawl over to collect my discarded sweats, then crawl back to the bed and lean against it while attempting to pull them on without throwing up.

As soon as I'm successfully vertical, I make my way to the kitchen one slow step in front of the other.

Hayes is facing his coffee science kit. I sigh, prop my hip against the short edge of the L-shaped bar, and simply watch him. I loved this — these morning coffees. His messy hair. Anal.

I mean... conversation.

Oops. Slip of the tongue.

"Good morning."

Hayes jumps a mile high. "Holy shit." He then turns around. "Morning, good. I mean… Good morning. Coughing? I mean… coffee? Heh."

Anal… Conversation… See… two words that sound pretty much the same.

"Coffee, yes… minus the coughing part. If I cough, I might vomit."

Hayes nods over and over and over again while turning around to face his temporary laboratory.

You know what I also missed? This awkwardness.

Tears spring to my eyes.

One, because I miss it.

Two, because he's only awkward around people he's uncomfortable around. Which means he is now uncomfortable around me, and that wrenches my heart. We had gotten past that. He fucked me in the ass. That was not awkward at all.

I step into the kitchen and hop up onto the counter, propping my heels on the slightly open drawer. As soon as I'm up there, though, he turns back around, coffee in hand, and brings it to me. "I heard you moving around in there," he explains, pressing the warm ceramic into my palm. "Sleep okay?"

The awkwardness drops a little, and I remain conflicted about how I'm supposed to feel about that.

"Yeah. Don't remember any of it, so I guess that's saying something."

He walks backward, never taking his eyes off me, until he can reach his own mug and pick it up. He takes a sip.

"Did you?" I ask.

Hayes raises an eyebrow. "Huh? Did I what?"

"Sleep okay?"

"Oh… ah… yeah. Sure."

When his focus drops to the black liquid in his mug, I tilt my head to the side and study him. Messy hair. Puffy eyes. "Big plans today?" I ask.

He shakes his head and takes yet another sip. Or, rather, gulp.

Unsure how else to handle this lack of conversation, I take a deep breath and just go for it: "Um… do you mind if I use your computer sometime today? I" — fuck, what do I need to do? — "need to knock out a few insurance things from my hospital stay. I was planning on going to the local library and using their computer, but seeing as you all are insisting I stay here and be babysat, I should probably pop onto your computer."

Hayes blinks repeatedly but ultimately nods dumbly at me. "Uh, yeah. Yeah, of course. Let me just clean up a bit in there first, then it's all yours."

I bob my head slowly and finally take a sip of my coffee. "Thanks." I try on a smile but am too flummoxed to make it not awkward and grimacey. "I… really need a shower anyway. Maybe I can pop in there after a shower?"

"Mm-hmm," he says around another gulp, fingers tapping against his thigh — a final gulp, because in the next second he slams the mug onto the counter and shuffles past me… with a salute.

I ease my coffee onto the counter and hop down, no longer able to stomach the bitter, ever-cooling liquid. Shower, first. Computer, after. Plus, all the answers to the difficult things in life often come under the battering of hot droplets.

And I sure as heck could use some inspiration.

CHAPTER THIRTY-TWO

Dammit. Dammit. Dammit. I am not fucking cut out for this investigative shit. Well, the investigating parts, sure. Behind the scenes. But talking to someone I'm investigating?

How the hell did she do it? Talk to all of us, all while digging into our personal affairs? How? Fucking how?

Where is Trenton?

He is supposed to be here dealing with her — with the talking part. My brain short circuits when she's around me. Alone. Zaaaaap. Fried. All my fucking brain cells gone.

I fall into my gamer chair and shove the palms of my hands into my eyes under my glasses before snatching my phone from my desktop and thumbing in a message to Trenton.

:Me: Where the hell are you? Get here. Stat. I'm losing my mind.

That fucker texts me back almost immediately with a laughy-face emoji. Then, follows that up with:

:Trenton: Tough shit HazerBeam. I played my part. Get her drunk. Worked for me.

:Hayes: That's the only thing that works for you.

:Trenton: Har, har, har.

The sound of running water coming from the bathroom calms my nerves. Remi is occupied. For now.

I toss my phone onto the desk, plop backward, and rock in the chair, eyes scanning the room. My focus lands on the black outline of her backpack on the floor next to my door.

No.

No, no, no, no.

She literally has nothing to change into right now.

Which means she's going to come out of that bathroom and walk around the house in nothing but a towel until she finds it. That, or she'll use Trenton's clothes. Or mine. Or none.

I shoot out of the chair, snatch up her bag, and pad to the bathroom door. I knock. She answers. I freeze.

Big mistake.

Remi opens the door, head stuck out of the shower, curtain held tight between her breasts.

"I have your bag." I hold it up high, in front of my face to block the view of everything I want—don't want—to see.

"Oh! Thanks. Just put it under the counter so it stays dry?"

I shake my head behind my barricade, but my throat and mouth say, "Okay."

But, no. I don't want to go in.

But, I do. Go in. And place the bag under the counter, shielding my eyes with a hand visor.

Just as I'm stepping my foot over the threshold, she just had to say my name. "Hayes…"

Nooo. "Hmm?"

"You fucked me in the ass."

I sway, choke, cough, tear up. All the things. I nearly fall over. She presses on: "Like… all the way. Balls deep."

"Holy shit. Stop."

"Why? I'm naked. It's not a big deal. Stop trying to not look at me."

Yes it is. It's a big deal. It's a very damn big — I glance down at just how BIG OF A FUCKING DEAL it is. I lift a finger to explain, but my tongue gains twenty pounds. All I can do is wave it at her. My finger, that is, not the huge fucking deal between my legs.

Then I escape. Quickly.

We get serious in street racing about girls making us stupid. I am the damn definition of it. She. Makes. Me. Stupid. Literally.

I remove my steam-blurred glasses, clean them off on my shirt, and put them back on. Then, I go to my desk, gather up all the incriminating evidence I have scattered all over the fucking place, and shove it all…

…in the tray of my printer. Yes. Perfect.

The water shuts off. I sprint into the living room, jump over the back of the couch, and curl onto my side to feign sleep.

CHAPTER THIRTY-THREE

Remi

A refreshing shower-induced brainstorming session is exactly what the doctor ordered. Up until I turned the shower on, all I knew was that I wanted to bring them together. To fix what I broke. The seed of my idea was simple: get them on the streets together again. But no matter how high I cranked the hot water, there were several pieces to the puzzle that I was struggling to figure out — the five W's, for instance. Then, in came Hayes. A knight in shining armor. He knocked at the perfect time. His flustered state and the many memories of us together that came with it, mixed with what Trenton said last night about the Golden Ticket event, watered the seed and made it sprout.

With Hayes asleep on the couch, I get situated at his desk as promised.

It takes me a few minutes to figure out the setup — where the browser and usb port are, for example, but not too terribly long. Despite having never used his computer, I still have a sense of déjà vu as I log into the car forum where this all began. "We want you out on the field, Remi. Recruiting." I whisper with a chuckle. "Well hello there irony, my old friend. Sleuth

218

and Recruiter Remi, at your service," I mutter under my breath, bowing at the waist and flailing my hand in the air.

The silly, dramatic smirk on my face drops when the page loads and a chat box containing messages between DoubleD and HazerBeam displays as open in the bottom right corner, having never been closed out. Hayes had typed a message but never sent it.

:HazerBeam: I have it bad for this woman. Beautiful, smart, knows her vehicles. Problem is, there are too many red lights flashing. I keep getting stuck at each one. My tank is running on E. Thought maybe I would ask for your advice…

Oh, Hayes.

I scramble to dig out my phone so I can log in to my account and respond, even if he never truly sent the call for help. The metal thumb drive flashes inside the clutch under his purple overhead lighting. I remove it, too, and set it aside.

The app loads excruciatingly slow on my phone. My nerves vibrate at a higher and higher frequency the longer it takes. Every wave dies as soon as the page opens, though.

My username and password no longer gives me access. I switch my focus back to the screen and realize now that my name in the chat box is greyed out.

Instead of sending the message, Hayes revoked my membership.

A layer of emotion clogs my throat, but I swallow through the obstruction… and carry on, distracting my feelings with the hope of redemption. From HazerBeam's profile, I easily find the one forum post that indicates the date when the main ticket pickups were supposed to take place. A few days ago. Which explains why Hayes was still doing damage control just yesterday. But, I also find another. One per week during my hospital stay.

Hmmm. The little yellow pieces of papers are out there. Someone, despite Hayes working damage control, has an invitation — one that contains all the information I need to organize a new event in its place.

Knowing there's not enough time to traipse around town interviewing strangers, and after having no luck searching computer files for the actual ticket, I decide to bring my sleuthing efforts to a new level; those important details will need to be found via other means.

As much as I dread the next step, I pull up a search on Rachal Halston.

The queue floods with articles.

I scan the titles and summaries searching for only what is needed — the date. Any other details or information needs to come directly from Crow, and I do not intend to pressure him to spill those secrets before he's ready. The date of their wreck is easy to find: October twentieth.

Four days from now.

Scrolling the queue back up to the search bar, my eyes catch on the line of images related to the wreck. Not just any image, but one of... Trenton.

Heart rate increasing, I click the image. When the article opens, though, the name under it says Travis. Not Trenton. How similar they look is uncanny. I get that they're brothers, but they could pass for twins.

Twins.

Oh, my God.

I eagerly type in Travis and Trenton Stokes, going far beyond what I intended this sleuthing session to accomplish. But curiosity gets the better of me. An article dated five years back is included in the first few suggested links... when they were all still in high school. The ages in parentheses beside their name are the same — both eighteen at the time. I exit out of everything and clear my portion of the search history.

Focus, Remi.

My goal doesn't have anything to do with digging into their pasts.

Only with changing their futures.

The next step is to find the location, and that piece of important information is only ever shared on a golden ticket. So I either need to get ahold of one...

...or... Hayes.

CHAPTER THIRTY-FOUR

S oft snores come from the direction of the couch. Hayes literally passed out. When I finished showering and getting dressed, his eyelids were twitching, forced into being closed. He was pretending. Apparently, exhaustion got the better of him, and he caved.

Works for me.

But first… I prop my phone up on the coffee table against a bowl of controllers, open the camera app, swipe to video, and click record. Then, I remove all my clothes, fall to my knees beside him, slowly undo his button and zipper, slip my hand under the waistband of his boxer briefs, and then… stroke him awake.

Not ten seconds later he stirs with a startle and a backward scamper toward the arm of the couch, finger lifted in defense — to which I also use to my benefit, slipping my mouth over it while straddling him and placing his unprotected cock at my entrance.

Crow gave in to our connection.

Trenton is unable to fight us.

Hayes will succumb, too.

He groans, and his head falls back, hands immediately flying to my hips to hold me, hovered above him. "Remi. What are you doing?"

"Fucking you so you'll give me the information I need to know about the Golden Ticket event."

His hands accidentally loosen, and I drop a short distance, the tip entering just enough to give us both a tease. This time when his hands tighten over my hips, it's not with nearly the same amount of purchase. His eyebrows curve inward as he tries to wake up and understand what I just said. "Ahh, hell... Wait... women usually do that gold digging type of stuff on the down low. Like, without actually admitting to it, right?"

"Lie? Trick? Betray? Yeah... I guess. But, that's not really my agenda here. I'm actually trying to earn your trust back, not whittle it down more."

He closes his eyes and slowly lowers me onto his cock with a delicious bite to his bottom lip. "No... see... you've pegged me wrong. My brain actually works when I am inside you. It's when my cock is seeking you out like a damn homing device that I am unable to fucktion. I'm not telling you anything. Nope." He thrusts his hips upward, and I clench everywhere.

Well, damn, I hadn't thought of it that way. I try to backpedal, to escape and reassess, but he grips harder and thrusts again.

His dark-blue eyes meet mine through his glasses. "But I have pegged you, Remi." Yes... yes you have... "You are the one who becomes stupid when being fucked." Hayes rolls his hips, his pelvis grinding against my clit just right…

… and just like that, the game is over for me.

His hands move to my ass cheeks, fingers splaying, spreading me. "I've been thinking this through all wrong," he pants, lifting me up to his tip and sliding me back down over him again. "I need to keep you busy. Keep my cock buried in you. Maybe then I can actually make some goddamn progress."

How? How is he talking so much right now? And why don't I understand any of it? I try humming out a question, but the effort is pointless.

Remi, Remi, Remi.

Girl… Take back control.

Come on.

My pussy clenches. I slam my hands down on his chest and spring off of him. He swipes for me, but misses. I fall to my knees, just as he sits up and is about to lunge for me, and pin him onto the couch with my palms against his thighs. Then, I open my mouth wide and descend on him, slick with a combination of my juices and his — ripe with our concocted musk.

Hayes tenses everywhere — thighs, abs, cock, tightly drawn up balls. His breathing comes in short, choppy pants. I have effectively rendered him speechless. For now.

I pop his cock out of my mouth with a smack. His eyes spring open wide, and I ask, "Where was the Golden Ticket event going to be held?"

"Shh," he susserates, slinking his fingers into my still-damp hair and drawing me in closer to his cock.

I swipe from base to tip with my tongue, all while keeping my eyes aimed upward and locked on his. "Hmm?" I hum over the tip.

Hayes lifts his hips, entering my mouth. When his cock touches the back of my throat, he shudders, and I lift my head again.

"You're taking advantage of me," he breathes low, fingers clenching and unclenching in my hair.

"Want me to stop? Refuse me an answer to my question," I state.

He groans, grabs the base of his cock, and swipes the tip along my lips. "The answer doesn't matter — we canceled it."

"Exactly. No harm, then." I glide him toward the back of my throat and out again.

"Wait…" he grunts, shifting under me. "How do you know that?"

"Trenton told me."

Hayes's already dark-blue eyes darken like a storm. One hand grips the back of my head, the other drops to under my chin. "Fucker," he breathes, tracing my jaw and slipping the tips of his fingers into my mouth to pry my lips open. "Open wide."

I do. So, so, so wide. Hayes stands, lines his cock up to my mouth, and drives inside me, thumb tracing the indentation of my cheeks, the movement of my jaw. He grinds again and again, drawing tears from my eyes. If he is going to give me information, he means to make it count.

And, if he is going to make it count, then so am I. I reach down and circle my finger over my clit in time with each drive. Hayes tucks his chin, his gaze angled downward, taking everything in: my mouth, my working palm, his controlling hand, the way his cock moves along the length of my tongue with ease, the jolt of my stomach every time he hits far enough back to make me gag.

My teeth are the only defense against him right now if he takes without giving — which would be fine under normal circumstances, but not this one. I give him a warning clench of my jaw and his rhythmic glide unevens for a couple thrusts. "Jesus," he pants, shoving into me, conjuring tears. I do it again… a little firmer. "Okay, okay. Christ. The old amusement park on the West End." He raises an eyebrow at me, head still tilted downward.

I try on a smile for size, but my mouth is filled with cock. The attempt pulls a moan from him nonetheless. "Harder?" he asks, eyes pleading, lids heavy. I cup his balls, and his knees unlock slightly. One hand drops to my shoulder, the other remains on the back of my head. I nod, looking up at him. He licks his lips, closes his eyes, and drops his head back.

Then, he fucks my mouth. Hard. Fast. Relentless.

And I finger myself to reach my own release…

…and for the sake of the recording camera.

WHILE HAYES IS IN THE SHOWER, I get back to work on his computer, feeling quite accomplished, if I do say so myself.

However, there is one more item of business I really need to take care of today: the matter of that strange, QR code looking thing on the copy of the photo of me and Dad.

I insert the thumb drive into the usb port on Hayes's computer and pull up the folder.

"Okay, Dad… What were you trying to tell me?" I whisper, zooming into the headlight of my bike. Once close enough, I remember that QRs are primarily mobile device friendly, so I open the camera app on my phone. Only to be immediately presented by a large cock being thrust into my mouth. The video plays silently, showing a small portion of the clip on repeat. My lips turn downward and nod in appreciation. I kinda worried I might hate seeing myself like that… but, hell, I pulled it off.

Shaking the distraction out of my head, I flick back to the portrait option, aim my lens at the computer screen, and my phone immediately registers the code; a notification pops up asking me if I want to open the link.

Considering the history with Porter tracing my phone, I open the browser on the computer, and manually type the link.

A cloud-storage page pops up on the screen, displaying a folder. I double click the trail. There's only one single file inside. A PDF. With a deep breath, I open the document.

At the top reads: Final Will and Testament of Troy Delancey.

My heart pauses.

The world stops spinning.

Everything around me... colors, sounds, sensations... become muted.

This must be the will Dad mentioned — the one Jude looked everywhere for.

All this time, the egg was hidden in my bike.

My daze pops, all the sounds, colors, and clarity return around me. Suddenly terrified I'll lose it, I save a copy to both the computer and my thumb drive.

Print. I... I need a print copy.

I frantically look around for the printer, spot it in the corner of the room beside his stereo system, and power it on. While waiting for it to boot, I impatiently drum my fingers on the desk.

As soon as the start-up whir stops, I click print on the document. The printer hums, then the *scrit, scrit* of the printer head moving side to side fills the room.

When everything becomes silent again, I snatch the papers from the printer, plop into the office chair, and begin scanning the sheets.

But the words on the paper don't match the words on the screen. I scan the paper again. An import document. I lean forward and scroll through the digitized version. No import stuff.

What the hell?

Wait…

I flip the papers in my hands over.

There. And again on the back of the next page.

My attention turns slowly toward the printer.

I scramble off the chair, fall to my knees in front of the machine, and tear out all the paper in the tray.

Documents. Several of them.

I study the ones in my hand again, flipping them back over to the import stuff.

The papers Hayes had with him the night of the meet.

This must be them.

If not more.

I tear through sheet after sheet.

Business information about Lance Industries.

Import paperwork.

Everything I know not a damn thing about.

Again, I look at the will.

My head throbs.

My vision shakes.

I have no idea what all this means. The words are like a foreign language to me. I was in school for Information Technology for goodness' sake, not Law!

Goddammit!

I fall back to my heels, papers strewn around me in an arch.

Then, I lose it. I crumple forward, head falling toward my knees, hands covering my face, hair creating a curtain around me, shoulders trembling, eyes purging.

Someone clears a throat behind me. I jerk to attention mid wail. The sob catches in my throat as I swing my head around to look toward the door.

Hayes is standing there, arms crossed over his chest, hip propped against the doorframe. "Time to talk, hm?" he says. All awkwardness gone.

"T-talk?"

He steps forward, falls into a squat, and moves the hair out of my face. "That's one of the reasons why we brought you here. You're not leaving. Tell me the truth. About everything."

CHAPTER THIRTY-FIVE

I shoot to my feet, zoom past him out to the living room and straight to the door. Locked. And not from the inside, either. Somehow, they'd locked me in from the outside. I check the garage door. The back door. Everywhere. All locked.

By the time I rage into his bedroom, Hayes is waiting for me, reclined in his chair. "What the hell is going on?"

The papers are all still strewn about on the floor. I regret taking advantage of him. He's level-headed now. Serious. Not the awkward, sweet Hayes I pine for. "You tell me," he responds, waving an arm over the documents.

I find a spot the farthest away from him and sit down with my back against the wall. In my mind, I rationalize that only a portion of the papers in here are my doing. "I found an updated will, hidden by my father. Used your printer to make sure I have a tangible copy."

He blinks repeatedly at me, confused. "That's how you found the papers I had? You were printing a will?"

I continue. "Yes… Those papers, are they the ones you had the night of the meet?"

His fingers twitch against his thigh. "Some of them." He falls silent for a moment before continuing. "How involved are you in Lance Industries? I know you said you're not interested, but what role did you play anyway?"

"Nothing," I answer honestly. "Infiltrating The Gulf Coasters was my first job."

Hayes's jaw moves over clenched teeth. "Who are the officers of the company?"

That... gives me pause. I hadn't considered what changes were made since Dad died. "Um... Jude is Chief Executive Officer, Porter is Chief Finance Officer, and... Aria Dixon has been the Chief Administrative Officer for as long as I can remember. Far as I know, she's still working from one of the offices back home."

Hayes leans forward, snatches up some of the papers, searches through them until finding the ones he is looking for, then plops several papers on my lap. "You are the Chief Administrative Officer, Remi. Have been since after your Dad died and you signed the agreements. The proof is right here. Why the hell are you still lying about it?"

My eyes track down the page, scanning past all the legal verbiage that I simply do not understand. To the bottom, where my name is signed. I flip the page. Another signed one. Again and again. Jude and

Porter's signatures are all there, too. All signatures include a date. The day after my father died.

Blinking dumbly, I tear my gaze from the documents and look at Hayes. "I... I remember signing these papers. They were supposed to be funeral documents and stuff relating to his death."

Hayes pulls a face, and again we fall silent. Only the creak of his chair bouncing as he rocks lightly can be heard until he speaks again. "Who was present when you signed them?"

Gaping like a fish, I flip wildly through the documents. "Porter. Porter had us sign these. He took care of everything. He acted as our spine in those few days following. Made sure everything was handled so Jude and I could mourn. You... you have to believe me. Please believe me. I have no idea what any of this means."

"You signed dozens of papers that you didn't understand?" he asks, tossing his head back with a growl. "Why?! Why would you do that?" His tone is accusatory and disappointed.

Rage and indignation swells inside me. I shoot to my feet and point an indignant finger at him. "I trusted Porter! I trusted that my dad had the right man under his wing! Aside from Porter's personal treatment of me — which worsened only after all this mess — as far as I knew, he was an honest, hardworking, business partner."

I begin to manically collect all the documents. All my family's personal affairs are being treated like trash on the ground. My tears are dried and internalized, and my body shakes harboring them, trembling with anger and confusion.

"Remi…" Hayes sighs, pushing something into my sightline. When I dart a pained glance up at him, he's on the floor with me collecting more of the papers and adding them to my stack. All except for a carbon paper… with my signature.

He places a hand over my vibrating one, slips the stack of papers out from beneath it. I'm left sitting there with nothing more than a carbon copy of my signature. "Where did this one come from?" I ask, watching him warily as he thumbs through the stack and pulls out two specific papers.

"I slipped it under the title for your new bike when you were signing it," he states, letting go of each of the two papers he plucked from the stack.

Fire explodes behind my eyeballs. Now, not only is my body shaking from repressed emotion, I'm also burning from the inside out. "What I did to you guys was unacceptable. Lying about why I originally showed interest in your crew and club. But this… this… is crossing a line, Hayes." Each word is delivered through nearly clenched teeth.

The two papers flutter to a stop beside said carbon copy. He doesn't acknowledge my accusation. He simply waits for me to read the papers.

With a huff, I snatch up all three and scrutinize them. I might not understand most of what the documents say — of their purpose — but I do understand what Hayes is trying to show me. Three papers. Three signatures. All mine…

…yet not.

The import document has my signature, but I did not sign it. I know… because according to the date on the ledger, I was doing something so, so much worse than putting a pen to paper.

I drop it like the fibers are covered in poison.

My mind scrambles to grab purchase on something — anything — I'm capable of understanding. A trickle of information that can lead me to the mouth of the river. "You got a copy of my signature so you could compare it? Th-that night of the meet you stopped me from admitting Porter's abuse to Jude. Why?"

Hayes's mouth ticks to the side, and he gives me a single nod. "Yes… and good question." I love how he can tell I am overwhelmed and confused but doesn't undermine my ability to understand. "My intent was never to dig up dirt on you specifically, but to dig up what I could in order to get Porter out of your life — to make sure he gets what he deserves. That's all I ever cared about." Hayes takes a deep breath and gets more comfortable on the floor in front of me. "My dad killed my mom." He keeps his eyes downcast, unable to look at me while he reveals his deepest, darkest secret. "He beat my sister and me, too, but she got away, only to run into the arms of one abuser after another. She's cut me out and moved to Washington. Won't let me help — for my protection." He scoffs at that last bit. "I pried into your affairs for selfish reasons. Because I can't let another woman I care about suffer like that. To be mind-fucked and taken advantage of." He turns his phone on, presses several buttons, waits for something to sound off in his ear, turns on the loudspeaker, then tosses the phone between us.

Jude's voice reverberates through the device, and my pulse skyrockets. "Jude here. We... have a problem." Hayes slides over yet another paper. My eyes land on a recent news article. The picture at the very top is of Boyd, the kid who owns the red Trans Am. The title beneath: Boy Missing, Foul Play Suspected. Jude's voice had drowned out, but my senses spike back into existence at his parting words: "Porter disappeared. Keep Remi safe." Jude's voice drops and catches. "Promise me you'll keep her safe. If... if she asks about me, just tell her I'm being her 80 percent." The line clicks.

Hayes steels his shoulders and pins me with a menacing glare. "Porter will kill you. And that's the other reason why you're locked in here. We're not out to seek revenge, Remi. We're trying to protect you."

CHAPTER THIRTY-SIX

The walls suddenly seem too confining, yet the locks no longer provide enough protection. Worried my heart might explode, my hand clutches at my chest.

A rush of facts hit me: Jude disappearing. Crow staying with me at the hospital. Lace paying my rent. Trenton getting me drunk so I had to go home with him. Hayes investigating.

I tip backward to lie on the floor and stare up at the ceiling. I have lived for days — weeks — under a false sense of security. Oblivious while gears turned and notches slipped into grooves, all while dirty oil seeped between the mechanisms.

What is real anymore?

Who can I trust?

How long will I live in fear?

"Dad had Porter and Jude running imports as teenagers. They would go to the sales lots, pay in cash, and drive the vehicles straight to the loading container warehouse. Jude and Porter were the ones always dealing with the imports. Jude was out of town that night. Porter told me I had to be present — to represent for Jude. But I didn't sign any paperwork, Hayes. Not once. As soon as Dad saw me there—" I shake my head, eyes filling. Sure, I had been keeping this from everyone else in my life, but I had been keeping it from myself, too. Any time the memory or imagery tried to present in my mind, I fought against it, grasped to replace the thought-train with something else. Something more bearable. "I didn't sign any papers," I whisper.

Hayes scoots closer. "What happened that night?"

"No." I refuse both of us that answer.

Hayes sighs.

"Stop. I... I'm not obligated to share personal information with you. Not this."

"What are you so scared of? Porter?" he asks, voice soft.

Again, I shake my head, trying to toss the sound of his voice out of my ears. "No. Listen... this doesn't impact you, Revelry, or The Gulf Coasters in any way. This is me. My secret. Mine." With every word, I point at my chest as if doing so will help affirm the truth.

"It does impact me!" Hayes rages. "Because it is eating you up inside, and I — we — care about you. God, Remi!"

"Stop," I sob.

Hayes holds his hands up, palms out. "Okay. Okay. Fine." He waits until I calm down again and my breathing evens out a little. "At least let us help you? With what we already know? Hm? This is fifty-shades of fucked up… You can't go it alone. You can lean on us. Promise."

I take several gulping swallows and blink all the haziness away from my eyes. "Yeah. Okay. But the moment you treat me like a damn child, I'm out of here." I push off the ground, collect all the papers, and tuck them under my arm. Hayes might have printed them all… but they belong to me.

My feet come to an immediate halt when I storm out of his bedroom door. Hayes runs smack dab into me from behind. Trenton is there standing, leaning against the wall just outside the room, expression bemused, yet hopeful.

Hayes nudges me to the side, steps around me, and swings a hard right hook into Trenton's jaw. Trenton doesn't move. Hayes stomps off toward the kitchen. I stand stock-still, stunned, papers crinkling under my arm and eyes darting from man to man.

Trenton chuckles and shrugs. "I was supposed to be the one to speak with you. He doesn't handle this sort of shit well."

My eyes spring wide, mouth pops open, and I nod solemnly. "He did great — yelled at me and everything."

"I heard." Trenton moves his jaw around and finally brings his hand to his face. "Damn… that fucking hurt."

Guys have such a strange way of delivering a point sometimes. "Okay… well… yep…" I give Trenton an awkward, twitchy smile and walk toward the dining room. Hayes was right: this is fifty-shades of fucked up. And, once again, I am sick and damn tired of not understanding anything. It is the shittiest of luck, too, that every time I try to understand, something thwarts me. Not this time, dammit.

Sharing a space with them may be requisite, but I will create my own little world within these walls. Inside here, nothing will hinder my attempts to piece everything together. My workload just increased substantially, and my time is steadily dwindling. Four days. Four days to get this all figured out and put an end to the madness. Every bit of it.

I toss the papers onto the table and swipe my arm over them in a big arch, spreading the papers wide across the surface. "Jude said Porter is missing. Where has he been all this time? And… why is Boyd missing now, too?" I ask, pulling that article out of the stack.

Hayes pushes a glass of water in front of me and a banana. "Jude had eyes on him. Porter was in intensive care for a while, then moved to a room, then transferred to a psych hospital a few counties east of here." I had lifted the glass of water and brought it to my lips, but stopped just prior to taking a sip. A cough-laugh erupts from me. Hearing that Porter was sent to a psychiatric hospital is the best news, even if he is no

241

longer there. "As for the boy, that is an unsolved mystery. That article is dated the same day Porter went missing, though. Seems pretty incriminating… for both of them." He picks up the paper and moves it to the top corner of the table. He selects all the funeral-related documents — or, rather, all the documents adding me as an officer on the board — and lines them up in front of me, sending a side-glance to check for my reaction and approval.

Shaking my head adamantly, I look up at Hayes, pleading — begging he overlook my stupidity. "I was bereft. Jude, too. Porter said we were signing documents all related to his passing. Neither Jude nor I have ever been good at the paperwork side of things. Jude and I both signed these under that same assumption. Does Jude know? Have you spoken to him about this?"

Hayes shakes his head. "I didn't want to jump to conclusions. Not static ones, at least. I have been running circles trying to piece everything together. But there are big, gaping, holes that even the most strenuous investigating won't reveal."

Oh good… so I'm not the only one that can't make sense of the Monet. "Why would Porter even want me to hold an officer position?"

Hayes shrugs and begins to collect the import docs. The hairs on my arms immediately stand on end and my throat closes. He freezes, eyes locking on mine. "No import stuff. Okay? For now. You printed the will on the back of these pages. Should we look at those?"

I nod and unclench my fingers from the edge of the table. Hayes pushes the officer stuff toward the top of the table and lines up the pages of the will in front of me. Starting at the top, I scan the document. My name is easy to find. I carefully read each section that includes it.

"Is this the most recent will?" Hayes asks, eyebrows furrowing.

"I… think so…" my words trail as I land on a part mentioning his request that I keep removed. "Ha! I jab my finger at the line. See? He always hated the idea of me being involved."

Hayes reroutes his attention to the line, knuckling his glasses up his nose, but when it looks like he is getting too immersed in the details, a sense of protectiveness comes over me, and I place my hand over the part his gaze had traveled to: Bequests. That section feels too intimate — like Dad perhaps meant it as a handwritten letter to me and Jude only. A final goodbye. Hayes respects my decision.

His shoulders lift and fall indicating a silent sigh, but he gives me a soft smile. "None of this matters, though," he says. "Every single word, plan, and promise is moot if a will came after this one."

"I… don't think any did. Dad filed the one with the courts earlier in the year, labeling Porter as the Executor. Maybe he filed that one under Porter's thumb? I found a trail to this one in the wreckage of my bike, so I assume this must be the updated one. Plus" — I drag my finger to the date — "this was just a few months ago, and it was only just prior to his death that an updated will was mentioned."

"Prior to his death?" Hayes asks carefully.

"The attending physician said he had mentioned an updated will during the moments he was still able to speak."

"Okay," Hayes responds with a small frown. "How long has Porter been involved in Lance Industries?"

"Like I mentioned earlier, since they were just teenagers, pushing imports. For Jude and Porter, that's where things started."

Hayes plops down into the chair beside me, leans his head back, and rubs a finger under his glasses. "This is complete speculation, but my guess is Porter knew Troy meant to bequeath something to you that Porter wanted — and that you would be getting whatever it is under the condition that you keep out of the business."

"…so he ensured I was in the business, by having me sign all the paperwork, then having the board vote me in when I wasn't available because of my state of mourning — using the signed documents as proof of my approval. Dad had the hots for Aria, though; he never would have removed her from the company much less replaced her with me."

Hayes straightens, nods, and smiles. "Speculation."

"Right. Speculation. But… figuratively speaking, if that is true, then Dad knew Porter was up to no good, which begs the question: Why didn't he just kick him to the curb?"

Hayes raises an eyebrow at me, indicating I already know the answer.

"Porter threatened him. Held something over his head."

"Not something… someone."

"Me."

I TOSS MY HEAD BACK WITH A GROAN and rub my eyes. "I've read these documents at least five times. I can't anymore. I'm going cross-eyed."

Trenton joined after it was evident he wouldn't get mauled upon entering the dining room. He and Hayes had been friends long enough for him to know just, exactly, how much time he needs when something goes down between them — a couple hours, apparently.

Three bottles of water and a banana later, I also at least had enough sustenance in my body to carry me through a couple of those hours. Still on my soapbox, I continue, "Plus, aside from yesterday, I have been stuck inside a building for weeks. Literally. I miss the rove of tires, rev of the engine, and the rush of wind."

Both guys lift their heads from the paperwork and stare at me. Trenton is the one to speak, Hayes having relinquished that responsibility as soon as Trenton walked into the room. "You want to leave the house? The one that is locked, both inside and outside."

I blink at him repeatedly. "Yes. I do."

"Alone?"

I roll my eyes and cross my arms.

Hayes leans back in his chair with a smug smirk.

Trenton flips him the bird.

I laugh.

I love when they're getting along and working together. But this orneriness between them is kinda fun, too. "Going alone isn't a necessity, but I'm not riding bitch on my own bike, so that part will need to be by myself."

"Where do you want to go?" the spokesman asks.

My grin widens, amused by this entire situation. "On a joy ride… Sir. "

Hayes chortles.

Trenton narrows his light-brown eyes on my dark ones. "You've been in lockdown for less than twenty-four hours, and you already have cabin fever?"

"Mm-hmm. Sure. Plus, I don't want to leave my bike at The Crowbar for much longer. How long were you planning on keeping me in here with the doors locked?"

Trenton pushes out of the seat, walks away into his room, and comes back jangling his keys. "Hadn't worked that part out yet… just that we made your very protective brother that shoots people a promise to take care of his sister. Guess we can protect you outside, too. Let's go."

Hayes launches up. "Really? Count me in."

Trenton shrugs.

"Shotgun!" I jump out of my chair, snatch my clutch off the bar top, and dash toward the exit. But the door is locked. From the outside. I spin on my heels.

Trenton has his phone up to his ear covering the muffled ringing on the other line.

Wait…

I step closer to the garage door… and hear ringing coming through the door, too.

"Rapunzel wants out of her tower; we're going with her," Trenton tells the person on the other line. The sound of locks unclicking soon follows, the door swings open, and Crow appears in the doorway.

I gape at him. He shoots me a wink. "How long have you been out there?"

"Since I carried you to bed early this morning." He jabs a thumb over his shoulder. "Slept on that cot over there."

Leaning to the side and looking past him, I discover that, sure enough, a cot is set up in the far corner of the garage, just past the Monte and Bimmer.

"Where's your car?"

"In the driveway."

I stand there, shocked into silence, for a few minutes. "Wow, you guys really went all out, hm? Hayes pulling research. Trenton getting me drunk. What was your job—"

Hold on. Was all that in the V Coupe — the love making at the junkyard — part of some sort of plan to make me amenable? I open my mouth, but his hand cups over my face. I chomp at his palm and fail.

Hayes yanks Crow's hand away from me. I fume. "So... the sex? You... you used me?"

"Sex?" Hayes grinds out. "You had sex with her?"

I spin on Trenton. "What about you, hm? The part that came after getting me drunk?"

Hayes opens his mouth again, glaring at Trenton, but then it snaps shut, and his tightly pressed lips slowly morph into a smile. Then a grin. Then laughter bursts out of him.

Trenton and Crow had started going head to head, but they freeze at Hayes's laughter.

"What the hell is so damn funny about this?" Trenton grinds out.

Hayes's laughter slowly dies, and he turns to me: "Go ahead… tell them what happened between us this morning."

"You, too?" Crow chastises.

"Ah…" I mutter. Well, shit. "No, that was all me. I kinda, sorta, bribed him… by giving him head. No big deal." I wave a hand in the air.

"So…" Trenton hums. "Let me get this straight… You were involved with all three of us… on the same day?"

I gasp and cover my chest, mocking offense. "Technically, two different days. But, uh, over the course of twenty-four hours… yes. Technically. We were good with that, right? Sharing and stuff?" I grimace.

Trenton and Crow engage in a stare down.

Hayes leans close to my ear and whispers, "I think we are about to find out." He shoves his hands in his pockets.

I watch in anticipation as both men battle with something that goes way beyond this. Us. Me. Maybe one day I'll understand, but I have a feeling right now is not that day.

As men tend to do, they actually don't say anything at all. This showdown is over just as silently as it started. Crow walks away, heading out toward the driveway. Trenton turns to me. "Who are you riding to The Crowbar with?"

Oooh, choices. "Hayes. Been a while since I've been in the Bimmer."

Hayes gives Trenton a beaming grin, pats him on the shoulder, "Maybe next time, sugar," he says in a terrible Southern accent.

CHAPTER THIRTY-SEVEN

G etting to The Crowbar is relatively anticlimactic aside from the fact that we're a damn entourage and recognized by just about everyone on the road.

"It's more obvious when we're all together like this," Hayes explains when at least one driver at each light salutes us. No one challenges them to a dig, though. Reading my mind the way he does, Hayes mentions something about that, too: "Trenton and I don't engage outside of organized meets anymore. Not usually, at least. And everyone knows Crow stopped racing."

Another item of note is that most people, aside from the occasional senior, moves aside when they notice one of the guys in their rearview.

We arrive at The Crowbar in record time. Just as Trenton had promised last night when I had asked a couple times before passing out, my bike was still there in the employee parking, still in excellent condition, and my helmet still hung on the handle bar.

I hop out of the Bimmer and run straight over to her, still disbelieving that Jude pulled this off... by selling Porter's car nonetheless. I love my new bike. I miss my first, but this is nearly a duplicate.

And because of that so-called cabin fever, I am itching to really test her.

One super nice thing about having a motorcycle is that it is independent naturally; the guys might coop me up, chauffeur me around, and follow me, but while on my bike, I make the rules. No one else. And, as I said... we're going on a joy ride.

Because, damn, I could use a little joy in my life right now. That, and I also need to do a bit more sleuthing. Sure, I would have liked to do it without them breathing down my neck, but that isn't exactly possible right now, and I'm not stupid enough to go out alone. They delivered the message, and I understood. I like the idea of being independent but am not stupid because of it. Or, at least, I'm not trying to be.

The guys all wait patiently while I store my clutch and shake out my helmet to make sure no insect friends took up residence inside it overnight. Before leaving, I don't bother to tell them my travel destination; I simply ride off toward the West End.

They follow me in a straight line, my personal guards, until I reach the closed down amusement park — the location my oral persuasion had earned me this morning.

For a second, I just stare at the monstrosity of the place. Movement in my mirror catches my eye, and I glance down in time to see Hayes approaching — most likely to discipline me and insist I turn back around. But he keeps going, all the way to the chain-link gate. He removes a key from his pocket, slots it in, and pulls the gate open. I instantly twist the throttle and zoom past him. First, through the parking lot, then straight past the ticket booths and into the main courtyard of the park.

It takes them a while to get to me, since their cars can't fit through the booth rows. They have to park, get out, and walk the rest of the way. Once they're bracketing me, though, I finally take off my helmet and really look around. "This place is amazing," I state.

"Yeah. Iconic. The imprint fades more and more every year that passes, though."

"What happened? Why did it close down?"

"Same reason why anything around here does: hard to keep up with the demand — increase in taxes, things of that sort. The owner sold it to build more condominiums, of course." Trenton scoffs. "The water park is still open, though."

"Guess the residential idea fell through? Seeing as several of the rides are still here?"

"They will be demolished one day. Most of the rides were moved to different parks throughout the US. A little piece of paradise now in places like Georgia and Connecticut."

Time to break into the topic of the Golden Ticket event: "Where do you all race?" I swivel my head around, studying the topography.

"In the parking lot. People set up concessions and stuff in the entrance booths."

I slip my helmet back on and snap the clip. "Cool. I want to take a look around."

"On your bike?" Crow asks.

"Hell yeah."

All three of them step aside, and I launch forward. The main courtyard has enough room for me to maneuver through, but the rest might be a little tricky, so I take it easy. At first.

One entire loop around the park is enough of a trial. The decaying rollercoaster and old, dome-shaped ride are my personal favorites — and both big enough to maneuver through. I zoom past the guys, giving them a two-finger salute, and start my second round.

I've never been big on stunts, but Trenton was right last night at the bar; since my wreck, I have become wobbly. Afraid.

A parking lot would do, but I was afraid the wide-open space would feel too free — too dangerous — until I get my tarmac legs back.

Here? Zipping under roller-coaster beams and through empty buildings? I could let loose a little. Corner posture a little deeper.

The first bend comes and I lean into it, holding my breath, but I straighten after about mid-lean, the curve relatively short. The main bend, though, the one that circles around the coaster, I let go. Literally. I lean into the turn until I can feel the concrete teasing my jeans. Threatening me. I drop my gloved hand — the same one attached to my scarred arm — and brush the ground. Then, at the end of the bend, I straighten her up.

Once upon a time, Hayes and Crow had shown off their donut skills. Now it is my turn. No one would see it, though. This experience is reserved for me and me alone. Five rides remain on the otherwise desolate lot: the old, wooden coaster, a dilapidating ferris wheel, a dome-shaped building designed to look like the devil, a large swinging ship, and a building that I assume must have been a haunted house once upon a time. Such a shame they only hang out in the parking lot for the meets.

Might be time to change that.

On the opposite end of the park, that large, ominous devil structure stands tall, mouth gaping wide as the entrance. Inside is a big, perfect circle. I disappear inside there. First, simply doing a tight circle around the perimeter, but then, I drift into a donut and let the bottom of my shoe graze the ground as I circle repeatedly before coming a stop in the center, heart pounding, the remnants of burnt rubber filling the dome and singeing my nose in the absolute best way.

As soon as the smoke clears, I dismount, dig out my phone, and make a very important phone call.

"Hello?"

"Lace?"

"Mm-hmm."

"This is Remi. Crow's... friend."

Her laugh is light and sweet. "I know who you are, hun. Welcome back."

"Heh. Thanks." I take a deep breath. "And thanks for covering my rent for the month."

"Favor for a favor. Foster owes me."

"Oh. Um... okay. So..." — I lower my voice, just in case — "I could really use your help with something."

"Whatcha got?"

"Well... three pretty incredible guys that could really use a stipend from the Universe."

"Girl! I love where your head is."

Yeah... Hayes appreciated that this morning, too. Anyway... I rush out my entire plan and what, exactly, she can do to help. She loves the idea and ensures her parts will be accomplished. All of them. I'm pushing all my chips toward her, because my hands are tied.

High on excitement and girly giddiness, I wait to drop the bomb last, though. "Oh and, Lace?"

"Yeah?"

"Remember that guy I warned you about?"

"Sure do, he poked his nose in here just like ya said he might."

Ah shit. I want to ask more, but there isn't enough time for that right now, so I press on: "Yeah? Well... maybe he'll do it again. Because I really need to make sure he gets a golden ticket, too. On the down low, you know?"

"I hear what you're saying. Consider it done."

* * *

TRENTON REMOVES HIS T-TOP again, Crow and Hayes roll down their windows, and I take advantage of Florida's lacking helmet law and take mine off for the slow ride back down The Strip. I even spook Crow by popping my front wheel for a couple seconds. As soon as we get to the end of The Strip, though, I put my helmet back on. I might have dropped a little of my fear back at the amusement park, but it still remains enough to where, despite the flexible law, I want my helmet on while navigating the higher-speed roads regardless.

As soon as we're back at the house, Crow rounds on me, flailing his arms and hounding me like the big ol' Papa Bear he really is not. For a moment, I wonder if Rachal had a similar reaction toward him a time or two in the past. The thought makes me smile.

257

"Okay, chill the hell out, Burke," I coo. "Next time, I'll pop a wheelie with the helmet on."

"No. Don't do that shit at all. You've been talking to Lace again, haven't you?"

Now, that part gives me pause. "Uh... why would you ask that?"

He storms off to his cot, mumbling something under his breath about "supers" and "idiots."

"Are you seriously just going to sleep out here indefinitely?" I ask.

"Yes," he answers, flopping onto the cot, crossing his ankles, and clasping his hands behind his head.

"For how long?"

He shrugs.

The rest of the day goes by uneventfully.

In fact, the next couple of days go by uneventfully, too.

Crow makes an appearance every morning, food in hand, and we all fall quickly into a routine. One that consists of him secretly nudging me under the table during meals, unbeknownst to Trenton and Hayes, because apparently I have become a no-touch rule. "Stop looking at me like that, Remi." "Close your legs, Remi." "Fucking hell, Remi." Over the course of my stay, they have reprimanded me many times. Sometimes, they just storm out of the room.

Fine. Their avoidance gives me more time to pull a shit-ton of hours planning the modified Golden Ticket event, unbeknownst to them. Which is hard. Almost as hard as it is being here and not jumping their bones. Almost.

I sleep in Trenton's room every night, since he works late hours anyway. But, for the sake of keeping things amiable between everyone, he sleeps on the couch. To my surprise and disappointment, he never sneaks in to see me. I do try to sneak into the living room, though. But Trenton sleeps too hard — no matter how much stroking, tapping, or laving I attempt, he never stirs. Of course, I then try Hayes. But after the first attempt — and failing — he now keeps his door locked every night.

Yes… I am that damn hungry for these men.

Since they all insist on torturing me, I decide to do the same to them. Well, to one in particular. Crow. Seeing as I am inclined to believe this unspoken rule has something to do with him. Just prior to falling asleep alone, yet again, I open my camera app, pull up the porn video of Hayes fucking my face, tweak a couple things, and send it to Crow.

Since he loves videos so much.

I probably should ask Hayes's permission, since it is his dick and all, but on the off chance he would say no, I equally decide against it. Plus, he saw the camera. I caught his eyes flicking down toward it more than once… and felt his cock swelling harder every time.

CHAPTER THIRTY-EIGHT

While in the middle of texting Hayes and Trenton that I've checked the perimeter, locked all the doors, and am going to pass the fuck out, a new message vibrates through — from a number I definitely recognize but haven't gotten the balls to officially save as a contact.

Remi's California area code pops up on the top of my screen, but I swipe it aside and finish messaging the crew before opening what appears to be an MMS download or something.

One thing is for certain, I do not envy either of them one bit for being locked up with her. Give me this cot any day as opposed to telling her no. I have tried doing that; it doesn't work for me. Out of sight, out of mind. Well… kind of.

I sit down into the middle curve of the cot, remove my ball cap, toss it beside me, pick up my beer, then open her text. While the screen populates her messages, I add her name as a contact, going ahead and biting the bullet.

:Remi: Sweet dreams.

Ugh, that girly crap. I tap the attachment, yawning while it loads. Probably one of those moving picture videos of her blowing a kiss or making a duckface or some shit. Which... would be kinda nice, actually. But I'll admit that to no one.

The file takes longer than expected, doubling my curiosity. Curling my finger around the neck of the bottle, I take another pull, my anticipation building with each movement of the loading line.

When the file opens — a still-shot of Hayes sleeping like a baby on the couch inside — I balance the phone on one thigh and quickly tap the play button before picking it back up, other hand still holding my beer.

Taking yet another small drink, nursing the cold liquid, I watch down the length of the bottle as Remi wiggles out of her shorts, bare ass toward the camera, removes her shirt, then gets on her knees and shoves her hands down his pants. He startles awake and tries to escape and I almost spit out my drink. Yep... no envy.

But then she bends forward and straddles him and goddamn the peek at her slit as she'd made that minor adjustment has me thumbing the video in reverse and pausing at least three times before I can bring myself to move on. Not twenty seconds into this, likely soft-core, video, and my jeans are already too tight.

I press play again, lifting my ass, palming myself, and adjusting. When I try turning up the volume, it soon becomes evident that she edited out the sound.

Hayes appears to attempt to stop her, but fails. But then the tables turn and she teases him with a stop of her own. I shake my head with a snicker, and take another gulp.

I've never been one for those story-telling porns — I prefer them nasty and raw — but the fucking torture on Hayes's face is pure gold. I'd give my left nut to hear what is being said. Remi appears to be working her charms, and Hayes is on the losing end.

Especially when she falls to her knees, her head bobs over his juiced-up cock, and his face contorts in the best type of pain. "Pansy," I mutter with a chuckle.

He weaves his fingers in her hair, and she descends slow and deep. I tip the bottle back and swallow my groan with the bronze liquid.

The foreplay stops, and they continue whatever conversation is calling the shots of this foray. The next thing that comes out of his mouth is simple and easy to lip read, though. "Open wide."

My dick lurches when Hayes stands, turns her sideways, and his eyes glance ever so briefly down at the phone. He may not have known she was recording at first, but he did then… and he gave zero fucks.

My man lines his raging cock between her lips, and she buries her hand between her legs. Whatever she set out to accomplish, must have been achieved. She looks up at him, cock-filled mouth, and gives him a winning smile, opposite hand snaking up to cup his nuts.

Cock throbbing, I finish off the last of the beer, unzip my jeans, and get down to business. Hayes fucks her mouth, while I rub one out to the sight of her gagging and fingering herself.

CHAPTER THIRTY-NINE

Remi

A hand covering my mouth startles me awake. My eyes spring wide and breathing amplifies. Lying on my side, the person hovers behind me. The room is bathed in a very dim blue-moon light, rendering me unable to make out much.

Terrified that Porter has come for me, I thrash. But as the muscular arm adjusts and pins me, I squeeze my eyes shut tight briefly, swallow hard, and remind myself that the entire house is on lockdown until someone hears from Jude.

Once I remember that detail, my body relaxes, and I wake up completely — every part of my body. The hand releases my mouth, and I flip to my back and then to my side to figure out which of my roommates my suitor is and why his hand is over my mouth.

Crow presses his index finger firm to my lips, and I blink up at him, nodding my understanding.

His hand drops to my shoulder, down my arm, and to my hand. He then cups my palm, pulls me out of the bed, and leads me out of the bedroom. I have to jog a little in order to keep up with his insistent tug, but I do my best to keep light footed past the couch, even though I swear there is nothing that will ever wake Trenton up after a long shift.

Crow inches the front door open, and we slip through. Then he quietly closes the door behind us. I wait until he is done dragging me all the way to his car — the Supra this time — before speaking. "Is everything okay?" I whisper.

"Mm-hmm," he responds, shutting me in and circling around to his side. He instantly starts her up and drives off. "No need to buckle up, we're going right around the corner."

"Train tracks?"

"Yeah," he breathes, fingers tapping against the steering wheel, teeth worrying at his lip.

A couple minutes later he parks backward, just like he did the first time we came here, gets out, and leans against his rear bumper. I get out and prop up beside him, hands curved over the rounded bumper, mimicking his positioning.

He doesn't say anything, but a couple heartbeats later, I feel the light brush of something along the side of my hand. My eyes dart down in time to catch his pinky lift and curl around mine. I curl my finger against his in response.

A low, droning sound fills the quiet night, and my attention darts back upward toward the tracks before flicking to Crow. He flashes me a smile and nods toward the track.

I return my attention ahead and wait. Not even an eight count later, the train engine is zooming by, carrying with it car after car. For every rail car that passes, Crow taps his pinky against mine, counting.

He inches closer until our shoulders are pressed together, and brings his mouth close to my ear to whisper-yell, "Hear that?"

I nod because of course I can hear it — the vibrating *whom*, *whom* and occasional screech of metal on metal overpowers every other sound.

"This is the only thing that stops the noise in my mind." His pinky still taps, working out a pattern he has memorized. "The thoughts. This drowns them all out. Just listen…"

I close my eyes, and he pulls his face away, but his pinky stays on mine, tapping. After a time, the sound becomes rhythmic, the tapping cathartic. Minutes go by. Several.

Then, the metal on metal slows with a quiet screech.

"Open your eyes," he says.

I do. Several boxcars line the track from tree to tree. Every single one of them is covered in beautiful swashes of bright graffiti. Sometimes the design is just a fancy name, while others are more creative drawings.

The sight is awesome — 100 percent illegal, but beautiful nonetheless. I have a feeling whoever actually owns the cars must not really care about the illegality of it, since one of the images, rusted and flaking, tells me no one has attempted to paint over them and restore the cars to their original color.

Crow turns around, jogs to the front of his car, pops open the hatch, and jogs back. After removing that hospital blanket from the trunk, he grabs my hand and tugs me away from the Supra. Hand in hand, we tromp through the ankle-deep grass toward the train cars.

He lets go of my hand, slides the metal door open, hops inside, and disappears into the darkness. Then his tattooed fingers pops out, proffered. I grab them and together we get me inside. The entire cab is pitch black, the ground cool and gritty under my bare feet. That is until the tips of my toes hit something soft, and Crow pulls me deeper inside until both soles are flat against the blanket. I blink down and wiggle my toes, dark against the white material.

Crow sits and guides me down with him.

"Come here often?" I ask, smoothing my hand over the blanket.

"Yeah. Well… I used to. Every week. Same day, same time. These boxcars stop here like clockwork." He strips off his shirt, lies down, and once again tugs me down with him. I lie my head and forearm on his chest, snuggling my body flush against his side. His arms wrap around me, and he takes in a deep breath. "I stopped coming after that first night I brought you here." His voice catches, and he pauses for a minute before continuing. "The noise in my head stopped that night… without the trains. And not even the trains could make me stop thinking about you."

I prop up on my chin and look up at him. He mimics the motion, tucking his chin and looking down at me. He then lifts the hand I have lying loosely on his chest and brings it to his bicep, encouraging my fingers to trace the tire tread tattoo.

"You know how I have a thing for taking videos and pictures?" His eyes flash with heat, proving he'd received and watched my video, but they cool quickly.

"Yeah?" I whisper, imagining the dips in his muscles are the grooves of tread.

"After Rachal's car was removed from the scene of the wreck, the only thing remaining was the tread marks from where she had hit the brakes and swerved. I stayed there all night, lying on that tire mark, playing chicken in the road, waiting for a car to come and send me to be with them. It never happened. The sun rose. I was still alive. They were still dead. The tread marks were still there. So, I took a picture and got that and the numbers on my fingers tattooed on that same day."

I lay my palm flat against his arm and squeeze.

"The reason I didn't die that night was because Trenton and Hayes had taken up post to the east and west of me and detoured traffic. All night."

My lungs seize, a vice clamps around my heart, and my stomach twists. I rest my head against his chest.

"Not long after they died and after finding out about Rachal and Travis fucking, I learned that Bree was his, not mine. He stole both my girls from me." He pauses, allowing me to piece together what he had told me the other day versus what he is divulging now. "I think I knew it before the wreck, though, you know? She… Bree… looked like him. Like Travis. I think we all suspected it."

Crow continues to be content talking, and I am content listening. His heartbeat is steady, comforting, and I know that he's sharing these details with me because he is truly ready. But then as he opens his mouth for the next part, his pulse increases and arm tightens around me. "Travis and Trenton could pass for twins; there's something like a nine-month spread between them. Even three years later, I still see my daughter when I look at him. I still see Travis, the fucker that took them from me. When I couldn't fucking stop the attraction and connection with you, all it reminded me of was my girl fucking one of my best friends. This time, instead of it being Travis and Rachal, though, I get to watch it play out between you and Trenton.

"Difference is, you were never mine. Not at first. You were his. In my screwed up state of mind, I wanted to fuck you just to do to Trenton what Travis did to me." He slaps at the side of his head a few times and squeezes his eyes shut tight. "Remi, I am so fucked up. Losing them screwed me up bad. I know in my heart that Trenton has nothing to do with this, but my head refuses that fact. That night on Steel Field with you? When Trenton suspected what I had done? You know what he did? He gave me his blessing. I wanted a fight. I wanted the girl. To steal her. Not to receive a blessing. Trenton… is a better man than me."

I finally speak. Because this has to do with me, not just them. "Trenton is not a better man than you. He's just a *different* man than you. What if it would have been him that wrecked instead of me? I find it really hard to believe that either you or Hayes would have spent much time away from the hospital. You probably would have been stealing his food just like you kept stealing mine. Regardless of who he looks like or what happened."

My own experiences as of late beg to be compared against his. I know continuing the topic of Rachal's supposed betrayal is super risky, but he's being open and honest and I want to be, too. "Do you think… maybe… Travis took advantage of her? Like Porter did to me so many times? That, perhaps, what happened between them was nonconsensual?"

A pregnant pause swells between us. Crow's muscles lock. After a while, though, he finally whispers, "No…" The response is delivered somewhat like a mix between an answer and a gasp of disbelief. His head shakes and he says it again with more conviction. "No. I would have known."

"Not necessarily. Jude is the closest person to me and he was clueless — blinded by friendship and a false sense of loyalty. Were you and Travis friends for as long as you and Trenton were by that point?"

Crow continues shaking his head, but his answer opposes the action. "Yeah."

"Right. You already were unaware they had sex; it makes sense for you to also not know the story behind how it happened. Look… Lace said Travis was crazy… and that you and Rachal were pretty tight. The altercation that night at the club could have been something as simple as her turning him down — her trying to take control." Crow doesn't respond, so I continue. "That day I showed up at your place, I told Porter to stop for the first time. He kneed me in the stomach then raped me because of it. Letting them say — and do — things is easier sometimes. Safer. At least in my fucked up head during those moments it always was."

His chest rises and falls several times under my head before words vibrate through. "I hate that you might be right. Gives me something to think about. Having dealt with that type of thing with Hayes and his sister, you would think it would be easier to spot right under my nose, though. Did Lace tell you how I got the nickname Crow?"

"No, and I hope you're not upset with her. She kept the details short and sweet. This is the first time I am hearing the meat."

After sucking in and releasing a large breath, his breathing slows a little, and he continues: "She gave me the nickname. Lace did. Because crows mate for life, and she always admired what Rachal and I had going. I thought about using my real name again after Rachal died, but I prefer Crow. Like my tattoos, it reminds me not to get in too deep. Everytime someone calls me that, it reminds me that nothing lasts forever. Crows mate for life, but life ends."

He has always been reactive anytime I call him Burke, and now I understand why — he interconnects the name Crow with relationships, and a relationship with me was the last thing he wanted. "Yeah, she never mentioned that part." I finally prop up on my chin and meet his eyes again. "She did share a little bit about why you started The Gulf Coasters. That's pretty damn cool."

Crow's shoulder inches up in a modest shrug. "People into the high-speed street culture are going to race regardless. The fact that it's dangerous and illegal makes it that much more seductive." His chrome eyes flick down to mine, and he drags his teeth against his piercing. "Provide them with organized events and a family — a home away from home — and they're less likely to act reckless, both on the street and in life. For a lot of those kids, the club is their only support system. The authorities here turn a blind eye because the benefits of ad hoc races far outweigh the consequences of impulsive ones."

"I really hope you keep it running. For the community." I drop my voice. "For Revelry."

Crow groans, but his heart rate and breathing evens out under my palm. "What if, when we're all group fucking, I lose my shit?"

The question is delivered so seriously, that I almost can refrain from laughing. Almost. A brief chortle barks from my mouth, and I cover anything else that tries to come out with my hand. "Sorry." I chuckle a little before clearing my throat and answering just as seriously, "You have the best traffic team you could possibly ask for. They kept you safe the night you slept on Steel Field Road; they will conduct enforcement if you lose your shit in the bedroom."

I love that his question is in the form of "when" as though he has already seen and accepted what this group dynamic really means. Crow was the wildcard from day one. With him along for the ride, I feel like we can overcome any type of roadblock together.

He leans forward and kisses me on the forehead before resting back again and flicking his tongue along his labret ring. "Next time, I'm coming on that beautiful face of yours."

Another bark of laughter lurches out of me. "Money shot? Sorry. Hard no. How about some double penetration… with Trenton as your wingman?"

His cock twitches against my thigh, and laughter trickles out of me.

The rail car jerks under us, and we both launch upward. Crow quickly bundles up the blanket and his shirt and holds my hand so we can jump out of the boxcar together.

CHAPTER FORTY

C row does a curbside drop-off, telling me that he needs to run down to the gas station and get a few snacks before turning in for the rest of the night, since his access to the refrigerator inside is limited. He makes me promise to lock the front door behind me. Then, he sits in the car and watches me until I'm safely inside. As soon as the door is closed, I spin around, pop up onto my tiptoes, and peer out of the peep hole like a giddy teenager having just been dropped off back home after the prom or something.

The type of teenager that gets dropped off back home, that is — not the one that holes up in a hotel room or at a friend's house to lose their V-card. Crow rolls away, and I twist the deadbolt, but before the lock fully engages, I am yanked backward against a large body. My squeal of surprise is muffled by a meaty palm.

Large body.

Meaty palm.

Neither of which belongs to Trenton or Hayes.

Adrenaline spikes through me, and I writhe and scream, but my captor unlocks and yanks the front door open and guides me outside before the house's inhabitants are any wiser.

As soon as we're on the curb, his hot breath hits my neck. "Remi, Remi, Remi."

"Fuck you!" I screech, but the words are unintelligible behind Porter's tightly pressed palm. He rushes me down the road until the first cutoff, turns the corner, and shoves me into the back of a rental. As scared as I should be, this gives me a giddy sort of satisfaction, and I break into a fitful of manic laughter.

He peels away, unamused, and spins into the next turn, causing me to slam against the back passenger door. Once he straightens the wheel, I yank on the door handle but to no avail — the child lock is engaged. So, I do the next best thing and scale the center console in an attempt to get to the front so I can unlock and get out of the passenger side door. What's another skin graft, right?

The light ahead that leads to the beach turns red, and I scamper into the seat and plop onto my ass. Porter ignores the traffic light and zooms straight through into the port and drifts around turns until we are in the very same warehouse where Jude had shot him.

He throws the sedan into park, and I unlock the passenger door, stumble out, and immediately push into a sprint. Gravely concrete and little bits of rock and random sharp things dig into the soles of my bare feet. I don't get very far before his arm snakes around me and I am slung backward onto my ass. He gathers my hair and yanks me up.

My hands fly to the bundled strands, and my fingers seek purchase on his hands, digging and clawing while he drags me. Given no choice, I stumble along to an unknown destination.

We move like this out of the warehouse and toward the water where a large cargo ferry is docked and shipping crates surround the area, blocking us from the view of any prying eyes. He then tosses me down behind a set of crates like a piece of trash. I stumble backward until my back bumps up against the cool metal.

"I loved you, Remi. Always have."

My eyes spring wide. "You are fucking insane."

"Seems while I was out of commission for a while, you forgot a few important things. Like why I fucking own you, for instance." I conjure a wad of saliva and hock a loogie toward his feet. He jerks backward, and my spit scarcely misses his shoes. "So, I'm here to remind you. Then you can pass the message on to your friends."

He lunges for me, but instead of yanking me up, he flips me over onto my belly and pins me down, the entire weight of his body on all of mine. In this position, I can't even move my arms. The only thing I can do is open and close my fingers outside of the grip he has on my wrists and move my head side to side, which comes in handy when he dips down and his tongue hits my cheek instead of diving into my mouth. That movement, though, painfully scrapes my nose against the concrete.

Porter stills my head and face by pressing his cheek against mine. "See that? Look," he says. "That little romantic date you and Crow went on almost ruined my fucking plans. But we made it… just in the nick of time."

A slither of repulsion slips down my spine at the thought of Porter having been in that field, watching us in the dark — the sounds of the train erasing the sounds of a stranger in the dark.

The crates are separated just enough to expose a crack that reveals the ramp of the ferry. Just like the night at the pier with my father, two men converge near the ramp and begin engaging in hushed conversation.

A memory of that night, of me behind a similar crate hiding, flashes in front of my eyes, and I slam them shut.

No.

No, no, no.

"Mmm…" Porter hums. "That's right. I want you to remember. Remember, Remi."

My chest heaves with each breath, compressed against the concrete. My shoulders burn from being yanked and held backward. But even through the discomfort, when Porter licks the rim of my ear and says, "Breathe. Smell the shrimp? The oil?" I do. I smell it… just like I did that night. With a whimper, I squeeze my eyes even tighter and writhe beneath him. A tear drops down my nose. "Listen," Porter whispers. "Do you hear the lapping of water against the ship? The quiet, deceptive conversation? The buzz of nearby construction?" He drops his voice to nothing more than an exhale of words, "So much like that night. There's even an import deal going on. Ironic, isn't it?"

The click of what sounds a hell of a lot like a safety releasing throws me back into the past. I can no longer feel the pressure of Porter against my back.

"Remi-Sue what are you doing here, Baby Girl?" Dad whispers, throwing his arm around my shoulders and ushering me away. "I told you never to show up at the port."

He darts a glance over his shoulder and quickly back down to me.

"Porter sent me to act as a witness since Jude is out of town and he might be a little late. He even set up entry ahead of time with the on-duty gate guard. I rode right in." Dad spins me to face him, fingers digging into my biceps. Voices — laughter — overpower the lap of water against the big cargo ship in the distance, and his eyes turn wild before darting over his shoulder again.

He reaches into his back waistband. Hands shaking, he opens and closes the chamber of his gun, releases the safety, and gently places it into my palm, wrapping my fingers around the grip.

"Dad… W-what are you doing?"

He spins me around again, shoves me toward the crates, and steps around them to the rendezvous spot. "Men! About time you showed up. Let's do this."

On the verge of a panic attack, I scamper deeper behind the crates, crouch down, and peer between them. Dad and the man grip forearms before both hands drop to their sides. The two engage in a quiet conversation, their susurrations mingling with the salty, foul-smelling breeze.

The man slips a gun out of the inside of his jacket, and pokes it into Dad's belly. I fall onto my ass, entire body shaking. My focus alternates from the gun to the crack between the crates and back again.

Dad never wanted me involved, but that didn't mean he didn't teach me. He taught me about cars and how to shoot. He always said he firmly believed women should always be taught how to shoot. I hated it. I liked the ice cream after being at the shooting range, though. But otherwise, I despised having to go.

I take a deep breath and position myself, propped up on one knee, elbow braced for support, opposite hand cupped under the grip, and I aim the gun at the man aiming a gun at my father.

Fingers damp and sticky, I flare them wide once before twisting them around the grip again and slipping my finger over the curved trigger.

This is fine. This is okay. He does import transactions often. Nothing will go wrong.

Except their conversation turns more passionate, and I have never witnessed any Lance Industries' grey-market business deals take place, so everything about it is obscure.

Dad's throat moves over a hard swallow, he drops his gaze to the ground, and shuffles seemingly nonchalantly to the side, angling his body toward the crates... and in doing so, revealing more of his adversary to me.

His eyes flick up toward the crates for less than a pulse beat. The blood drains from my face. "Dad... No," I whisper. "Dammit. No."

The man's safety clicks. I shoot, and Dad goes down, the sound of the recoil ricocheting off the surrounding crates.

In real-time, my body lurches in sync with the pop of the memory bullet, and I snap back to the present, body shaking and drenched in cooling sweat and revealed memories. Porter's hand presses against my cheek and pushes the damp hair off my face. "I shot him," I wail. "I killed him. He trusted me. Taught me. And my bullet hit him."

"Shhh," Porter hushes, tucking the hair behind my ear.

Again, I am thrust into a memory — one of Porter showing up and everything that ensued.

I knelt, frozen, staring at my father. The man left — stumbled off into the night. Porter had arrived two minutes too late. He jogs up to Dad, looks around, then falls to his haunches and begins running his palms all over Dad, searching for the wound. With blood-covered hands, he pulls his phone out, dials a number, then yells panicked words into the speaker.

I stumble out from behind the crates, gun dangling from limp fingers.

"Oh, my God, Suzi!" Porter shoots to his feet and darts over to me, quickly taking the gun from my hand. He scans my body from head to toe, hands assessing, searching for harm.

"I shot him," I wail. "I killed him. He trusted me. Taught me. And my bullet hit him instead of my mark."

Porter stills, hands frozen on my cheeks as he probes my eyes with his. "W-what?"

Through shaky, sobbing breaths, I explain everything. Porter's hands drop from my face, and he stumbles backward, head shaking side to side.

He spins on his heels, rushes back over to Dad, untucks and lifts his shirt, and engages in the horrific act of fingering the wound. But my feet are frozen; I can't move.

Porter finishes, jogs back up to me, grabs my wrist with one hand, and places something hot and wet into the palm, curling my fingers over the item. "You have to get outta here, Suzi. Go. Ride wide open. Don't look back. He... he's still alive, and the ambulance will be here any minute. But you can't be here when they get here." He grabs my jaw and shakes my face. "Look at me! Do you hear me? Get out of here. Get rid of your bullet. Go home. I'll come for you as soon as I can."

I blink away my daze, adrenaline spiking inside me.

The ambulance is coming.
They will save him.

That night, I rode wide open for the very first time. Sped through lights, leaned tight into turns. I was invincible...

...because as far as I was concerned, my life was over anyway.

I went home, hid the bullet, and curled into a ball in the corner of my room, much like I am balled against the concrete now. Hours ticked by. My room flooded with tears. My father's blood dripped off my jaw — the blood from where Porter had grabbed my face, souping with my salty emotions.

Space and time seemed ever-looping, going on forever and ever, until my door creaked open and Porter scooped me off the floor and placed me in the tub, bath drawn. I remained mute while he bathed me, caught my tears, and shushed me — promising me a new world of safely kept secrets. I had lost my dad; I couldn't lose my brother, too.

"Your secret is safe with me, Remi. You know that," Porter swore. That was the first time he ever used my first name. We both knew our world shifted that night. That night, we fucked out our fears, hard and raw.

The weeks following were wound tight, twisted with grief and the stress of tying loose ends. I took my new-found aggression out on Porter, and he let me — ever the punching bag. But with that favor came more promises and more secrets. A mutual partnership. I used him. He used me. The sheets whispered words of betrayal while wrapped around our writhing limbs.

THE PRESSURE RELEASES FROM MY BODY. Frozen with debilitating despondency, all I can do is tuck my knees toward my chest and cover my face with my hands, both to provide protection between my skin and the concrete, but also to catch the tears.

Knowing Porter is here with me now, insisting I relive this memory, to remember just how much I owe him, and realizing what comes next — the fucking — a switch flips in my body. My tears dry, I uncurl from my ball, and propel to a stand. I have suffered enough at his hand. This part of the trip down memory lane will absolutely not happen. I refuse.

But when I fully stand, chest heaving, eyes blinking for clarity, Porter is nowhere to be found. Instead, a shimmer of yellow flickers at my feet, drawing my attention downward. A golden ticket.

I pluck the small paper off the ground and hold it up to the light. All the numbers line up with my plans. Lace came through. She printed some hastily designed tickets I emailed her, and made sure Porter received one. A bleeding ink dot encourages me to flip the ticket over. "See you there. Don't forget whose side you belong on," I read under my breath.

I take a shaky breath, steel my shoulders, walk to the water, and toss the ticket into the sea.

"See you there, Fucker," I agree aloud.

Let the race begin.

I IGNORE THE BLARE OF A HORN as I walk away from the port and across the main intersection, cheeks and nose burned from the harsh concrete, bare knees covered in grit, hair plastered with sweat, face streaked with dirt and dried tears, Trenton's baggy shirt whipping up in the wind and displaying my underwear to the late-night world.

Worried somcone will actually stop and offer help, I pick up my pace, mind whirling. Just before I turn the corner onto Trenton and Hayes's block, I skid to a halt.

The event is in countdown mode. I have busted my ass these past few days weaving the perfect night. A night meant to fix everything. A night where, for once, I get to perform a selfless act. As selfless as selfless acts go, that is. Considering no act is truly selfish.

My eyes dart to my filthy bare feet.

If the guys find out what happened tonight, the Golden Ticket event will never happen. They won't let me out of their sight. Not even at night during sleeping hours. I absolutely cannot let them see me like this.

The journey back suddenly becomes an obstacle course — the front door my biggest challenge, assuming they didn't wake up when Porter was dragging me out of there, and Crow didn't double check the locks and sneak in to make sure I made it into the bed.

As I approach the house, all the lights are still off. Crow's Supra is in the driveway. I run my hand over the hood in passing and note that it is cool. He did as promised and had been back for a while.

I wrap my fingers around the front door handle, turn, and pull, but the door stays shut. My eyes dart up and find the outer deadbolt near the top. Crow had locked us all back inside, which undoubtedly meant he would notice it being unlocked in the morning. One of the reasons, aside from keeping me from getting out without them knowing, was to also know if someone had attempted entering from the outside.

But I have no choice. I pop the lock, inch the door open, and slip inside.

Trenton is snoring quietly on the couch just as he had been when I left with Crow. A tremendous amount of relief washes over me as I click the interior deadbolt shut, tiptoe past him, and stow away into the bathroom.

Once that door is shut and locked, my body drains of all its adrenaline and a severe shakiness overcomes me from head to toe.

I struggle to get my shirt and underwear off and step into the shower without falling over. And once in there, I don't even bother to wait for the water to warm before flipping on the shower head. Cold water hits my skin, returning some much-needed, real-life, present-day sensation to my body. The water muddies and pools at my feet, and I slosh it down the drain with a couple of swipes of my soles against the basin.

As soon as I am clean, I get out, wrap myself in a towel, shove my dirty clothes into my backpack under the sink, and take out replacement pajamas and my meager collection of makeup.

Dried and dressed, I finally meet my reflection in the mirror while flipping open the concealer. The concrete stamped a smooth scrape on my nose… and cheek. Talk about irony. With a huff of morbid laughter, I dab the spots and blend. I hope my makeup is up for the challenge, because for three days I will need to keep these final secrets from them.

Three, long days.

CHAPTER FORTY-ONE

Like clockwork every morning since my sleepovers started, Crow storms through the front door hollering, "Grub!" Trenton, Hayes, and I are already at the table, coffees — and a water for Trenton — in hand. Crow deposits the food between us all, moves to the kitchen, removes his Cawfee cup from the cupboard, fills it with the remaining coffee, takes his seat across from me as usual, and scoots in.

Trenton, Hayes, and I fight the good fight for our food in the middle. As always, though, they are faster than me. I simply pluck up the remaining bag and open it to see what sort of surprise I get this morning.

The sandwich container seems to weigh five pounds. I sneak a peek at Trenton and Hayes's packages, but they both stick to the rules and keep their containers covered. This is a new game between us as of late: Crow brings three different sandwich types and guffaws at the person who gets the "specialty" item. Generally something nasty, or just something one of the participants dislikes in general.

One was a mushroom and onion smothered sausage burrito. Trenton got it and gagged every time he had to eat one of the mushrooms. Crow got lucky that day, because both Hayes and I quite like mushrooms.

"On three," Trenton slams his fist down onto the table.

Crow points his finger at me, and I say, "One." His pointing arches to Hayes who says, "Two." Then comes Trenton's turn. Trenton concurrently launches out of his seat, swaps his with Hayes, and yells, "Three!"

Hayes scrambles to take his original box back, but Trenton pops his open. I hurry and follow suit. Hayes falls into his seat grumbling and pops his open, too.

Since I'll eat just about anything, the true entertainment is watching their reactions, so I wait to peek at mine. Hayes's eyebrow raises, and he gives Trenton a self-satisfied smirk, lifting up a super thick and juicy burger. Trenton dons a similar smug look, though, as he double fists an omelet — who needs a fork? Their attentions turn to me, and I grimace, now quite concerned.

But then Trenton gasps, drops his omelet, and tries to make a swap toward my meal instead. Crow's hand darts out so fast that Trenton gets clotheslined and bounces back into his chair. I peer down at my sandwich.

"Aww, see, that's playing dirty right there," Hayes states with a mouthful of food, pointing his finger at my box.

I slip my finger under the monstrosity and lift it slightly so I can better understand the sandwich layers… Two gooey, glazed donuts with a piece of deep-fried, boneless chicken in the center. My opposite hand immediately darts to my stomach.

"So, instead of someone getting the short stick today, someone got a prize," Trenton assesses. He then nudges Crow in the side with his elbow. "I expected rain and grey clouds again. Is that a ray of sunshine I see peeking through?"

Crow's knee bumps mine under the table. "Guess the cot is doing wonders for my mood," he mutters, very non-sunshiney, cupping his hand over his jaw and narrowing his eyes on me.

There's absolutely no way this monstrosity is fitting in my mouth, so instead of attempting to take it all at once, I swipe a finger along the gooey top and pop it into my mouth, giving it a little twist to make sure no stickiness remains before doing it again.

Crow's foot parallels mine, his jeans brushing against my calf. A swash of sadness splashes over me when his touch first reminds me of Porter's visit a couple nights ago and the importance of making sure these guys are none the wiser. But then I remember what came prior to that — the impromptu date with Crow.

Focus, Remi.

I brush my knee inward in response, he scoots further down in his chair.

That familiar electric zing connects us, and my other knee closes in, only to be stopped by his between them.

His chrome eyes spark, and the corner of his mouth quirks behind his tattooed fingers. He then drops his hand and rests it loosely on the table. "Anyone else notice how hungry our girl is?"

Huh, what?

Hayes, Trenton, and I freeze, three mouths full. Their eyes move from Crow to me and back again. I tear off a piece of the top glazed donut and pop it into my mouth with the food already in there. "Good thing I have something so big to put in my mouth," I state quite classily around stuffed cheeks before picking up my coffee and washing down the sweet bite with the bitter liquid. Mmm, the perfect combination.

I take advantage of Crow's very helpful change of topic and break right into something so much more important than all their penises inside all my orifices. "I have been in here for going on four days without so much as an open window of fresh air. No one has heard from Jude since the message" — which is a problem I intend on addressing last minute, setting bait while crossing my fingers — "news is quiet, and Porter is a ghost."

The lie tastes terrible on my tongue. I tear off a piece of salty chicken and a chunk of donut and pop the combination onto my tongue hesitantly. The sweet and salty is phenomenal, though, and in a matter of seconds I'm overcome with focusing on said bite, words temporarily forgotten. "Mmm, damn," I mumble around the delicious mix. "This is really, really good."

A smirk pulls on Crow's face. Trenton and Hayes roll their eyes. Lie swallowed with a bit of coffee to push everything down, I continue. "I'm dying to get out of here. I really want to see the amusement park at night."

"There's nothing to see there at night," Hayes answers. "No lights."

"Even better." I grin, pick up my donut sandwich, and take an actual, open-mouth bite now that a good chunk of it is missing.

My gaze flutters from Crow to Trenton and back to Crow again. Both boys adjust in their seats. Hayes leans back and flicks glares at them warily, sensing foul play.

After swallowing, I explain further: "When we were there a few days ago, I spotted a section of fencing behind the coaster that could be spread wide enough for your cars to get through. We can park in the courtyard and screw around a bit." I finish off the remainder of my coffee, place it on the table, and bring my plea home: "Plus, it's out of sight, which makes it safer. We just need to get there is all."

Hayes crosses his arms over his chest and narrows a glare at me. "You have really thought this through…"

"Yep. Haven't been able to get it off my mind. Been dreaming about it, too. Guess that's what cabin fever does." I give a nervous chuckle, feeling the sudden pressure of his curiosity. "Take me out," I whine. "I promise to make it worth your while." I waggle my brows, lean forward, pressing my breasts against the edge of the table to plump them up a little. My focus trains on Crow. Because ever since opening up the other night, he has officially become the weakest link.

He leans forward, matching me tit for tat. Well… minus the distracting tits part. His brooding, dark, pierced presence isn't any less distracting, though. "Fine…" His tongue swipes along his piercing, and I nearly gush on the spot. "But I get my money shot… and Trenton has to watch."

Hayes chokes on a bite of his burger.

I don't catch Trenton's expression, though, because I'm too distracted by Crow's thumb as it swipes along the corner of my mouth, moves to his, and he sucks off some glaze I'd been collecting.

CHAPTER FORTY-TWO

H ayes knocks on the bathroom door for the third time. "Are you sure you're okay?" he asks.

"Yeah. Promise." For the past thirty minutes, I stared at myself in the mirror, unable to walk out of the bathroom. Because as soon as I do, the timer starts; tonight, I will be arrested for the murder of my father. But, I refuse to go down alone — Porter is coming with me. "Just dealing with some road jitters. I… I haven't ridden much since my wreck." The lies come easier and easier with every passing second.

Trenton's voice comes next. "We got you, Pet. Come on out, okay?"

"Okay, okay. Yeah. Just… give me five more minutes?"

I flip around, lean against the counter, and open the messages on my phone with shaky fingers.

:Me: Jude… I know you're not risking communication with me, but it's an emergency. Please, please respond. I need you. Porter came back, stole me out of their house, and took me to the pier. I'm meeting him at the old amusement park. I'm ending this. Tonight. But listen… don't tell the guys, okay? We're on our way now. Just… get there.

:Me: x

That last part is the biggest risk of all but added for good measure. The X was always our code with Dad if we needed help. But, if Jude calls or texts one of the guys, freaking out, they'll reroute, and we will never get to the park. That, or they'll go by themselves and leave me here.

:Me: Hey, Lace. Everything ready?

:Lace: Yeah, girl. Everything is set. We just log in to this app and the QR code does the rest, right?

:Me: You got it. Easy. See you soon.

One more person to bait… Then, the meet can begin.

:Me: You want me? Fine. Devil's Dome at midnight.

After placing my phone into my clutch and stepping out of the bathroom, Trenton's arm immediately curls around my shoulders, and he jostles me against him. "Hey… we'll hang and get some fresh air, okay? When you're ready to come back, we'll come back. You call the shots."

I would love to come back. For life to become normal. But that's not in the cards for me — hasn't been since that night at the port in California. The time has come for Jude to get closure, for Revelry and The Gulf Coasters to shine, and for Porter and me to get our comeuppance. Time for all the puzzle pieces to fit snugly together. After tonight, no more lies. No more secrets.

The entire ride over, my mind spins like a tilt-a-whirl going over everything again and again and again. By the time we are close, I have a headache from hell — ironic seeing as I staged everything to go down in the devil's belly.

I take the lead on my bike. Even a quarter mile away, the traffic is backed up — vehicles of all sorts coming from every direction, heading to the meet of the year. Light from tall, portable, diesel towers can be spotted webbing over the old, decaying rides even from this distance.

During a moment when the traffic is congested enough to stop completely, I anticipate one of the guys getting out of their vehicle to chastise me, but none of them do. Instead, they make me sweat it out, no doubt waiting until we park to spew the lecture.

Opposite of what I had suggested about entering at that spot behind the coaster, I swing around to the main lot. The four of us roll through a parting crowd up to the very front and park in a line paralleling the gates — gates that have been converted into "Golden Ticket" booths. Lace and her girls designed some sparkly posters, effectively turning the decrepit signs into fun, faux ticket stands.

The crash of waves on the beachside across the street is overpowered by the rev of engines, sound system competitions, and laughter. Setting aside what will happen later and appreciating the present scene is easy to do when the atmosphere is springing with joviality like this.

Behind the cloudy, cracked, and busted booth windows are Lace's co-workers — all there to honor Rachal and Bree, to support Crow, and make sure the racing community thrives.

The four of us tighten inward, but no one talks; we all stare up at the booths and watch as people file in, Golden Tickets in hand. With a soft smile on my face, I turn to the guys. Their expressions are hard, though, immediately tugging me back down from my fluffy cloud of pride and grounding me.

Reminding myself they are unaware of any possible danger lurking, I feed on that mentality, grab Crow's hand, and pull him to the end of the closest line. For now, we get to have fun. For now, together, we are safe amid numbers.

Until midnight.

The four of us all file in. Hayes is the first to speak: "How did you pull all this off?"

I take in a deep breath. "A lot of phone calls… a lot of poking around on the forum…" My focus drops to the concrete, unable to look him straight in the eye while he likely pieces together that I learned about him banning DoubleD and had to borrow his profile. "Lace helped tie everything together," I share, lifting my attention to Crow.

Crow drags a hand down his face. Trenton stuffs his hands in his pockets and finds something incredibly interesting to look at on the gravely asphalt, the imprint of his fingers twisting around in his pocket.

We step forward a few paces in line. A gust of wind from the gulf stirs up my hair and carries with it a blended scent of sweet and spicy smoke. On one side of the gates, a restored vintage truck, a lot like the one in the junkyard, has a handbuilt grill setup in the bed — two metal barrels welded together into a T-shape with handles made out of smoothed, thick tree branches. Barbeque smoke swirls from the cylinder chimney. On our opposite side, a group of people are circled around a colorful, bubbling hookah, blowing out Os from their mouths.

"I knew you were talking to her," Crow groans.

"Sorry?" I grimace, attention returning to the group. "You know… I'm a little confused about that. When you assumed I was talking to her the other day, I had only just started. What made you think I was communicating with her all along?" The first time he

300

said this was right after the very first time I asked her for help.

"You got the sudden, unacceptable, urge to stunt. I figured she told you about Kal's crew and the rally next week, and you decided to practice."

Ahh, I remember her talking about a rally… and Foster mentioning someone named Kal. "Oh… nope. Completely coincidental. Stunting isn't really my thing. Leaning into a tight turn and little hops hardly count. Rallys aren't really my thing, either. Too many cruisers for my taste."

The line shifts again, and we step forward to close the gap. My phone vibrates against my ass, causing me to nearly jump out of my skin. I pull it out of my pocket.

Jude.

But instead of texting, he is calling. Damn, bro. Follow instructions.

I drop the call and open my messages.

:Me: Devil's Dome at midnight, Jude.

"Speak of the devil," I state, waving my phone in the air so they don't suspect anyone other than Lace messaging me, considering everyone I talk to as of late is standing with me right now. "She's just checking to make sure we're in line."

:Jude: What the actual fuck, Remi? Answer your damn phone. I'm coming, but I need to know you're okay before that. I need to hear you.

:Me: I'm okay. I promise. The guys are with me.

I rush to open my photo app and hold it above us. "Quick, group selfie time!" We all bundle together. I make a sexy duck face at Crow, and he gives me a look of disgust but otherwise bends down to my level and flips up his middle finger at the camera. Trenton crosses his arms over his chest and lifts his chin. Hayes gives the phone a half-smile, hands shoved in his pockets.

As soon as the flash goes off and I return my focus to the screen, Trenton continues the topic we were discussing, "Keep hanging out with her, and you might change your mind. About the rally, that is. Not the cruisers. Hell for Leather members all have superbikes."

My eyebrow rises. "A superbike club? They one-percenters?" I ask, sending the selfie to Jude. My gaze lingers on the image, heart twisting. Before blacking out the screen and slipping my phone back into my pocket, I brush my thumb over the picture reverently.

"Not according to the one-percenters." Crow rolls his eyes.

"Right." I laugh. "I would imagine not."

"But, yeah, you could say that. They're not from here, though. They only come twice a year for the rally… and for Lace."

A screech of tires yanks our attention behind us. Between two of the parking lot rows, an unofficial dig was staged. Two vehicles are duking it out — a Vette and some sort of import too customized to distinguish the make and model at this distance. The Vette wins by a longshot.

We all turn around to face the line again only to discover a large gap has been made, and the entry counter is waiting for us.

Lace beams and gives me a wink as soon as we are in her sightline.

"Wink at her like that again, and we're gonna have problems, Lace." Crow narrows a glare at her, leaning his elbows on the counter. "Remi is taken."

Oh… wow. My lips glue together into a tight line, eyes crinkling in the corners. Trenton tucks his chin and side-eyes Crow. Hayes's eyebrows shoot sky high.

"Treat her right, and maybe she won't hafta come crawling to me," Lace tosses back with a grin, sliding her cell phone across the counter under the small, arched opening to between his elbows.

The comment has me committing to a friendship with her on the spot, but my heart climbs up my throat and lodges there, right along with the air I had just inhaled, as Crow studies the screen and his hands drop and clench at his sides. Lace shoots me a look of uncertainty, and I give her a tight nod. "Just scan the QR with your phone and follow the instructions," she states.

Crow digs out his phone, and I slowly release my held breath.

Trenton and Hayes follow suit.

I scan the code last.

We all take turns stepping through the rusty turnstiles. After waving goodbye and giving Lace a thankful smile, like most everyone else who enters after scanning the code, I find a clear spot to step aside so we can follow the steps on the screen.

The app goes through the basics first: name, crew title, attendee status — racer or spectator — email, secure payment method. As soon as we each type in Revelry for the crew title, the payment button shades out, having been set to turn off for their crew. They might be willing to answer a few questions, but I highly doubted they would put any financial details into a Midnight Runners' application.

Of all the things I had to do to prepare for tonight, making sure the app Porter made worked without a hitch was definitely the most challenging. Especially the bit about where the funds would ultimately be funneled through and pool. I put a helluva lot of my schooling to practice hacking into what Porter so tightly designed.

I lift on my tiptoes and take turns looking over each guy's shoulder to see who picks what for the attendee status, paying extra close attention to Crow's progress. Trenton selects racer. Hayes chooses spectator. Crow hovers his finger over the spectator button, but I dart my hand under his and press the racer button before he can stop me. Then, I hide behind a laughing Trenton. "Maybe they'll pit us against each other," he states in response to a grumble from Crow. "Now that would be something. I would lose, but getting Crow wound up would be worth it."

Crow huffs and starts to press the back button, but I dart out from behind Trenton and pop up in the circle of Crow's arms, blocking him from viewing his phone.

"Trust me," I respond, grinning. "Let's take this thing to the next step, hm? There might be some *money* in it for you. Give it a *shot*." Damn, I am really desperate for this to all play out as needed, but a lot rides on interactions, too.

Crow tightens his arms around me, and his eyes drop to my mouth, tongue snaking out to flick his lip ring. "You better not be playing with me right now." He shifts his hips and the hint of a growing erection rubs against me. Before it grows too substantially, his hold breaks, and he brings his phone back into his sightline.

I drop my focus to my own screen and attempt to take care of my part while darting nervous glances at him over and over again. Instead of adding my personal information, I pretend to be Jude and quickly zoom through the next steps. As a spectator, Hayes is done for now, which means I should be done, too. But acting as Jude and adding him as a racer means I am required to fill out all the details of his vehicle, too.

While Trenton and Crow go through the various prompts — car make and model and year, engine, mods, etc. — so do I. After a few minutes, a thank you screen pops up. I shoot Jude a quick text letting him know that I signed him in on the app and pocket my phone, glad that part is behind us and we can finally mosey around. Crow and Trenton finish soon after.

So far, everything looks awesome… except for the skeptical and dubious expressions on their faces. While the crowds continue to file in, I turn to them, straighten my shoulders, and address the elephant in the room — er, amusement park. "I have never given you guys a good reason to trust me, especially where meddling in car stuff is concerned, and I know this ultimately means I have kept you in the dark about something again. But… think of it as more a surprise than a betrayal this time? I swear that everything planned for tonight is well-meaning."

Crow speaks on behalf of their disbanded crew. With a firm nod, he says, "Yeah. Okay."

"Ready to have some fun?" I ask with a girly squeal. The setup is pretty damn exciting… and it's time to live like today is my last. Because it very well might be.

CHAPTER FORTY-THREE

Soon after our adventure begins, Crow screeches to a halt to take out his phone and snap a picture of the unique photo opp two separate crew managers setup for attendees. A massive, lifted truck, jacked up to the point that the suspension lift must be at least five feet off the ground, is parked at the center of the innermost courtyard. But what makes the scene even more grand is that a vehicle is parked beneath — a lowrider. The slammed truck sits flush against the ground, body and tires nearly seamless.

Hanging from the tow hitch of the hefty domestic truck, is a large set of metal balls, designed to mimic the look of giant ballsacks. Super classy. The humorous pairing of the two vehicles continues; across the topmost part of the small import's windshield is a decal that reads "Under Compensating."

Fucking truck guys.

The camaraderie between the two crew managers makes me feel all bubbly inside, though. Hopeful. Usually, the "bro truckers" and "hellaflush" crews are in their own separate cliques. Taking it to another level, they are generally of different cultures and races, too — stereotypically speaking.

Crow steps up to the managers, gives them each one of those manly embraces, and thanks them for participating. Their respect for him and the program is evident and makes my heart ache in the best way. He was right to create this community club; this single display alone speaks volumes about the efficacy.

Hayes and Trenton are just as distracted by the scene as Crow. Knowing there is still so much more to see and fun to be had, I wedge between the two and nudge against each of them with my shoulders. Hayes never did drop the dubious expression, but a hesitant mix of awe and excitement spark in his gaze, contradicting the cynical flattening of his brows. I slot my fingers between theirs and squeeze. They both squeeze back.

"I was a little limited with whom I could contact and what I could get away with, but I did toss out a few suggestions. Most of this is as much of a surprise to me as it is to you." One such suggestion, however, was for sure supposed to happen. Eager to show the guys, I tug them ahead, whistling at Crow in passing. They stumble forward at my incessant guidance. Crow gives the managers one more handshake each and jogs to catch up with us, pushing through the crowd that steadily grows around the two trucks.

Just beyond, we step into a bona fide car show, the backdrop a large, swinging pirate ship attraction. I realized after a bit more research that having the actual meet inside the park was a bit unrealistic, but we could at least bring a little show inside. Not just any car show, though.

Trenton lurches to a stop, eyes roaming over all the vehicles lined up with their hoods open and engines rumbling. He squeezes my hand so hard, I fear something will break. Then, he bends down and crashes his mouth against mine. I laugh into the kiss. Trenton lets go, jogs ahead, and starts perusing the line. Crow replaces him at my side, groans, and mutters, "There is the real betrayal."

My cheeks ache from smiling so hard. Crow, Hayes, and I stand side by side, three import owners amid a crowd of gearheads fawning over a dozen or more domestics. Despite the facade of his loyalty, Crow practically vibrates with need to walk over there. After all, the bias of a true enthusiast is often slim.

I grin up at him. When his desperate eyes meet mine, I slap him on the ass and shoo him away. He mumbles, "Well, if you insist." But with as fast as he makes his way over there, one might wonder if a quarter is wedged between his ass cheeks.

Hayes stays beside me, still a bit despondent in spite of the excitement swarming around us. I have not been remiss to notice that he hasn't stopped thinking, investigating, assessing since we arrived. Not that I blame him. Hayes handles all the finances for The Gulf Coasters, after all. With a big to-do such as this, he is likely trying to figure out how an event like this works since it's very clearly functioning the way the Midnight Runners' meet went a while back but is being promoted as The Gulf Coasters and Revelry.

His focus drifts sideways toward a Midnight Runners decal on the domestic closest to us. I break the uncomfortable ice: "Confused and curious?"

He pushes up his glasses with a knuckle.

I need someone on my side. I got them here, and while coming clean to Hayes right now will certainly put a damper on this "fun" part of the evening, I still want their backing — need their support. I step as close as possible to him, look up into his eyes, and swallow hard. "The catch?" I ask. He nods. I blow a raspberry between my lips and steady myself as my nervous system begins to give out a little. "There's no easy way to say this…"

I peek over my shoulder, seeking out Trenton and Crow in the crowd before turning my attention back to Hayes. Then, I explain almost everything: About Crow and I sneaking out the other night and what happened after with Porter—about how Porter had held a certain secret over me as blackmail and said he would be here at this meet; How I truly pulled everything off for tonight and about texting Jude to let him know; That in addition to wanting nothing more than to see Revelry and The Gulf Coasters thrive, I had some unfinished business to take care of. How Porter needed to be dealt with.

"And why didn't you tell us any of this?" is his quiet, rushed response, eyes flicking toward Trenton and Crow before returning to mine.

"Because I am terrified," I admit. A chill skitters over my arms. "Porter is right; what he's holding over me is that bad. But, I refuse to let him keep that traction — to drag Revelry and Jude under, too." I take out my phone and show Hayes the last two messages. The one to Jude, and the one to Porter. His eyes widen and lift to mine before dropping down again to check the time. We still have a couple hours. "I am ready, Hayes — ready to be done living in fear."

His shoulders droop. My high-current nervous system appreciates that he doesn't appear shocked... nor does he act betrayed. Hayes knew. Maybe not everything, but he knew there was more to the agenda tonight as soon as we rolled up. His hand comes to the back of his neck and he rubs it. "At what cost, Remi?"

Twenty-five to life in prison?

Damn, those words are scary.

Running from the question, and the answer, I take a couple steps away from him. He grabs my hand and stops me from turning my back on the conversation. "At what cost?"

My hand trembles inside his, and he clenches his fingers, squeezing me tight, gifting me his courage. "I really have no idea what the outcome will be exactly.

I have my speculations, my hopes, but… please… just let me keep them to myself for now?"

He blinks a couple times, presses his lips into a firm line, and nods. Again, his focus darts over my shoulder. When it returns there's an urgency in their dark-blue depths. "Crow and Trenton?" His eyebrows curve inward, and his hand squeezes mine ever harder, this time in desperation.

"No." I shake my head adamantly. "You all will play a role — I hope — but I would never put any of you in a situation beyond your capabilities." I chose those words carefully and practiced them every night before going to sleep. Is the situation unsafe? Yes. Is the plan a risk? Yes. But this plot is just as much about trust and aptitudes as it is hope and redemption. "Look, I know I fucked up and made some terrible decisions. But I could really use a few people in the stands."

Hayes's eyebrows flatten. "Did your plan take into consideration that I have every intention of killing Porter the next time I see him? I made a promise to myself, Remi — to my mother. Never again. Jude or me… one of us will shoot, one will bury."

The blood drains all the way to my toes and seeps into the old, unused ground. Trenton and Crow appear at that very moment. I clench my fingers against Hayes for support, blink repeatedly, clear my throat, and plaster on my most convincing grin.

CHAPTER FORTY-FOUR

After that ominous comment from Hayes, I expect the next couple of hours to drag — for him to continue on in his locked-down state. But my honesty had the opposite effect on him; he relaxes and allows himself to enjoy the entertainment.

Instead of the remaining, decaying rides acting as the main attractions, each ride entrance has a different type of activity going. In front of the Devil Dome, a live band is playing. Just outside of the old Haunted House, a sound-system vendor is set up, speakers running on generators and competing with the nearby band.

At the chainlink entrance I had mentioned to the guys, vehicles are being let in to run on a mobile dynamometer that's setup under the largest climax of the coaster's track so they can test just how impressive what they're running is — and so spectators can get a hopeful tease to help sway their bids once the races start later.

With every minute that goes by, my anxiousness cranks a notch. With every new voice I hear in passing, I find myself stealing glances over my shoulder. Instead of being on my own in my fear, though, Hayes backs me. He walks nearer to me and pays closer attention to everyone around us.

All that fear and anxiety fades to the background when we arrive at the Ferris Wheel, and I sneak the guys under the yellow caution tape meant to keep people away from the actual ride. I pull out all the dramatic stops, pressing my back against beams, slinging my head side to side, and acting as the lead of a super stealthy mission.

The guys... all follow me... walking normal. I get a smile out of Trenton, though. When we're on the opposite side of the base, hidden from any prying eyes and shining lights, I gear up for my final fun surprise of the evening. Hopping over the rusted-shut door of the most accessible capsule, I let my actions dictate for the guys to follow.

Once we're all inside, instead of sitting down on the bench, I climb over the back of the seat, balance on one of the rim bars supporting it, and peer at them over my shoulder. "I know Revelry is all about that high-speed life, but how do you guys handle heights?" I ask with a beaming grin, gripping the nearest spoke with one hand and holding my other out for whoever of the guys is willing to accept the assistance.

Hayes cups his hand with mine, and I pull him up. Not that he needed the help, but the symbolism mattered. Hayes turns around and holds his hand out, and Crow swats it away, climbing up on his own and bypassing both Hayes and me, scaling the bars toward the next capsule.

Trenton looks like he has seen a damn ghost. "Fuck that," he stammers.

"That was the idea," I chuckle.

"Th—wait, what? What idea?"

I flash him a grin, wink, and leave the rest to his imagination. Hayes and I turn around, and he helps me up the bars, ever the protector. When the three of us are in the second capsule, we all look over the seat back down at Trenton who is still standing there gaping.

"Come on," I holler at him. "You climbed out my window, you can do—"

"When did he climb out of your damn window?" Crow chastises, affronted.

"When everything went to shit after the meets," I respond, knowing well enough that the answer still doesn't make any sense. Maybe one day when we're chatting on the phone with jail glass between us, he can ask again. I'll have more time to explain.

Crow doesn't dig deeper, though. He stares down at Trenton, shoulders curving. Then, he shocks both Hayes and me by hopping back over the seat like a practiced parkour enthusiast and scaling down until he hits the first bar.

He extends a hand. Their eyes lock. And in a heartbeat, this becomes so much more than Crow helping Trenton overcome a fear.

Trenton launches his hand out, and the two friends grip forearms. My eyes… damn them… All the sparkling lights from the amusement park spanning below us blur and flare. Hayes wraps his arm around my shoulders and squeezes. "Thank you," he whispers.

"Heh. Anytime." I sniffle.

I set out to reassemble a disbanded crew — a family — and prevailed. Watching Crow lead Trenton up the beams, and Trenton trust him enough to keep his eyes closed the entire time, is both humorous and beautiful. A shaky-legged Trenton joins us in the second car, immediately followed by Crow.

But from here, we still aren't quite high enough. "One more?" I ask, more as a directive than a question.

Trenton blanches.

Crow punches him in the shoulder. "Hell yeah!"

Hayes laughs.

Trenton topples over into the seat clutching at his chest. Partially to be goofy, partially because he probably thinks his heart might very well explode.

"Just one more. Promise."

Trenton nods and stands. "One more. Then never again."

I want to remind him that we'll have to go back down, but figure we can cross that bridge when we get there. "Yep, one more," I reaffirm.

He takes a deep breath and actually leads the way, eager to get it over with, no doubt. Within just a couple more minutes we're in the next capsule, all of us agreeing this is high enough — Trenton especially.

I curve my hands over the edge facing the park and peer out at everything. The hundreds of people and cars. The lights. The movement. The happiness and excitement. "Wow," I breathe out, reaching my hand back and swiping at Trenton. He accepts this time, and I gently pull him forward until we're side by side. He's a little wobbly but studies the view below nonetheless.

Hayes and Crow bracket us, Crow on my other side and Hayes next to Trenton. "Have you ever seen your club from this vantage point?" I ask — not to truly get an answer, because I'm fairly certain they've never climbed a Ferris Wheel during a car meet. "The scale." I look at Crow and give him a soft smile. "The impact." I drop my voice low, worried my next comment might be crossing a line, but willing to take the chance nonetheless: "Pretty amazing what Rachal and Bree see from their perspective, hm?"

His jaw moves over clenched teeth, and the whites of his eyes redden under the moonlight. "What you guys do for this community is amazing. Getting all these people here was the easiest part of my deceptive plan." I turn on the dramatics again, exaggerating the word *deceptive*, hoping humor will lighten the emotional moment. It works. Crow huffs out a jittery chuckle. "That respect is hard to earn. No outside club or crew would ever be able to compete against this sort of loyalty."

I let go of Trenton's hand and step back, leaving Revelry to look down on all their supporters without me muddying the moment. Capsule swaying a little with my movement, I sit in the corner of the opposite side and look over The Strip and to the endless gulf beyond. The moon is full and bright. Not a cloud in the sky. The light towers sprinkled throughout the event still reach at this height, too. Both combined gives us enough visibility to not kill ourselves as we move about.

The guys skip conversation and stay looking over the park for only a short time before turning around and joining me in the seats. Hayes sits beside me, leaving Crow and Trenton to pair up on the bench across from us. The three men share a look, silently communicating. Even Crow joins in this time, somehow decoding the wordless conversation.

Hayes leans in close and whispers in my ear low enough that Trenton and Crow shouldn't be able to hear. "All this effort" — he opens his arm wide — "tells me you think that this is it. That when whatever happens with Jude and Porter is said and done, our time together is over. Do I have that right?"

"Yeah," I whisper. But when I continue, I speak loud enough for Crow and Trenton to hear my answer, too: "I just wanted to make sure you all know how much you impact me personally — how much I truly have come to care. How thankful I am for all your support despite the odds being against us from hour one."

I lifted my gaze to the men across from me. Crow watches Hayes and I interact, hand covering his jaw. Trenton is leaned forward, elbows propped on his knees. Hayes adds to the conversation, mouth even closer to my ear, breath fanning against my skin: "Guess we better make this last hour count then."

"Really?" I gasp, attention darting to his so fast we nearly bump noses. I had hoped something special between us in this Ferris Wheel capsule is where things would lead, but after telling Hayes about the caveat, I figured that was the real end — the rest just a temporary epilogue.

He leans back, arm stretched out behind me, and asks the group, "Did any of you bring protection up here?"

Thank goodness for the night, because otherwise they would see the red flush that covers me from cheeks to chest. With as bright as the moon is, they might be able to see it anyway. I grimace, and a nervous chuckle bubbles out of me.

Trenton straightens, and his head falls back. "Sonofabitch. No, of course not, we're in a damn Ferris Wheel!" Crow drops his hand from his jaw and flashes his pearly whites. "I always have protection in my wallet."

He does. Trenton and Hayes have always gotten theirs out of drawers in their rooms. Or, in the instance Trenton and I were intimate in his car, from the glovebox.

When I glance at Hayes, he's nibbling at the inside of his cheek, clearly thinking through the same conclusion to which I had arrived.

"But if our girl keeps to her promise…" Crow continues, words trailing and being replaced by the upward tick of his lips, and his teeth toy with his lip ring for a heartbeat before he says, "I won't need any."

Oh… crap. The money shot. D-did I promise that? My mind hits rewind, and my heart thrums at full speed to match the pace of my thoughts chasing the recollections.

I lift a finger and point it at him accusingly. "I never promised such a thing. I mentioned double pen—I mean I promised to make tonight worth your while." Oh god… I have never been nervous around them. Always trusting. Always hungry.

Trenton's momentary disappointment fades and an amused grin pulls at his features. "Something happened to the first part of that sentence. Can you repeat? Not sure I caught it all."

Hayes chuckles beside me. All three men are quite clearly entertained by my flustered state. Then, he has the audacity to join in on the bullying: "She told me that she was willing to try anything once." He shrugs, and his fingers lightly meet my shoulder.

Trenton groans and drops his head into his hands. "I knew coming up here was a bad idea. Cock blocked by a damn Ferris Wheel."

"I got it covered," Crow says, lifting his ass off the seat and digging into his back pocket. All attention turns to him as he pulls out not one but two condoms and plops one into Trenton's lap and tosses the other at Hayes. When my eyes meet Hayes, he winks at me. He knew Crow would have more than one.

O-okay.

This is happening.

In a Ferris Wheel.

With all three of them.

Hell yes.

But also... holy shit.

"May I have this dance?" Crow asks Hayes. Hayes stands, and the two swap places.

Hayes and Trenton immediately bring their heads together and begin whispering. Plans, no doubt. Ones that include Crow this time. Usually they don't need a briefing prior to stuff like this, but I guess since Crow is involved and a certain wish list of activities are on the proverbial table, a little planning is requisite.

Crow grabs my hand furthest from him and tugs me onto his lap so that my knees are straddling him.

He glances briefly over my shoulder before turning his gaze on me. His smug grin disappears, eyes flick between mine, and his throat constricts over a hard swallow. "Thank you for the cure," he chokes out.

I want to tell him that I still have some poison left, but when I open my mouth he covers it with his. The kiss is gentle and sweet, and he pulls his head back shortly after. "I know something is going on — that you have more surprises in store tonight. Trenton knows, too. But right now? We only care about this."

My eyebrows rise high.

He shrugs. "The domestics were great and all, but we had some things that needed to be discussed." They were definitely looking at those domestics for a really long time. I had begun to wonder. "For instance, how something like this would work without our dicks touching. Because I like him and all, but... not that much."

A laugh bursts out of me. "Y-you seriously talked about that while looking at cars?"

He chuckles. "Yeah. Was over pretty fast. I said, 'Touch my dick with any part of your body and I'm out.' He said, 'Deal.' I am kinda afraid he might touch my dick on purpose, though, just to keep you to himself."

My laughter grows and so does his, but his fades sooner and he gets all serious again. Crow's hands come up and cup my face. "I was kidding about the money shot." He gives me a half smile. "I think you're just as nervous about that as I am about doing this stuff with Hayes and Trenton involved."

My heart quadruple jumps. "You're nervous?"

Oh good... it's not just me then.

He lets out a shaky chuckle. "Hell yeah." Then he wiggles under me, and the swell of him rubs hard between my legs. "Apparently my dick isn't, though."

"You just gave away both your condoms," I remind.

Crow raises an eyebrow and his thumb comes to my bottom lip. "I haven't stopped thinking about fucking your mouth since you sent me that video of you and Hayes. I might not get to come on your face, but I really fucking can't wait to have you look up at me with your mouth full of my cock."

Too damn bad mouths don't throb like vaginas do. Kinda unfair seeing as he's talking about putting his cock in my mouth but it's my pussy that is responding. I wiggle against him, seeking friction. His hands drop to my ass, and he slips his fingers under the hem of my shorts to cup my cheeks.

He brings his lips to mine and whispers, "So... double penetration, hm? How is that going to work?"

I know he's not asking how it actually works, but rather how it will with them, up here, in a wobbly Ferris Wheel capsule. I shrug up a shoulder and chase his lips with mine, but he teases me by pulling back slightly. "I don't know," I whisper. "But I trust Hayes and Trenton together. I'm nervous, but not worried."

Those nerves nearly reach the top of the circular structure when a second set of hands swipe against either side of my neck and pull my hair off my shoulders. Crow's eyes dart to whoever approached then fall back to mine. "You can tell us to stop anytime. If something is uncomfortable, let us know. Okay?"

My breath hitches when the man holding my hair twists it slightly. "Okay," I force out on an exhale. Damn this is already intense and we haven't even started.

CHAPTER FORTY-FIVE

Crow moves his hands to my waist and encourages me to stand. I situate my feet between his. My hips come to about eye level. With a jittery breath, I pull my shirt off while Crow unbuttons and slides down my shorts and underwear.

The weather is nice, but the ever-incessant breeze from the nearby gulf makes my nipples pebble. The double crinkle of condom wrappers floats to my ears from behind, and the clicking of a zipper resonates from below. All three men prepare as quickly as possible, Crow getting done the fastest since all he had to do was whip himself out.

When I reach down to wrap my fingers around him, he grabs my wrist and shakes his head. "All three of us are about to take a lot from you."

Hayes's voice joins in. "You'll be doing enough by just existing between us, if you start participating too much, you'll get over stimulated, and we'll lose you too soon."

When my attention returns to Crow, he shrugs. It makes sense. But both of us are sorta in uncharted territory so we just have to go with it.

Between my thighs dampens, my fingers tingle, and my mouth waters. I ache to feel, touch, and taste, but heed their advice. They have no trouble beginning to ravage me, though. All three men engage at once: Trenton, who steps to my side, curves his finger under my chin and draws my mouth to his; Hayes twists my hair and drags his mouth along my neck; Crow cups my sex and slips his fingers through my folds. My hands dart out to his shoulders for support.

Trenton twists his tongue with mine and Crow inserts his finger, twisting to somehow match the mating of our tongues. Trenton breaks slightly and whispers against my mouth, "Crow is going to take you over the edge the first time, fast and hard, loosen you up a little." My pussy clenches around Crow's finger as he inserts a second, and my breaths increase, fanning heavy over Trenton's words.

Hands drop to my hips, and Hayes presses my ass up against him, causing Crow to have to follow the movement. Hayes is bare and uses the crease of my ass cheeks as friction for now, teasing, giving me a hint of what only moments from now should bring.

Trenton gives me one more deep, hard kiss then directs my face to Crow. Crow's chrome eye spark in the moonlight and so does his piercing as he drags his tongue across it and his eyes flutter down to my lips. He drives his fingers inside me and straightens to connect our mouths.

Knowing we are short on time, and there will be a good portion of this experience that might need extra, I relax and let Crow do exactly what Trenton tasked him to. Trenton's hands cup my breasts, Hayes grinds against me, and Crow moves his fingers in and out with a slow, rhythmic motion, curving just right.

The G-spot stimulation makes me spiral hard and fast, per Trenton's wishes. Hayes curves over me, his mouth brushing against my ear. "Mm, damn, I love how easy you let go for us."

Legs trembling, chest panting, arms like jelly, I make a mental promise to challenge them if I'm ever given another opportunity. Because, he's right — I am too damn easy where they're concerned. Tonight, that is a good thing, though, otherwise our precarious timeline wouldn't allow us to join in this way right here, right now.

As soon as I come down from my first high, Hayes moves aside and uses his hands on my hips to guide me over to an awaiting Trenton. Crow's fingers slip out of me with the swap, and I watch as he brings that hand to his cock and rubs himself with two long strokes, eyes locked on mine as Trenton takes over and sheathes himself inside me, reverse cowgirl style, from his lying down position along the length of the bench.

The position is a little tricky, fitting my one foot between him and the seat back, but possible. Trenton lets out a low rumble as I move over him to get adjusted. With my opposite foot still on the ground, I practice lifting and descending along his length. He grunts when I successfully complete the motion. But on the next upward climb he removes himself and realigns with my other entrance. I swallow hard, eyes snapping to Hayes. Hayes gets on his knees between Trenton's feet, cock in hand, and gives me an encouraging smile. I nod, and Trenton lowers me onto him. Having already orgasmed once, my muscles are already looser, more relaxed — but I am also more sensitive.

Trenton enters deeper. My body tenses. The capsule swings slightly. Crow steps to us, grips my jaw, turns my face toward him, and crashes his mouth against mine. My body immediately relaxes again, melting into his kiss, and Trenton is able to sink all the way inside.

Crow disengages. Hayes pulls my focus back to him. He presses his hand between my breasts and guides me backward, Trenton still filling me, until my back and head are flush against Trenton's chest and shoulder. Crow balances his shins on Trenton's upper arm, casting a quick glance toward his friend first for approval. When Trenton's head nods beside mine, Crow brings his cock to my mouth. I open wide, limited by my movements and at the mercy of his directive.

Crow slips the tip of his cock between my lips. The positioning of his cock so close to Trenton's face amuses me, but I keep my mirth to myself, lest Crow get spooked.

He's not scared, though — any clinging nerves seemed to have been carried away on the wind as soon as he began to slip his length into my hot mouth. "Holy shit," Trenton groans into my ear. Crow meets a little resistance due to the angle, but Trenton assists by slipping his hand along my shoulder and to my neck. His fingers wrap around the column of my throat, and he whispers, "Relax. Take him. All of him."

A tremor of scorching need shoots through me, spurred on by his instructions and the lurch of his cock buried deep inside me. As though Hayes senses the return of my desire, his fingers brush against my clit and through my folds.

Chest heaving, that overstimulation Hayes spoke of already trying to muddle my mind, I close my eyes and try to compartmentalize each sensation. The pressure of Trenton's hand against my neck and his cock inside my ass, the girth of Crow between my cheeks, and the thick fingers Hayes inserts right at that very moment. But it is no use. I wiggle against Trenton, get a little savage on Crow, and buck over Hayes's hand. I can't tell the difference between the sway of the capsule and the sway of my body. Nor can I stop. My insides betray me. Everything bundles tightly, and I implode, contracting and clenching everywhere all at once.

Beside my head, Trenton whimpers and groans. "Goddammit. Oh fuck. Remi..." But then his voice becomes muffled and my eyes spring open, mid-orgasm, only to find that Crow has slapped his tattooed hand over Trenton's mouth.

Trenton's chest heaves under mine, and he scrambles to wrench Crow's fingers away. I come down just as fast as I went up, but just as replete.

"What the fuck?" Trenton hisses.

"Did you nut?" Crow asks, cock still in my mouth.

"No! Your grimy hand was around my mouth! Major mood killer right there."

Crow slips his cock out to the tip, I loop my tongue around it and collect the precum, and he dips and back in, head falling backward, a low and long groan vibrating from his vocal cords before he breathes out, "You're fucking welcome." Crow's cock inside my mouth is the perfect assistant for keeping down my percolating laughter. His head straightens, and he thrust nice and slow inside my mouth again. "Hayes, put your cock in our girl before Trenton combusts and it's too late. I want to see her completely filled."

I side-eye Hayes, face still turned toward and being used by Crow.

"Ready?" he asks.

Crow slips out of my mouth so I can answer. "Yes," I respond breathlessly.

Trenton adjusts under me, and all those tingly sensations from the last orgasm spark to life again. Hayes adjusts his glasses, grips his cock, and aligns it with my pussy. Our eyes lock and he broaches my entrance. The sensation is immediately unlike anything I expected. It feels like his cock is hitting a bone, or a place inside me that has gone untouched up until now, and it certainly feels like he shouldn't be able to go any deeper.

Yet he does. My eyes slam shut tight, and I turn my face back toward Crow. "What can I do to help?" he whispers closer to my ear than I anticipated having envisioned his cock so near my face. The offer is so unexpected, I forget for a heartbeat that I have two cocks inside me and one waiting to be and my eyes open, meeting Crow's immediately.

Both Hayes and Trenton pause their movements, waiting for my response to Crow. But I can't speak. My tongue is thick and thoughts are heavy. I blink repeatedly at him and close my eyes again. With them still like this, it feels good. Too good. But my lack of experience has me beginning to worry that should any of them move it will no longer feel good.

"T-Top." This comes from Hayes. A verbal response isn't returned, but a physical one is. Fingers curl some wayward hair around my ear, brush against my cheek and skirt along the shape of my lips. When I part my lips, Trenton, based on which side the fingers came from, swoops a finger inside my mouth and loops it around my tongue before removing it and pressing his palm down the length of my body until his damp fingertips can rub over my clit.

The cooled sensation works. My worry fades and is replaced by more want, more need. I hurt… in a good, albeit overwhelming, way. My pussy aches. Throbs. My stomach clenches. Hayes moves deeper inside me, and Trenton moves this time, too. It was just entering that was the difficult part. Now, it is no longer uncomfortable. "More," I breathe.

Hayes acquiesces.

Trenton grinds his hips.

A moan vibrates through me.

I am able to open my eyes again. Crow is still squatting, watching me, eyebrows curved in concern. "It feels really good," I breathe out shifting slightly, testing my boundaries.

Crow's long, black eyelashes flutter. "Yeah?" he asks, still unsure.

His genuine concern, when he's always so tough and dark, does something crazy to my psyche. My body coils everywhere. "Oh, God. Yes." Crow's focus drops to the mouth that said those words, and his tongue snakes out to drag across his lip ring.

Hayes begins to move slowly inside me. Trenton circles his hips.

"Crow?" I breathe.

"Mm?"

"I-I am ready… but…" Oh, wow, talking is challenging. "You are probably going to have to do all the work." I rush out the last part, worried my diaphragm will soon stop working, "And… and I don't think I'm going to last long." To make my point, a moan whines out of me.

His chrome eyes widen. A breathy chuckle trickles out of me.

Crow hustles back to his position, using Trenton's arm as support, and I open for him. He immediately enters, ready to check off his wish list item.

These men definitely have things under control. But that is a problem now, because I need them to lose control with me this time. I can't keep going. I'm so full. So relaxed — every muscle. And so. Damn. Sensitive. I need to come, and I need them to come with me. Which means I need to push them over the edge. And to do that, I need to focus — to participate.

I cup Crow's balls with one hand and his cock twitches against my tongue. "Careful," he groans. I keep my eyes closed, because I happen to know that one specific on his wish list is to have me looking at him. So, I will save that for last.

I reach down with my opposite hand and circle my fingers around the base of Hayes's cock like a ring, providing him even more sensation. Then, I move my hips into a circular grind.

Hayes's hands move to my breasts, and Trenton rubs my clit, sneaking the tip of his finger into my pussy along Hayes's length in order to collect a little more lubrication.

Ready. So damn ready. I flutter my eyes open and lock them on Crow. "Jesus," he pants, driving inside me. He is surprisingly more gentle than Hayes was the other day, and damn, that turns me on. I angle my head back a little. A whimper trickles out of him and he convulses, having a damn hard time keeping his release contained.

The circling of my hips becomes more desperate. Hayes gains confidence in my body's ability to handle him, and his movements strengthen, giving me the opportunity to lift my ass a little and descend on Trenton rather than just grind against him.

Trenton's fingers leave my clit and flutter against my hip. I know this sign language between them this time, though, and am ready for it. I give Crow's balls one more good roll, remove my hand, pierce him with a sultry glare, and tap at my cheekbone.

All three guys freeze. Crow's eyes bug. "Really?" he squeaks, then clears his throat. He'd done an excellent job keeping his cool, but now his chest rises and falls under his black shirt. I smile up at him, mouth full of cock.

335

He throws his head back and a shudder wracks his body. "Mm, fuck," he groans.

Hayes and Trenton move back into action, and we stage our race.

Hayes thrusts. Trenton grinds. And Crow fucks my mouth hard and fast until his balls draw tight and he pulls out. My nerves spike again, but I close my eyes and show Crow the trust I show Hayes and Trenton.

Fingers meet my lips. "Open your mouth," Trenton grunts, attempting to pull himself firmer against the bench in order to thrust inside me concurrently. I obey. A rumbly groan precedes the first hot spurt falling onto my tongue. Another quickly follows.

Both Trenton and Crow moan in unison. Crow won the race, but I come in second place, body shaking, consumed. Something hot and dense hits my cheek and again on my chin. My orgasm builds and builds and builds until I am flying high above the Ferris Wheel. Trenton and Hayes tie for third.

When I float back down, I have three men there to catch me. Hayes had already pulled out but I was so high and so languid that I didn't even notice. Crow's arms hook under mine and he helps me off of a softening Trenton. I am moved into Hayes's lap and Crow begins hastily untying and toeing off his boots, and fighting to remove his pants like ants somehow climbed up them and he can't get them off fast enough.

The sight is odd, and immediately grounds me, since we're all supposed to be putting our clothes back on, not taking them off. In fact, Trenton and Hayes seem equally confused. Trenton begins putting his jeans back on, while side-eyeing Crow's every move. Hayes is already cleaned up and dressed, hand curled around his used condom. Both arms are wrapped around my naked body, and they tighten at Crow's odd behavior.

Crow undresses his bottom half in record time, tosses his boxers to the side, then pulls his jeans back on and slips back into his boots. With each step, my head tilts further to the side. Then he snatches the boxers back up, wraps his fingers in the fabric, and drops to his knees in front of me. His free hand cups that side of my face, and his chrome eyes flit all over my features.

When his thumb drags along my cheek bone and down to my jaw, everything around us fades away. His other hand, the one now wrapped in material, lifts to my other cheek and he brushes it against my skin. Only then do I realize what he's doing — remember that his cum is marking my face.

The next spot he wipes is on my chest, eyes locked with mine. The cum that had landed on my chin must have dripped off, the consistency changing due to the heat and motion of our bodies.

His mouth meets mine, lip ring dragging along my bottom lip once before he puts a hairsbreadth distance between them. "Was that okay?" he asks. "I tried to get it all in your mouth, but apparently I race better than I aim."

Damn. Trenton is supposed to be the funny one. Not dark-hearted Crow. A watery chuckle leaves me, and I blink away the stupid veil of blurry vision his care conjured. "Well... I'm glad you missed. Wouldn't quite be a money shot otherwise. Then, I would still owe you."

He groans. "So you're saying if I would have gotten it all in your mouth, you would've let me try again? Dammit."

Hayes clears his throat near my ear and everything around us poofs back into reality. Crow blinks several times, finishes wiping down my face and chest, and stands. "It's a quarter to twelve," Hayes whispers. And just like that, the reality below the Ferris Wheel spikes into existence again, too.

CHAPTER FORTY-SIX

After working our way back down to the bottom of the Ferris Wheel, we climb and jump over the chainlink fence that runs parallel to the gulf, jog to the shore, and quickly clean up as best as we can. Crow saves the night again by bundling all the garbage items in his boxers and tossing everything into one of the public beach trash containers on our way back to the event.

Hayes and I share a look as we cross the street. The euphoria of our group experience dampens with every step. Crow mentioned that he and Trenton were aware of a caveat, but not what it consists of. They walk along behind Hayes and me in silence, knowing what comes next must be just that — the caveat… the climax of my plan.

I walk to the opposite side of the park, pulse picking up with every step. The crowd becomes thicker, and we have to push our way through sweaty, dancing bodies to the ride behind the band. I bend under the yellow caution tape, and the guys follow.

The Devil's mouth yawns wide. Decaying, chipped teeth bracket each side. A long, lithe tongue snakes out, mimicking some twisted version of a red carpet entrance.

Hayes enters first, hand out behind him to make sure I stay behind while he gets the first peek inside. When the coast is clear, his hand drops, and the three of us file in. There are a couple of those light towers set up, as per my request, their telescopic feature retracted in order to fit inside. I sure as hell owe Lace and her friends; they'll be getting paid a pretty portion of the profits from tonight, and they got to keep their clothes on while doing so, but I still owe them.

Arms wrap snugly around my waist and squeeze. "This has all been amazing. Thank you," Trenton's voice hits my ear. I smile, content for half a second, but the smile drops, knowing the moment is just that... a moment. I turn in the circle of his arms and give him a chaste, sweet kiss on the cheek before wiggling out of the embrace.

"Don't thank me yet." I give a half-hearted chuckle.

Trenton peeks over my shoulder, connecting with one of the guys behind me, then his attention flicks back down to me. "I was an assho—" My phone vibrates, and I nearly jump a mile high. All four of us reach for our phones at the same time. My lungs seize. Hayes darts a glance my way as his screen highlights his face.

I turn my attention to my own screen.

A notification from the QR app.

The breath I had held comes out in a big whoosh.

"The racing portions of the meet start after midnight. With the app" — I wave my phone in the air and walk toward the center of the dome — "everyone can vote and place bets on the assigned races. Sign-up closes at twelve, but, as vehicles get paired, people can start tracking and betting a few minutes before."

Trenton holds his phone up with a snort. "They paired me with a Bronco."

Crow laughs and peeks over at Trenton's screen.

"If you click on your opponent's name, you can see all the stats he — or she — entered," I explain.

Trenton taps at his phone and his eyebrows lift high. "Well, shit. Coyote swapped and turbocharged. Should be a good run then."

I look at my own phone, thankful for the momentary distraction, pull up the same pairing, and study the stats of both vehicles. One of the first things I noticed, and loved, about the Monte Carlo, was that it is a sleeper. I never got the opportunity to ask him what all those fancy gauges and stuff do, though. According to what he entered into the app, he has something called a "clutched supercharger." I raise an eyebrow at him. Sure, I know a bit about cars, but that one is lost on me. Something having to do with driver demand, no doubt.

"Clutched supercharger?" I ask.

Trenton positively lights up. "Yeah, been working with an aftermarket company testing a new concept on the down low. Electromagnetic clutch that engages when the supercharger is needed. The control panel on my dash engages the clutch on the supercharger and boots up a different tune in my PCM. When that happens and when the car starts seeing boost, a pressure switch in my air intake energizes my secondary fuel pump so the engine won't starve."

Shuffling of feet sound outside the entrance, and my eyes dart to the time. Midnight exactly. I swipe out of the QR app and open my documents folder. Then, I sidle up against Crow.

Since Hayes already knows what to expect, kinda, he turns his back away from the front, shoves his phone into his pocket, and drops his hands loosely at his side, fingers slightly curled.

Trenton's attention remains locked on his screen. That is, until a figure enters into the belly of the devil, Crow grinds out a "Motherfucker," and Hayes launches.

Hayes freezes on the spot, mid lunge, thanks to an unexpected human shield Porter has pressed tightly against his body. A hostage, gun dug into his temple, face bloody. My mind races to catch up — to see past the swelling and blood to the features beneath.

Hayes slowly backs away, hands raised in a defensive position. But his eyes make the barest of flickers toward Trenton. Trenton was the one closest to the entrance. Porter and his hostage stumbled in right past him without noticing.

"The kid," Crow grinds out under his breath.

No one moves. At first.

Porter's eyes flash wildly around the room. Keyed up, he is caught completely unaware when Trenton yanks the gun out of his hand and kicks him at the bend of his knees, causing him to fall forward and lose his grip on Boyd.

Hayes bends down, picks up the gun, and shoves Boyd toward Crow and me. Crow points an accusatory finger at the whimpering kid. "You stay out of the damn way." Boyd nods and shuffles backward.

Hayes shoves the gun into the back waistband of his pants and throws the first punch.

Porter is a helluva lot bigger than Hayes, but Hayes has trained and toned himself. Whereas Porter has a beer belly and overall natural bulkiness. If he weren't such a horrible human being, he'd pass as attractive and cuddly. Such a waste of a pretty picture.

Both Crow and Trenton launch to Hayes's aid, but I step in front of Crow before he makes any contact.

His eyes are wild, teeth bared. I push him in the chest, since a gentle nudge wouldn't be persuasive enough. "Wait. Listen." I grab his face between my palms and force him to look at me. "I need you. I need your help." His nostrils flair and eyes dart from me to the brawl behind me and back again, confused, riled up. "I set him up." Recognition slowly dawns, and his rage toward Porter's appearance turns to me instead. Before he can chew me out, though, I hurry and finish, now that I have his full attention. "Record everything for me? Make sure it gets to the right people… and stays away from the wrong ones?" This is it. My eyes sting and bile churns in my stomach. My life is over.

Crow's mouth slams shut, and a clarity sparks in his chrome gaze. He stumbles backward into a curve of the large dome. There's a quick flash of light from his phone, but then he all but disappears against the dark background.

It's interesting, having this all begin to play out and become witness to the part of my plan where I knew I wanted Crow, Hayes, and Trenton here. Because I knew they would have my back, no questions asked — yet.

Confidence blooming with my support system surrounding me, I walk over to the brawl, put my fingers between my lips, and whistle. Trenton and Hayes stop kicking Porter in the ribs and stomach. Porter heaves, curling into a ball of hurt.

"Get him up and hold him still."

Trenton yanks Porter off the ground, twists his arms behind his back, then drags him to kneel in front of me.

Chest heaving, eyes blurring, I step up to Porter and peer down my nose at him. Then I wind my fist back—

Hot fingers wrap around my wrist, and I nearly fall backward from the unexpected stop. An equally hot, trembling body presses up against me from behind, a finger slips into the pucker between my thumb and forefinger, and Hayes pulls my thumb out of my clenched fist. Chest rising and falling against my shoulders, he adjusts my finger and thumb positioning. "Forward punch. Keep your elbow in, no swinging. Bring your opposite shoulder back, and twist in your hips and leg like golfers do with a driver. To hit harder, pretend like you're punching past him."

I nod, and he steps away from me.

Ticking off all the boxes he suggested, I pull back and punch forward and into Porter's cheek. Then, I double over, clenching my throbbing fist. "Ow. Oh, my God," I breathe out. The hit steals as much of my breath as the contact appears to have stolen Porter's.

Jude enters, raging. "Remi!" he screams. When he spots me doubled over, though, he runs forward and his body collapses over mine, bringing us both to the ground.

Our arms come around each other and we hug, on our knees, for an indiscernible amount of time. My face stays buried in the crook of his shoulder while his cheek is adhered to the side of my head.

"So. Fucking. Sweet." Porter eventually says, spitting out a wad of blood. I shoot to my feet, knowing exactly what is going to come out of his mouth next, and yell, "Gag him, quick!"

Trenton moves like lightning, slamming his hand against Porter's mouth as a temporary measure while Hayes tears off a piece of Porter's shirt, shoves it into his mouth, and ties it around his head.

Porter gets off by threatening to reveal my secrets. That power will be stripped from him tonight. Right now. Because I intend on revealing it myself.

I push off the ground and distance myself from everyone, walking backward until I'm in the very center of the dome again, all spotlights on me. My eyes immediately hone in on Jude, and my eyebrows curve inward. "Jude... I am so sorry. So so so sorry." My voice hitches.

"Remi. Stop," he responds.

Holding a hand up, I insist, "You stop. Let me do this." I take a deep breath, dart a glance at Crow in the darkness, close my eyes, then let the truth spill. "It is my fault Dad died. I shot him—"

Arms are around my shoulders, the words squeezed short from the compression of Jude's body around mine. "Don't do this to yourself, Remi. It wasn't your fault." He steps back, holds up a finger begging my patience, digs something out of his pocket, and holds the item—two items—out to me in his open palm.

Two bullets.

I shake my head, eyebrows pinching together in the middle. The words he had stopped are gone; no words exist. My brain ceases to work. My mouth ceases to form words.

Jude continues, louder this time. "Dad and I had the same type of gun. Same bullets." He points at the smaller bullet on the right. "This bullet" — he points to the opposite metal — "did not come from one of our guns."

I still struggle to understand. But one thing I do conclude is that somehow Jude knew. He knew I was involved.

"How long?" I ask.

Jude skirts around my question. "I know your heart, Remi. I refuse to lose my sister to the system because of an accident or misunderstanding." I open my mouth to speak again but he overrides my speech with his. "I only just discovered all this recently." Again he taps at the opposite bullet. "This bullet — the one that was removed from Dad's body — came from a different gun."

CHAPTER FORTY-SEVEN

I rear back, realizing now that Jude is holding the bullet Porter had dug out and handed to me that night. "Wh-when — where — did you get that?"

His dark eyes meet mine. "Remember when we moved in, and I helped you pick up all the pictures that fell out of that box? This bullet fell out, too. I didn't understand what it was at the time, or why I found it in your stuff. It wasn't until your friends handed over the bullet you removed from Porter that I started piecing things together. I just wish you had told me. Trusted me to be your 80 percent." I explode into tears. He pockets the bullets and grips my biceps hard. "Listen to me. I wish you had told me, but I understand why you kept it to yourself. That's a heavy burden to bear." He wraps his arms around me again. "Hey… Shhh… It's okay. I understand."

Jude shushes me until my mind can grasp all the things. When I am finally able to speak again, I ask, "Is that why you disappeared? To figure that out?"

Jude nods. "Partly, yes. But… uh… first…" His focus slides to a different curve of the dome and back to me again. Only then do I remember that Boyd is in here, in a terrible state no less. "At first, I was chasing the kid down. After Hayes pieced together some cam feeds from your wreck, Trenton pointed out the spot

348

where you pulled your clutch and your rear tire locked. Boyd never stopped. Not to see if you were okay, nothing. It was fishy as hell. He just kept going. Thanks to Revelry's connections, I was able to get access to all the traffic cams in the area and eventually find him…" Jude's words trail, and he gives me a small grimace. "I interrogated him."

Dad had always made it a hard rule that Jude never speak to me about the jobs he had to do. The persuasion. The deals. The burying of bodies if someone misbehaved on a grandiose level. I still found it hard to believe some days that Jude was anything but a cuddly — but slightly unhinged — teddy bear. Jude continues, "Then, he disappeared. I had gotten enough information from him, but when Porter turned up missing, too, I got on the first flight to California so I could pull on our local resources to get the port feed, have it tweaked for clarity, and things like that before he got ahold of anything else. I am still working with a few people behind the scenes to figure out who owns the gun that this bullet belongs to. If you ever get to the point that you want to, we can watch the video together. But, for now, in summary: your bullet hit the guy, not Dad. The guns went off at the exact same time, the sound of your gun recoil masked by his and vice versa. His bullet hit Dad. Your bullet hit the guy. From your angle it could have easily looked differently."

Darting my attention to Trenton after a brief glance down at the gagged Porter, I deliver a silent message. Trenton nods curtly before removing the gag. Porter is positively chomping at the bit to speak. His grating, obnoxious, voice fills the space right away. Even on his knees, bloodied and restrained, he still acts like he wrote this screenplay. He scoffs and spits out some of the blood that had trickled from his nose to his mouth. "Imagine my surprise that night, my luck—" he sniggers, eyes watering "—when you pulled the trigger and thought it was your bullet that took the invincible Troy Delancey down."

The blood drains from my face. "Y-you knew my bullet hit the other guy, and y-you let me believe I killed my father?!" My rage is an unfair combination of anger, relief, and abhorrence — a squeaky, trembly, unintelligible mix.

"You were supposed to simply watch it, to be witness to the fact that some faceless man took down Troy. To use that boiling rage inside you as a vendetta. To partner with me and take the company by storm — make it so much more than Troy and Jude ever had the balls to. But the story was so much better with the daughter taking the blame. Your voice and signature as a witness, replaced by your silence as the perp was fucking gold."

I peer into the darkness toward Crow, hoping with all hope that he is still there, recording everything.

Jude joins my side, his profile practically vibrating in the glow of the spotlights. He unsheathes his gun. Porter flinches. I step forward, drop to my haunches in front of him, pull up the document saved on my phone, and turn the screen, holding it within a few inches of his face. "I found the updated will."

"What? Where?" Jude whispers.

Porter narrows a glare on the highlighted portions of the screen.

"Care to read it aloud for all to hear, Trenton?" I ask, knowing full well Porter will refuse the instruction.

Hayes and Trenton switch places. Hayes's steps are a little wobbly, though. As soon as the swap is made, he pulls the gun from his waistband and holds it up to the back of Porter's head, execution style. His eyes drift over my shoulder and lock with Jude's. Hayes releases the safety and Porter swallows hard, his red face whitening.

I toss the phone to Trenton who then clears his throat and punches his chest with a closed fist before cupping his mouth and announcing the highlighted lines to the invisible, roaring crowd — ever the perfect spokesman. "Remi-Sue Delancey is not permitted to own, be an officer on the board, or engage in any part of Lance Industries." He then holds a finger up, ear-to-ear grin spreading across his face. "I, Troy Delancey, bestow and bequeath any interest which I may have in

LI Imports at the time of my death to be sold and all funds given to Remi-Sue Delancey."

Trenton chucks my phone to Jude for him to review the document... and to keep him distracted, mind-whirling with something other than killing Porter... on camera. He then moves to Hayes's side and speaks to him low. Probably also encouraging his best friend to refrain from carrying through with that promised killshot.

I had fallen asleep studying that will every night since the day I printed it — desperate to understand. To read between the lines. The import portion of Lance Industries was where Dad owned the most shares. "He knew you were up to no good, Porter. He wanted to secure my inheritance, and to make sure the company was left to Jude clean — minus the gray water tank, the imports. And he did it all behind your back."

Porter turns the best shade of red and purple. I twist the proverbial wound a little: "If you want to run a million-dollar import company, looks like you'll need to start from the ground up, because the board will sure as shit not agree to sell it to you."

Hayes clears his throat and lifts his chin, no longer silent, commanding the space: "From prison... for murder, among other things," he states matter-of-factly.

Jude's attention springs upward. "What? Why?" Jude had already determined who really shot Dad that night at the pier, and while Porter might have staged it, that guy pulled the trigger.

Hayes takes a deep breath and explains on the exhale, "Eleven days prior to the night of Troy's recorded death, a POA was filed with the courts. In California, it takes ten days for the POA to clear. Ironic, don't you think? I pulled the hospital paperwork. Troy had suddenly and unexpectedly slipped into a coma — he was hurt, but not fatally, prior to that. The POA, knowing Troy's wishes for never wanting to survive by artificial means, instructed the facility to pull the plug."

Do what?!

"Every good idea needs a Plan B." Porter smirks. "The damn bullet didn't get the job done. I administered the drug and pulled the plug, and I would do it again."

My piercing, psychotic scream fills the dome, and I tackle Porter, arms flailing, lungs screeching, blackness overtaking my vision. "You! You killed him! You killed him! You killed him!" I repeat those words, unending. My newly learned punching form flies out the window. I pummel, kick, slap, pull, push. Nobody stops me. I, somehow, remain untouched as I take out years of rape, gaslighting, manipulation, and the death of my father out on this man. This villain. This devil in disguise.

Until I no longer can. Until my muscles are weak and my lungs and abs are sore and overused. As soon as I go silent and collapse on the old, dirty ground of the devil's belly, I am scooped up and moved backward. Farther and farther away to the darkest curve of the dome.

The room turns into chaos. Flashing lights. Deep, yelling voices. An arm wraps around my shoulders in the dark and pulls me in close while my senses return to sane. Somewhat.

"Porter Davis you are under arrest…" The rest of his rights trail as my mind fades and everything turns to mumbles. Hayes begrudgingly relinquishes the gun to the police, eyebrows flattened as he bores a final, cold glare at Porter. I watch, detached, as Boyd is looked over and carried away by paramedics and Porter is detained, read his rights, and removed from the dome.

When the room goes silent — Porter, Boyd, and the authorities gone — I whisper, "What just happened?" The police showing up was not planned. I knew my fate would end with the authorities involved, but I never intended on them crashing the event.

"I transmitted the feed directly to the precinct," Crow responds. The metal of his labret ring catches on one of the webs of light as his mouth curves into a grin.

I turn to Hayes. "The signature? All that time, you were researching what really happened during that import deal?"

Hayes nods and rubs the back of his neck. "The timeline of everything was fucked up. I didn't have the resources to get the recordings like Jude did, or I would have. After you told me that you thought you were signing funeral documents, I looked deeper into the medical side of things. Those are a lot easier to hack into. Documents filed with the courts are usually somewhat public, too. Plus, that first time we took you to the port and you had a panic attack, threw a major flag."

Still trying to comprehend, I turn to Jude. "And you were looking into the bullet. What else?"

"The night of the meet, when I was looking for your phone, I stumbled on our financial books hidden in Porter's room. The numbers were a lot different than the ones Porter had been reporting to me. All this time, he was showing me a copy. A doctored version. Come to find out, it was those same, falsified reports that he had been providing the board and the Security Exchange Commission, too. I called an emergency meeting with the board, showed them all the proof — port videos included — and voted him out before he could do anything else. Since you were out of commission in the hospital, it canceled the need to wait on your vote. I hated leaving you, but I had to use your coma to our benefit."

My hand darts out to seek purchase on whoever is closest. Crow. "S-so what was the difference? With the books, I mean," I ask, wobbling.

"Lance Industries is thriving." He beams.

"W-we aren't going broke? The company is okay?" I ease myself to the ground, leaning back against the paint-flecked, dust-covered, curved wall. The only reason why we agreed to move to Florida was because Jude and I thought that by doing so we would be covering Dad's assets and keeping his name clear.

The big picture starts to form in my mind, and I let out a shaky chuckle. "While you two were doing all of that, I was following a trail to the updated will and hacking into the app Porter designed." I look up at all four guys. "All three of us were sleuthing at the same time. Working together. Yet apart. Keeping secrets. Solving problems. All for the same end goal."

CHAPTER FORTY-EIGHT

"Was Boyd working with Porter all along?" "Boyd was starved for attention. He wasn't really working with Porter, just being manipulated by him." Jude explains, "Kid has an addiction to muscle relaxers. Porter became his supplier in exchange for his help with a few things, all while keeping him drugged up enough to where he never truly understood what he was doing. The day of your wreck, he was simply tasked to challenge you. Porter spun it in a way that made the boy believe you were pining over his car. That you wanted the race. Porter screwed with your bike, Remi — tampered with the transmission fluid. My best guess is he did it before our meet, and that's really why he was late showing up."

The recollection of Crow telling me that my transmission was fucked up springs to mind. "How did you figure out it was the transmission?"

Crow responds to this part, "We put her in gear and spun the motor. Something was off with the input shaft. Since the back tire was locked up, we had to cut the drive belt. Before doing that, we checked the fluid. The drain bolt was stripped and the tank was empty."

"So... then once I hit a certain speed, with the fluid drained, the parts in the transmission got super hot, and just as I was about to shift up, the input shaft sheared in two and made the engine rev higher?" Damn, if Dad could hear me now, he would be hella proud.

"Seriously?" Trenton groans. "Am I really the only one here that gets a painful boner when she pulls shit like this?" And just like that, the buzz of anxiety in my veins decelerates to more of a hum. Trenton clears his throat when Jude scrunches his nose at him, and responds to my assessment, "Uh… Right… And the guts of the transmission seized up which made the tire lock."

The amusement lingers. Crow scuffs at something on the ground with the tip of his boot, trying to hide a smile. Hayes lifts his glasses and pinches the bridge of his nose, lips half-cocked. Jude holsters his gun and tosses his head back, hands on his hips. "Do you know how damn hard it was to not put a bullet in his head?" he grinds out.

"Really damn hard," Hayes answers.

Jude's head flops back down, and their eyes lock. I can tell by that glare that he's wondering just who the hell Hayes thinks he is that he can relate. But his raised eyebrows relax and curve into what I might label as… gratefulness. "Sometimes other means are far superior to snuffing out a life," he says, blowing out a heavy breath.

My heart pangs at the very Troy Delancey-like comment. An image of Dad sitting in his leather chair flashes in my mind. A breathy chuckle leaves me. "A life in prison with all his control stripped away is definitely far superior for Porter. I hope someone in there gives him a taste of his own medicine and he gets to experience all he did to me."

Jude grimaces. We all laugh, regardless of how twistedly inappropriate laughing at such a thing might be.

The sounds of the Golden Ticket event outside make their way back into reality, and our attentions swivel toward the dome's entrance. Jude reaches into his pocket, digs out my phone, and hands it to me. I push off the ground and dust off. "What is Boyd's fate?" I ask.

"Well, my trigger finger does itch," Jude replies.

I tilt my head at him and narrow my eyes. "Give him a chance?" I alternate glances between Revelry and Jude. "Give him a family." Crow's eyes dart from the ground and up to mine. "Maybe he'll clean up if he has a good support system."

Jude slings his arm around my shoulder and starts leading me out of the dome. "Fine. But I intend on at least letting him know how close he came to taking his last breaths."

"Deal." Because there's no talking Jude out of it anyway. Poor kid has no idea what's coming.

Jude jolts to a stop, and my attention darts away from the approaching exit to his face, but his focus is now on the hand now curved over his shoulder. Trenton and Jude lock gazes. "Mind if we keep her in here for a few more minutes?"

Jude drops his arm from our embrace, turns to face Trenton, then very obviously looks down at his gun and back up again. Trenton gives a nervous chuckle but otherwise says, "Worth the risk."

Jude double blinks, pauses for way too long, then nods. "Yeah... because there would be no talking her out of it anyway." I press my lips together. Damn, I love us as siblings. He speaks up loud enough for Crow and Trenton to hear the next part: "Hurry up, though, because I'm getting tired of my phone vibrating about some damn race that I have somehow been registered for." He flicks me a side-glance before spinning on his heels and hollering over his shoulder, "See you at the line."

Do not grimace. Do not grimace.

Crow fumbles to get his phone out of his pocket.

Because if Jude has been getting those messages, then so has Crow. But due to the circumstances, Crow must have been ignoring them.

Not anymore.

He turns the screen on and glares at the notifications. "Y-you paired me and Jude up?"

"Nah… the app did." I hold my hands up in defense. "I mean… I might have added some extra code in there… to tip the scale a little. Maybe." Annnnd, here comes the grimace.

Crow points a finger at me, hides his lip ring between pressed teeth… but remains speechless. His finger drops, and he messes around on his screen. I also might have maybe added a code that would prevent him and Jude from declining or backing out of the race. And my guess is the pot is getting pretty high at this point. If the bugging of his eyes is any indicator.

Trenton clears his throat, drawing my attention back to him. "What I was trying to say earlier before Porter showed up was… sorry. Sorry I was such a shady asshole for a while there."

"We exchanging apologies?" I ask with a wink. "I get it. I really do. Being in the rink means you're gonna have to take a few blows. Maybe we can make it up to each other later… bypass the cutman."

"Oh ho… yes, yes we can." He grins wide. "But, I was kinda hoping I could do a little remedying right now?"

Oh, God. But… but…

Butt.

I shift from foot to foot, still very much feeling the lingering strain from how we remedied things in the Ferris Wheel.

My shock turns back to Trenton when he drops onto a knee, digs in his pocket and pulls out… a string. "I had to borrow this from the elastic waistband of Crow's dirty boxers earlier, but it'll do for now."

Crow jolts to attention, his gaze finally leaving his phone. "Say what? I told you I didn't want you anywhere near my dick. Those get near my dick, or have you forgotten the purpose of underwear?"

Hayes crosses his arms and leans against the dome wall, grinning ear to ear. I can almost imagine him holding a coffee and taking a sip as Trenton lifts my hand and starts trying to twist the string around my finger.

"Remi Delancey, will you talk to me about cars, drink Hayes's nasty coffee, and give Crow money shots for as long as we live? Or at least for as long as you want… starting tonight? Right now. Please?"

He struggles hard with the string. Hayes steps beside us, puts a finger in the middle so Trenton can loop it into a little bow. Crow rolls his eyes.

"Depends," I say.

Trenton reels back. Hayes chortles.

"About damn time you met your match, T-Top," Crow spouts, smug grin in place. "You need to hear 'no' a hell of a lot more often."

"What can I do to sway you?" Trenton pleads, still on his knee.

"Crow?"

"Nope. Hard no. Not doing Crow. Pen pals, then?"

A laugh bursts out of me. "No… I was addressing Crow."

Crow pockets his phone and joins our proposal group. "Not taking orders. You get what I give." He flicks that damn tongue ring.

"Race for me," I state, all amusement wiped off my face.

He points a finger at me, but then brings his hand up, rubs his jaw, then drops the hand to his side. "You… are up to something."

"Yep."

He takes in a deep breath, lets it out slowly, then groans. "Fine."

CHAPTER FORTY-NINE

When it comes to planning such a momentous event and occasion, many things are at the whim of luck or happenstance. As luck would have it, instead of being in the back of a police car during the race I set up between Crow and Jude, I am still here. Better yet, standing between both cars, black-and-white checkered flag in hand.

Lace and her friends were tasked to stage and drop the flags, but I claim this one. Jude and Crow line up. I point at Jude and give him the hand motions to pull forward a little. Since we're in a parking lot, the digs are shorter than they would be on Steel Field. If both cars were stock, Jude would win off the line. In this race, though, Jude was required to give Crow a blessing on the app to use nitrous in order to make it fair.

Who wins is inconsequential. The point is for them to earn each other's respect — to put any ideas of a takeover or the need to defend their turf behind them. They might not understand that right now, but they will. High on adrenaline, buzzing from the dig, Crow and Jude will see the benefit of a mutual camaraderie.

Hopefully.

The person in charge of announcing the races introduces each. Their names, make, models, and mods. Their crew titles. Their standing. First, I meet a dark-brown gaze until Jude nods his assent. Then, chrome eyes meet mine. Crow gives me a smug grin. With an eye roll, I wait for the head nod — seems he forgot the protocol for a hot second.

Until his eyebrows flatten, his jaw tenses and grinds, and the nod comes.

Heart in my throat, air captured in my lungs, I lift the flag high, close my eyes, and drop it fast and hard, bending into a squat in the same motion.

The air that whooshes past me from their launch almost tips me over, but I clench my fingernails into the asphalt for purchase. Then, I shoot up and turn 90 degrees, dropping the flag to my feet and pushing the hair away from my eyes. The track is short, about half the size of a preferred drag race. The cars are so fast, that the race will be over in less than ten seconds. Something I was completely not expecting happens: a white parachute pops out and flutters behind the Supra. Apparently, Crow had a kit stored in his trunk, only to be taken out and mounted when needed.

Sure, I know he used nitrous against me in our race, but if this parachute is any indicator, he must have used a baby shot against me in comparison. Brake lights flash in unison, and someone chucks me a walkie-talkie. The walkie-talkie sparks to life. "The Supra was winning by a gap until he released the chute early! They crossed the line at the same time. Tie!"

The person manning the sound system repeats everything the guy at the end of the race straight says, adding a bit of flare to the delivery.

Tie?! No way.

Again, the walkie-talkie *chhhs*. "Hey, Announcer?" Crow's voice comes over the small speaker.

"Yeah?" the guy responds.

"Hold the radio up to the mic, man."

"You got it, bud."

A *tap, tap, tap* sounds over the loudspeaker. "This thing on?"

The crowd cheers.

"Any of you ever race for a girl?" This… comes from Jude.

My face flames red.

The crowd laughs and several people whoop.

"Yeah? Well whoever just agreed shouldn't be behind a wheel. Sure shot way to get yourself killed. Women, that goes for you too. Start racing for the peen, and it'll never go well."

Oh. My. God.

I lift the radio to my mouth. "Guys… stop."

Jude comes back on the speaker. "So, yeah… Crow and I here want to deliver a message." Oh no. "Remi Delancey? Raise the flag."

With a nervous chuckle, I bend down and scoop up the prop flag high into the air. The crowd turns their attention on me.

"I want to protect my sister and keep her in my life. And... apparently Revelry wants her, too. For other reasons."

Several people in the crowd whistle and cat call.

"Remi?" Oh shit. This comes from Crow. "We raced for you, and we both won. Think you can handle sharing?"

I have never been more embarrassed — for the best reason ever — in my entire life. I raise the radio to my mouth again. I would love to spout out that having three cocks in three orifices at one time is a pretty damn good indicator that I'm quite the sharer, but my brother and a crowd of people are listening, so I stick with, "Guess we'll have to see what the street says. My Duc against your Supra. No nitrous."

The crowd goes a little wild. Crow continues, his voice immediately garnering their attention. "Well, in that case, you have already earned the win. There's no way I could best you without my nitrous."

There's a shuffling — an exchanging of hands — and Jude comes back on. "Apparently you've already earned his heart, too."

The line goes dead, and the announcer picks up the slack, wooing the crowd back into excitement. A few seconds later, the red of their brakes flash again and they park. A couple minutes after that, I'm nudged to the side by Lace, so she can take my place and line up the next race. Trenton and the Bronco.

She and the girls look super sexy in their matching stockings, short skirts, and tiny tops. I really struck gold — or impressed the Universe — meeting her. She gives me a wink and returns her attention to the Monte Carlo and Bronco, curling her fingers at Trenton to get him to scooch forward a little.

The Bronco is missing a hood — the coyote swap he mentioned unable to fit properly, clearly modded even beyond simply adding the 5.0 engine. Trenton doesn't seem bothered. Lace lines them up like a pro and definitely looks much sexier than me getting it done. Trenton and his opponent are off the line before Jude and Crow can make their way back up here. In another ten seconds or so, the winner is called over the speaker.

The Bronco. Barely.

Hayes comes to my side, finally able to get to me after the production and the immediate race staging after. "Ah, shit. Trenton will be whiny all damn night, then take it out on that aftermarket company tomorrow."

A watery smile breaks free. Crow and Jude approach, pretending like that whole embarrassing — and super sweet — announcement was a figment of my imagination. Jude gets closest to me first. The four of us wait quietly until Trenton joins us again.

When Trenton approaches, he is tapping angrily at his phone screen. "How do you set a rematch on this damn app?" he asks.

I sidle up to him, take his phone away, and slip it into his pocket. He glares down at me, but his glower soon turns into that affable grin I love so much. He slips his hand into mine and rubs the line of that string ring with the pad of his finger.

Jude gets super weird. He looks off in the distance, sighs, and swallows hard. Then... he addresses Hayes. "So... Lance Industries is looking for a new CFO."

Crow and I turn an unhealthy shade of white at the same time. My heart thrums hard and palm immediately dampens.

Jude turns to Crow and Trenton. "And I could really use some trustworthy partners. Even keel. I have been tracking The Gulf Coasters since learning about you, and you guys really need some business backing or else your ticket will expire soon. And, well, we have a few open spots on the board." He meets my gaze and smiles. "Because Remi probably plans on selling real estate or something."

I gasp, trying hard not to let the emotional situation get the better of me. "Actually, rumor has it, those girls at the strip club make a killi—"

"No." Both Jude and Crow answer at the same time.

Hayes and Trenton laugh. The light humor is short lived, though. Jude asked a big question. Even the gulf breeze seems to still, awaiting a decision from Revelry.

Crow, Hayes, and Trenton all share an esoteric look, speaking in that wordless code honed by years of practice. Crow cups his mouth and jaw. Hayes rubs the back of his neck. Trenton squeezes my hand tight. Then, Crow drops his hand and extends it toward Jude.

The men lock grips, their eyes meet, and they shake. "We'll sleep on it," Crow answers.

And... for tonight, that is good enough for me.

THE END

ABOUT THE AUTHOR

Adell Ryan is a hubby/wife pseudonym. Adell writes unconventional love stories about fierce women and their numerous male suitors. Because let's be honest, we need more than one to satisfy our multi-dimensional needs. Right? Ryan simply puts up with Adell's crazy fantasies and toots her horn regularly. Occasionally he'll add in a shoulder pat, and a deep, sexy "Damn that's good stuff."

That southern boy (bless him) stole this northern girl's heart and they live together in the deep south, raising their three boys. When Adell isn't writing she's homeschooling — primarily working on dictation, making sure they say 'creek' instead of 'crick' and 'fire' instead of 'fer.' She also dabbles in photography and graphic design. Oh yeah, and reading. Every. Night. Much to Ryan's dismay. Sometimes she puts the steamy stuff down and gives him a quick kiss on the forehead though.

To be the *first* to know about new releases and exclusive behind-the-scenes stuff, join the fun in her FB Group: facebook.com/groups/authoradellryan/

You can also check out her website at https://www.adellryan.com and sign-up for her newsletter.

Still not enough? Find her at the listed social media platforms as well!:

Goodreads	Instagram	Pinterest
BookBub	TikTok	Patreon

Printed in Great Britain
by Amazon